HEARTBURST

*a time travel rom-com
for broken weirdos*

THEORY KNIGHT

__Heartburst__
Copyright © 2025 Theory Knight
All Rights Reserved

This book or any portion thereof may not be reproduced without the express written permission of the publisher, except for the use of brief quotations in a book review and certain other noncommercial uses permitted by copyright law.

This is a work of fiction. Names, characters, places, and incidents either are products of the author's imagination or are used fictitiously.

First edition 2025

Published in Canton, GA, USA by *thewordverve* (www.thewordverve.com)

eBook ISBN: 978-1-956856-74-3
Paperback ISBN: 978-1-956856-75-0

Library of Congress Control Number: 2025934785
Cover design by Getcovers www.getcovers.com

Paperback interior design by Robin Krauss at Linden Design
www.lindendesign.biz

eBook formatting by thewordverve

♫ **Spotify Playlist for Heatburst** ♫

https://open.spotify.complaylist/4lqsCEpSmALWsrxg9u56Fv

CHAPTER 1

Lilac

♫ **"Back in Time"** ♫
by Huey Lewis & The News

I was working on a decade of mourning when adventure beckoned.

It was early Saturday afternoon. I was in my craft room/ sticker workshop on my never-ending quest to feel something again. Perhaps following an art therapy painting tutorial, and drinking calming tea, wasn't the most exhilarating approach to jolt my system alive, but I'd tried pretty much everything else.

Sunlight was still streaming through the skylights, flooding the white room with light. I lived in a heritage building with twelve-foot ceilings. I was not sure what this room was used for originally, but my dad painted everything white for me. The idea was to create a tranquil sanctuary to provide a sense of peace, serenity, and security. There were floor-to-ceiling cupboards with doors, a wrap-around counter space with drawers underneath, and an oversized fold-out desk. It felt like a cloud. It was like a Care Bear craft room. I hadn't done much creating in here. I was so tranquil, I felt nothing. It was not the room's fault. After the intense pain of Lan's death faded away, I went into a numbness that had never lifted. My best friend—gone. And by her own hands. I felt nothing. There was no good, no bad, I just went through the motions, acting like I knew a human should act. I printed her artwork as stickers for my side hustle and followed painting tutorials stroke for stroke.

When Lan died, her mom threw out all of her art to the street on garbage day. Her portfolios, sketchbooks, notebooks, journals . . . everything. Lan usually texted me most of her digital art, so I had a pretty complete collection. She didn't exactly leave me the rights to reprint her work, but I know she would have, if she had believed it had any value. I doubt her mother would remember a single piece—she thought it was a complete waste of time. It was good, and it was not just me who thought so, I had consistent orders coming in. Other people appreciated her artwork too. If she'd had more time to develop her style and create more, she could have been living off her art by now, or at least her art and her music, between the two I know she could have made a living.

I heard voices. It sounded like they were coming from a vent, though I'd never noticed one on the floor before. I ignored it for quite a while because I always had this feeling like maybe recovery was in a magical combination of strokes. I'd almost become superstitious about following the tutorials exactly. There were hundreds of comments below each video talking about the miraculous healing abilities of the process, and I wanted to get there. If I had any strong feelings at all, it was the desperation to get better.

The voices grew louder, so I had a casual glance, looking for a vent. Nothing.

Well, that's a little bit mysterious.

The voices carried on. I finished up the section I was working on and paused the tutorial. I put my brushes in water, washed my hands, then had a look under the counter. I didn't see anything, but I could still hear voices. I opened the bottom cupboard door and the voices were louder. It sounded like cowboys, talking about construction. The cupboard had a sliver of light along the bottom back edge. I got on my knees and pushed gently on the back wall. It opened a little, as though it was hinged at the top. The voices were even louder. I emptied the few items in the bottom cupboard and put my head inside to peek through the sliver. I didn't want to be spotted, but I was really surprised my cupboard opened into the neighbor's house. It didn't sound like my landlords, Buck and Jan, but maybe they were doing some more renovations. I wondered if they knew this cupboard opened directly into their apartment.

They haven't had the place for long. They probably have no idea.

I wedged as close to the opening as possible. It opened into the top of a room. I was lying on my floor peeking into the top of a room about twelve feet from the floor. I only had it open a sliver, so I could see shadows of the people who were talking, but not their faces. I didn't really want to be spotted, so I just took in what I could.

I was totally disoriented. I closed my eyes. I wasn't looking into the apartment next door. I was looking into the shop underneath the apartment next door. But if I was looking into the shop next door and downstairs, it should have been the shoe store, but instead, it was a large, empty, wood-furnished room. I put my head down to think. Even if I was on the other side of my apartment, looking into the shop under that neighboring apartment, it should have been the Chinese restaurant. Even if by some strange geometry I was looking into the shop right below me, it would be a furniture store.

I heard sounds of the cowboys leaving, the door close and a lock click. I pushed the back wall open a little more, to get a clearer view of the room.

It was wood from floor to ceiling. The floor was wide planks of wood, freshly waxed. There were tables and counters of wood—

all freshly made and stained. The walls had built in shelving, older than the furniture, but well cared for. It looked like an old-fashioned candy shop, or something you'd have seen in *Anne of Green Gables*. I leaned through the hole as far as I could without putting myself off balance. Below me was more of the empty built-in shelving to the floor then about four feet of space, and then a wooden counter—like a cash counter running the length of the room—from the front window to the back window. Except for the wooden tables, display units, and counter, the entire shop was empty. It looked like someone was opening a new store.

I couldn't remember any renovations happening in the shoe store. I anchored my body in the cupboard and leaned down far enough so I could look out the front window of the shop. I saw three horses tied up to a wooden railing in front of the shop. I stared at them in disbelief. I backed out of the cupboard and went to my kitchen window to have a look at the horses. I didn't see any. I ran out of my door, down the stairs, and around to the front of the building. There were no horses and no railing. I looked in the window of the shoe store. It was jam packed from floor to ceiling with shoes, and a sign in the window announcing: "New Arrivals." I looked at Buck and Jan's shop, a furniture store, and it was business as usual. There were people coming out of the Chinese restaurant looking satisfied. I went and looked in the window just to make sure. There were still tables and booths and Chinese pictures and lanterns.

I stood in the middle of the sidewalk and closed my eyes for a few seconds.

Am I dreaming?

Please don't melt down. Please, hold on to what's real. Go back to painting. Just be calm. Calm is better than full on breakdown.

It was surreal. I walked back to my apartment above the shops, touching everything I passed to feel the textures to ground me. I thought about sliding my hand on the new section of banister to get a sliver, but I wasn't that dedicated. I was pretty sure I was awake, and slivers are terrible. I sort of wanted to avoid my craft room but was also insanely curious about what I'd seen.

Just paint and ignore it. Do not break down.

But really, it feels . . . good. I feel curious. This is huge. I feel . . . excited.

Scratching a mosquito bite until there's a big painful sore feels good too . . . while you're doing it, but there are consequences when you stop.

So . . . don't stop.

I went back in, but cautiously. Even from the door I could see light coming from inside the cupboard that should be dark. I left the craft room and called my brother Kent.

"Howdy." Kent's usual salutation.

"Hey, how's it going?"

"Good, and you?"

"Good. Has today been weird for you?" I asked.

"No . . . are you okay?"

"Yeah, I actually feel pretty happy today."

"Good for you, I'm happy to hear that."

There was a long pause because I still needed his help, but I didn't know what to say.

He broke the awkward silence. "So, what are you up to today?" He obviously knew I'd called for a reason and wanted to get it out of me.

"I just feel like maybe it's a weird day, like—things seem weird, you know?"

"Did you eat gluten?" It sounded like he was trying to decide if this was about gluten or mental wellness.

Gluten makes me hallucinate, everything else of late falls under mental wellness. Usually, if I've accidentally eaten just a little gluten, it was fairly easy to pull me out of the hallucination with a little conversation. "Not that I know of."

"What did you see?"

"Nothing. Really, I just wanted to talk." I felt stupid.

We had a fruitless conversation ending with him saying he better get going, he had work to do. It was fair, because I was lying to him and he knew it. I hung up the phone and grabbed a mug from the counter, slamming it down on my fingers. It hurt . . . a lot. I called my mom and tried to sound more normal. I hoped she would pull me back into reality. By the time I got off the phone, I was 99 percent sure I was totally lucid.

I went back to the craft room. There was still light coming from the cupboard. I sat on the floor, looking through the open panel to the wooden walls on the opposite side of the impossible shop. I sat there for about twenty minutes, contemplating my insanity. I'd been well for quite a while. I was stable anyway. I hoped this wasn't a new symptom of my depression. I'd never hallucinated on anything but gluten before. I sat there for a long time, crying. I thought about Lan and how I couldn't help her, and now, even though I'd been doing so good, I was losing my mind.

Of course I couldn't help her, I can't even help myself.

Crying is something. At least I FEEL sad.

I blew my nose, exhaled all the fear and sadness out, got on my hands and knees, and popped my head into the room below. It was empty. I looked out the front window again, the same three horses looked at me, nodding their heads. I took it as encouragement to come out. I eyed the shelving in the wall below me, and decided I would have to exit feet first, so I turned around, cursed myself, and climbed through the cupboard into the room below. The climb down wasn't bad because the shelves were empty and very well made. I climbed all the way to the bottom and ducked behind the counter to regroup.

The room had a strong smell of wood and oil. I crawled along behind the counter until I reached the front window. There was a two-inch gap, letting me see out into the street. Unfortunately, my view of the street was mostly blocked by the horse tied up right in front of me.

Suddenly I was tired of hiding. I figured if I was hallucinating, I would just have to accept and roll with it—what was the sense of being scared in your hallucinations? Maybe the only way to conquer it was to embrace it and go forth fearlessly. I ducked under the fold up section of the counter, unlocked the front door, and walked out onto a sidewalk in front of the street.

The smell in the street was strong. Horses, horse poop, and dirt. It was hot and sunny, just like it was outside my apartment. People walking down the wooden plank sidewalks were dressed straight out of a western. I had on a T-shirt and cut-off's, with bare feet. I felt a little out of place, but really, they were out of place; after all, it was *my* hallucination.

"Howdy," I said, nodding my head to the dirt-encrusted cowboy walking toward me.

"Howdy." He tipped his hat but looked confused.

I kept walking, imagining he probably turned his head to get a rear view too.

Maybe I'm dreaming this whole thing. Maybe I'm in my bed right now.

This is just a dream, I will not be made to feel uncomfortable in my own dream!

Even though I kept trying to make myself feel brave, I didn't feel brave. I felt out of place—like everyone was looking at me. In a weird way, it felt good to feel uncomfortable. It was something.

I wanted to climb back up the shelving into the safety of my apartment. I forced myself not to, because I didn't want this to become a reoccurring thing. If you don't face things, they come back. Besides, maybe I was on the verge of a breakthrough. Maybe this was some kind of vision with a message of closure.

When the wooden sidewalk ended, and I had to cross the rocky dirt road in my bare feet, I balked a bit. If there hadn't been so much excrement, I probably could have done it. Looking back the way I'd come, there was a much horsier street the next block up. Looking to my left, there were empty dirt lots, crudely surveyed. To my right there was a church, with a very small church yard, and a bench. Straight ahead there were a few houses, spread out with spindly little trees. It was still Virden, but it looked like my town had been about a hundred years ago—not just by what I could see, but what I could no longer see—the comforts of home in the twenty-first-century. I knew, however, that if I kept walking straight forward, I would come across Gopher Creek.

I decided if I had this dream again, I'd make sure I put shoes on so I could cross the street.

I suppose I could just go back and get my shoes.

I walked back toward the empty shop, just to regroup, not to go hide in my bed until the crazy passed. This time, I paid more attention to the shops in between. There was a hardware type store with various tools and nails. I looked through the window and a bunch of dirty faces look back at me. I wanted to face my fears, so I waved, but kept moving. Next up was a barber shop. The barber was using a straight razor.

How cliché.

They paid me no mind, so I kept on walking. The horses tied up along the way seemed mildly interested, I guess because there was nothing else to look at.

Suddenly, I heard a loud racket. I fully expected Dick Van Dyck to start singing "Chitty Chitty Bang Bang." Coming down the street was a huge car my uncle would have loved to have seen.

Ah, if only he was as mentally imbalanced as me.

It was black with silver finishings. It made my little Toyota Camry hatchback look like a Delorian. A man with a bowler hat, round metal glasses, and a waxed moustache was driving. Beside him was a proper looking lady in a hat with a parasol, squinting at me. It was hard to tell if the dusty road was making her squint, or if she was trying to look at me. I preferred to believe it was the microscopic feces irritating her eyes, and not my lack of proper attire. The horses seemed more disturbed by the noise than I was. Along the entire block there were probably fifteen horses tied up, and all of them were shifting hooves, nodding heads and flapping tails. I was impressed with the car, but the ride looked bumpy. Everyone I could see on both sides of the street was staring at the car.

I suddenly felt invincible and incredibly friendly. I ran into the street. I imagined I would jump on the back and say something like, "Would you mind giving me a lift to the crick?" When I made it to the car, I realized it wasn't the kind with a suitcase mount on the back. I spooked the driver who swerved, spooking a couple horses. There was a great commotion.

Why are passing opportunities irresistible to me? If my choice is do nothing or go now, *I always pick* go now! *It's definitely my biggest toxic trait.*

The next thing I knew, I was laying on a hard couch looking up at a wood plank ceiling. There was a beautiful and capable looking woman about my age, wiping my face with a cloth.

"You're awake." She looked both relieved and curious.

I wasn't sure what to say because I wasn't sure what was going on, so I just took it all in.

"Motorcars are dangerous." She looked irritated with the thought, but caring toward me.

"Where am I?"

"You're in the back room of the post office. I was sorting the mail back here. Some men carried you here, from the street, you had an accident," she spoke gently.

I imagined how much trouble I must have been to carry. It made me laugh a little to think of men carrying me into the post office. I was confused again.

When did I get to the post office?

"What am I doing at the post office?" I sat up. Everything was old fashioned, yet brand new.

Obviously, this hallucination isn't over.

"I asked them to bring you here. I don't think you should get up yet." She gently pushed my shoulder until I lay back down. "You have a bit of a gash on your head. It hasn't stopped bleeding yet. My friend is coming to dress it for you. She was a nurse in the war."

"Thank you." I wasn't sure what else to say.

"Where are you from?"

"Um," I wanted to say Virden, but it sure wasn't *this* Virden. "I'm traveling. Do my clothes give me away?"

"Well," she paused," I just haven't seen you before. You didn't have any shoes on when they carried you, do you know where you put them down? I'll fetch them for you."

"Oh . . . thank you. I'm not sure actually. I haven't seen you before either, I've only been here a rather short while. It's a rather complicated story, and I'd rather not speak of such things."
That's a lot of rathers . . . Is this the extent of my old-timey language abilities?

"That's fine. Are you hungry?" She held up a piece of buttered bread.

I was pretty sure she would not know what a gluten allergy was.

I can't have allergic reactions to food I eat in dreams.

"I wasn't until you asked, but that looks really good." I held out my hand to take the bread. She gave it to me on a plate.

"Here you go."

"Thank you."

I took a bite from the corner. It was amazing. It had a slight crunch to the crust, but inside was fluffy, sweet, and buttery. The butter was the creamiest butter I'd ever tasted. The woman was laughing at me, which made me realize I was making all sorts of noises of delight. I couldn't help it. The bread was like cake and the butter like creamy icing.

"This is amazing. I mean this is the best bread and butter I've ever tasted in my life. Where did you get it?" I asked.

"I made it this morning before work. . . . I've never seen short pants before." As soon as she said it, her face turned red.

"Oh, yes. I saw some women in New York wearing them. I just shortened some of my brother's pants for myself. They're much cooler in the hot weather," I said, hoping it was a good cover.

"You've probably never seen this before either." Don't ask me why, but I lifted my arm to show her my hairless armpit.

She jumped back like I'd just mooned her, or worse.

"It's very popular in . . ." I was going to say Paris, but I was pretty sure it *still* wasn't popular in Paris. ". . . in Toronto."

"Oh. Well. Not in Virden. Everyone thinks you're in your underwear." She laughed. "To tell you the truth, you're the most interesting thing to happen in Virden in a long time. Where did you come from?"

I had no idea about train schedules or busses, or even if they had busses. I figured everyone probably knew what everyone else was doing. It was going to be hard to come up with a good answer. I took another bite of bread, then held up my finger, "asking" her to wait while I chewed and tried to think.

"She came with me," said a tall, strikingly handsome man around our age. "I brought her with me today from Brandon— she's my wife."

———◆———

The woman looked surprised, but I can tell you I was more so.

My whole body flushed. Not just my face, I could see my skin go pink, right down to my toes.

There's the jolt I've been waiting for. Do not wake up. Do not wake up. This is getting interesting.

"Zeta, you've got customers at the counter. I can look after her." He urged her out of the room.

He watched Zeta leave, then turned back to me.

"I know who you are. Well, not exactly, but I know where you've come from. You're from the future, from Virden in the future. You came through the portal in the bottom cupboard in the apartment above the accountant's office." His eyes twinkled at me.

I choked on my bread and butter. "What do you mean?"

"I came through the same portal, eight years ago." There was a devilish charm to his smile. No man ever looked at me like that before, not even in my dreams. I mean I'd seen the look before but never directed at me.

"Eight years is a long time, do you ever come back?" I couldn't help but wonder how to interpret a dream about going back in time, meeting a person who left my reality eight years earlier and asking them if they ever go back.

Is my subconscious considering a break from reality, or considering rejoining everyone else's reality, and letting go of whatever protective isolating mental state my outside self might be in right now?

None of this is easy.

"I did for the first several weeks, but no, not after . . . a while." He looked out the window. There was no distant view to look to, the window faced a brick wall, but he wasn't looking at that either, he was looking into his past, which was the relative future, a long way off. "I need to use your computer."

"Okay, let's go." I shoved the last bit of bread in my mouth and followed him. I waved goodbye to Zeta.

"But wait, the nurse!" she said.

"I feel much better, I think all I needed was a bit of rest and your healing bread!"

We walked out the front door and I made a mental note to repay her kindness if I had the chance.

"Where're your shoes?" he asked when we moved toward the street.

"At home. I didn't exactly know I'd be time traveling." . . . I smiled at him.

"May I?" he asked.

I had no idea what he was going to do, but whatever it was, I had no objection.

"Please." I smiled.

He lifted me like we were newlyweds crossing the threshold.

This is the best day of my life.

"When I first started coming, the shop was used for storage, so nobody was ever around. It will be more difficult with them putting something active in there. I'm not sure when they plan to open the new shop. I'll have to see what I can do . . . maybe I can buy us a little time." He wasn't even struggling with his words as he carried me across the street.

Let's make this legal, for realz.

Breathless and struggling to stand on my own when he put me down, I tried to make conversation. "What year is it?"

"Nineteen twenty." He opened the door to the empty shop.

"What's your name?" That probably should have been my first question.

"Sam."

"You probably have twenty thousand emails in your inbox, Sam." I laughed.

"Probably. I'll wait here. Can you bring it down?" He smiled.

"Sure." I climbed up the shelving and handed my laptop down through the opening. "Internet works down here?"

"It did for me before."

I don't have anything super sensitive on my computer, except everything and all my passwords. I climbed down from my apartment and peeked over his shoulder at what he was doing. He was googling people.

"Dammit." He slammed his fist down on the counter.

Yikes.

"What?" I asked.

"Sorry. I have been trying to change some things in a future timeline. It appears I was unsuccessful. I need your help." He smiled and pleaded with raised eyebrows.

"O . . . kayyy." I was a little concerned, but curious, it felt good to wonder.

"We need to get you some clothes and shoes, but first you need to put this back." He closed the laptop and handed it to me. "Do you have a dress and some simple dress shoes you could put on?"

"I do."

I kind of liked his take charge attitude. My get-up-and-go had gone-up-and-left when Lan died.

I hurried back up to my apartment, left the laptop on my desk, and changed in a mad rush. I didn't want him to disappear. Climbing back through the portal I asked, "Is this okay?"

"Perfect." He smiled.

We walked a few short blocks with people staring at us all the way. I heard the word "wife" in many not-so-subtle whispers.

A bell rang as we went through a door. A petite lady came to help us. The shop was full of fabric, lace, hats, and frilly things. There were a few ready-made dresses. She looked at me like I was a Sasquatch. I felt like a Sasquatch. Sam didn't seem to notice. Who was I to care if they'd never come across a hormone fed woman from the twenty-first century before?

The lady huffed and puffed and measured me all up. Sam made the arrangements for pickup.

"Good, let's go." He ushered me out. Half a block down the street, he unlocked a door, and we went up a staircase to a large room above a shop. It was similar to my apartment, only there were no rooms, it was just one big open space. There were tables with books, and notes, and all kinds of projects on the go.

No sooner did we get through the door than there was a knock on it.

"Sam, I heard—" A genetically blessed man stopped short at the door.

"Clive, this is . . ." His eyes widened, which I took to mean he just realized he didn't know my name.

"Lilac. Pleased to meet you." I outstretched my hand.

"How do you know each other?" Clive shook my hand but didn't look at me.

"She came through the portal."

Clive sat down.

"He knows, he's the only one who knows," Sam said to me.

"Can I see?" Clive asked.

"Would that be all right?" Sam asked me.

"What, come through the portal? Sure." I was fake married to one hottie, but then another hunk of a man was begging to come through a portal into my apartment. This was my favorite kind of dream.

"Just remember, the story is—she's my wife," Sam said to Clive, then to me, "I needed an excuse to be alone with you, this is 1920."

"What excuse do I have to be alone with her?" he asked. "You'll have to come through the portal with us."

"I'll go with you to it, but I'm not going to try to go through. You don't need me with you in the future," Sam said. Clive raised an eyebrow.

Sighing, Sam said, "It didn't work."

"What do you mean?" Clive asked.

"The same thing happened."

"Oh," Clive said.

"What happened?" I asked.

"I'll tell you later. How about you take Clive on a tour. I need to think," Sam said.

"Sure." Whatever he was upset about when he was on the computer was obviously a big deal. Emotional. I could give him all the time he needed.

We walked back to the portal.

"Could I use your laptop while you do the tour?" Sam asked.

"Absolutely." I climbed up and retrieved the laptop. I handed it down to him and he went right to work.

Clive came up through the portal.

I wish I'd known I was having company.

My place wasn't messy, but not totally company tidy either.

It took us ten minutes to get out of my craft room because he wanted to know what the iPad, printer, and Cricut were. I gave him a little demo. His mind was sufficiently blown. Super simple things, like my couch, were so foreign to him. He couldn't get over how comfortable it was. The dishwasher, fridge, and stove impressed him. The washing machine and dryer were almost too much for him. The real insanity was TV and video games, the incredulous look on Clive's face was priceless.

Even though he appeared interested, I notice he never looked at me directly in my face or in my eyes. He had a handsome profile, but I couldn't get a good look at his whole face. Like a sign in a dream—you can't quite read it, because the light is too bright or the paint is too washed out.

"Did you just move in?" Clive asked.

"I've been here a year and a half, I guess."

"Who's this?" He pointed to the picture of Lan on my fridge.

"My best friend, Lan."

"I thought she must be important, it's the only picture you have up, even though your studio is full of paintings."

I looked around. He was right, I hadn't even noticed. I had a postcard of the Eiffel Tower laying on top of the fridge. I pulled the magnet from Lan's picture, overlapped the two pictures and used the magnet to stick both to the fridge.

"There, I just doubled my pictures." I laughed.

Clive visibly shuddered when he saw the Eiffel Tower. "Have you been to Paris?"

"No, but I feel like if I could go there, I could get bet—"

Wait, stop. Clive and Sam don't know me as damaged. I'm not "broken" with them. Hold on to that freedom.

"I want to go to Paris to write a book," I said.

"I've been there. It's not a peaceful place to write a book. But hopefully by now they've cleaned up after all the bombing."

I took down the Eiffel Tower postcard. "Were you there . . . in World War I?" I calculated.

"There's more than one?" He hung his head. "I thought it was the Great War—to end all wars."

I was not ready to lay the problems of the world on him. If he was physically upset by a picture of the Eiffel Tower, he could hardly handle the enormity of what had happened since 1920.

"Where would you go?" I asked.

"The Sandwich Islands."

"Sounds delicious."

He laughed. "My great grandfather worked for the Hudson's Bay Company at a post in the Sandwich Islands when he was young. For my grandfather's whole life, he told him about the strong people, fertile land, good food, and pleasing weather. My grandfather told those stories to my father, who then told them to me. I'm sure there couldn't really be such a paradise, but I hope to find out. I think if you want to write a book, you should go to the Sandwich Islands, not Paris. It took him many months to get there, but you will have more to write about the journey."

I was curious. "Now I have to know where this is."

I grabbed my iPad and looked up Sandwich Islands Hudson's Bay Company. "It's called Hawaii now."

I showed him on the map, then zoomed out to show him where we were in relation.

"Mmmmm, many months," he said.

"Not now it isn't. We can fly out of Winnipeg today and get there by tomorrow morning."

Clive looked at me for the first time, right in the eyes, like he was searching for lies. I had to catch my breath, feeling an instant connection.

It's not a connection, he's just gorgeous.

"Tomorrow?" he asked.

"Yes."

He whistled. "Not in any plane I've ever flown."

"You're a pilot?" I was a little obsessed with aviation. Or, I used to be, before Lan died. When I used to care about things.

"I was." He didn't elaborate, and by his stiffness, I sensed not to press further.

"Do you want to see pictures of the Sandwich Islands?" I asked.

"Yes," he said.

We sat on the couch, side by side, our feet up on the coffee table, looking at pictures of Hawaii.

"It's everything he said it was, perhaps more," Clive said. "I knew it was real."

It gave me a high, showing Clive all of these things. I absorbed his joy somehow. "Come look out the window."

He looked, but didn't say anything—his eyes wide as he took it all in.

"Wanna go for a walk out there?"

"I need to tell you something." He looked out the window while he spoke. "I wanted to believe Sam came from the future, but sometimes I worried I was just as delusional as he was, like we were both caught up in a fantasy. I'm relieved it's all true. I want to go to the Sandwich Islands. I want you to show me everything, but since this really is all true, and what he was trying to do didn't work, we have work to do."

"What do you mean?"

"I think it's better if Sam tells you." That little bit of intrigue suddenly made me ten times more attracted to his facial hair. I doubted Clive's interest in my facial hair, though.

Ha ha. Doesn't matter, I'm married to Sam.

Back we went through the portal, to 1920.

⁌━━━●▬━━━⁍

"There are some things I'd like you to print for me, if you wouldn't mind. I made a list in your notes app." Sam clicked on them to show me.

"Okay."

At the top of the list, he'd written: History of Sam Gabler.

"Is your name Sam Gabler?" I asked.

"Yes."

"I learned about a Sam Gabler in school. The first guy to patent genetically modified seed."

"That's me." Sam seemed delighted.

"You gave it for free use, but nobody knew what to do with it, so it was another sixty years until genetically modified seeds became a thing. There's a statue of you in the park. You and Boston Pizza are Virden's claim to fame."

"I did Boston Pizza too."

"What do you mean?"

"I mean, when I was going back and forth through the portal, at first there was no Boston Pizza, the next day, there was."

"How did you do it?"

"I don't know. All I know is, one day there was Boston Pizza, and everyone acted like it had always been there. The only connection I can make is the founder was from Virden," Sam said.

"Thanks. I like Boston Pizza."

"I can't believe there's a statue of you!" Clive's strong hand pushed Sam's muscular shoulder.

Good grief, stop looking at them.

"It's probably covered with bird poop," Sam said.

I shrugged. "All statues are."

"Does it look like him?" Clive asked.

Sam struck a superhero pose.

"I'll let you be the judge." I laughed. Truthfully, he was much better looking in person.

I looked down the list. There was a subheading, *Expired Patents*, with a whole list of crop seeds.

"What are these expired patents for?" I asked.

"Did you learn anything about GM seed companies in school?"

"Just that they're a nasty bunch." I remembered a documentary we'd watched.

Sam stood up. "There's nothing inherently wrong with genetic modification, I'm just trying to stop it from being a huge money maker, to take the nasty out."

"Of all the problems in the world, why that one?"

"It's not some big secret, but it makes me angry, and when I'm angry I can't focus. Just give me time to think," Sam said.

"Right, sorry. Either way, it's a good problem to tackle. GM seed companies make huge profits and regularly bankrupt the little guys." I had this tiny attraction to his anger. I used to get angry, but I didn't have it in me anymore. I wished I could feel passionate indignation again. If he would tell me why he was mad, maybe I could feel blood pulsing in my veins again.

"We get another chance. You're here and we've got time. We can still fix this." Sam smiled at me, inspiring me to do whatever he had in mind.

"Fix what? Sorry!"

Whoops. It's hard not to ask obvious questions.

"I need time, but I promise I'll tell you. Just know you're a life saver, literally. I need to go think about the information I reviewed today. Thank you for everything Lilac," he said.

"I'll try to get as many of the items on this list as I can."

"Thank you, I really appreciate it." He hugged me, all my soft bits squishing out between the angles of his hard angry body.

Get a grip.

"Hey, could you bring some Coke and ice next time? . . . I miss the silliest things."

"I could bring it right now."

"No, but next time."

"Are you sure you don't want to come up?" I tried to be enticing to my new handsome husband. "Phone some of your family or something?"

Sam's face turned hard. "No. Thanks . . . It's been a big day, and I have lots of planning to do. I'm excited you've come. Is this your only computer?" Sam asked.

"I have an iPad, but this is my only laptop."

"Okay. Thanks. I think it'll be easier for you to get the things on the list with the laptop," he said, handing it to me.

"I can bring it back when I'm done," I suggested.

"Clive, do you want to come back with me now and watch TV? I'll make you dinner."

"Thank you for your kind offer, but I'm going to stay and help Sam with the game plan, but I'd like a Coke and ice too, I want to try everything!" Clive grinned.

Double rejection. This feels normal.

"I'll bring them for sure," I promised.

This is the most lucid dream I've ever had. What did I have for lunch?

I climbed back into my apartment and turned around just in time to see the back door closing behind the men. I pulled the panel back in place, shut my cupboard doors, and I sat in the middle of my craft room and cried.

I'm crazy for sure.

CHAPTER 2

Zeta

♫ "I Love You" ♫
by Sarah McLachlan

Porca miseria! Wife? Why did I wait so long to tell him?

I watched Sam walk out the door with his wife.

I should have made him a priority.

Maybe they're not married yet. When I came, Phillip didn't marry me for a few days. She doesn't look like a picture bride, though. At least, for me, I tried to look pretty when I arrived to meet my husband to be. A waste of effort on Phillip, but still, I tried.

After work, though—yes, I did. I went to Sam's. To refine the point, I went across the street from Sam's to the rooftop and watched Sam in his place, alone. The wife woman wasn't with him. At midnight, I was satisfied she would not be coming. I went to him.

"Zeta?" Sam opened the door appearing tired but looked happy to see me.

"Sam, I was on my way home and I saw your lights on. I came to wish you and your bride felicity. It came as a surprise that you . . . were married. I'm happy for you."

"Uh, thank you. I . . . you know I . . . I thank you." He turned red in patches coming up from his neck. I'd seen him like this before. "Has there been any news on Phillip?"

Tell him. Just tell him now before it's too late.

But this woman has come. She deserves happiness too.

But not with my Sam.

"Nothing solid on Phillip."

Coward, I'm a coward and I deserve to lose him. I made him wait too long.

"May I give your bride my best?" I could feel a blush coming over my face as well. We'd been doing this dance for so long, it was silly to still feel this way.

"She's not here tonight . . . yet . . . between you and me . . . she's not here. But just for tonight. She will be here," he stammered.

"We go back a long way, Sam. I'm proud of you. You make me proud to be human. You've faced injustice and personal loss, and I don't know all the details exactly, but you dominated it. Now you're married. Congratulations." I turned, crying all the way down the stairs, and the whole ride home.

I just about have everything I've been working for. But Sam was a part of that, and I let him go because he thinks I'm married and still waiting for Phillip to come home from the war.

CHAPTER 3

Lilac

♫ **"Daddy Cop"** ♫
by Zander Hawley

I was completely disoriented. My craft room was littered with the contents of the cupboard, and if I didn't clean my brushes soon, I'd probably ruin them. It felt like only minutes ago that I'd been peacefully painting.

That could not have been real. My family is going to be so disappointed in me. Mom has done so much to help me. She got me my job, this place. Why do I have to be crazy?

I was crippled with anxiety; I lay down on the floor and cried myself to sleep.

When I woke up, I was still totally disoriented. It was dark and I was on a hard floor. I realized I was in my craft room, and then I remembered. There was only moonlight coming in from the skylights. I looked at the cupboard door. I couldn't bring myself to crawl inside and look to make sure it really was a portal to the past. I felt like I was losing my mind.

I walked through my apartment feeling lonely and scared. Everything looked sad and dark. I wanted to call my mom or Kent again, but for sure they would know something was up, and I hated making them worry, so I decided to watch TV. I made a nest on the couch and watched *Columbo* until I fell asleep.

The next morning, I decided not to look through the cupboard door. It wasn't how I wanted to start my day. Instead, I called up Uncle and asked if I could look at some of his stuff. He's a great collector of old things. I thought it would feed my fantasy, which was bad, but incredibly irresistible all the same.

"What do you want to see?" He was already walking from his house to my car when I arrived, grasshoppers springing out of the way in his wake.

"All your treasures." It was true, I did.

"I don't think you could handle so much glory in one day," he teased.

"Well, we gotta start somewhere," I said. "I wanna see your really old stuff. What do you have older than, say 1920?" Just to be totally random and not connected to my delusions at all.

"Before 1920? Lots of things. Do you want to see arrowheads or aboriginal artifacts? Or are you thinking cars and bikes?"

I was thinking about things I could fit through the cupboard door. If it was real, and it was feeling very real, maybe I could somehow financially benefit. Maybe I could figure out what things to bring from the past to the future for profit, but also, if I had money or things I could take into the past for profit, it would be beneficial too.

Maybe I watch too many movies.

"Um, do you have any . . ." I hated to ask, it seemed so blunt. ". . . money?" Sometimes you've just gotta say what you want.

"From before 1920? I'm sure I do. Come with me."

We walked out to the biggest of his outbuildings. There were antique tractors, old cars and bikes, all in various stages of being refinished and rebuilt. Along the back wall was a counter running the length of the wall, just high enough to comfortably put my elbows on it. *The perfect height for working.* There were three shelves made from 2x4s running the length of the wall. Jars, sealers, tins, and cans lined the shelves. There were watch parts, screws, nuts and bolts, buttons, fuses, and keys. Pretty much everything you could imagine fitting in a jar, had a jar. He pulled out a scratched, rusty crackers tin, pushed a space clear on the counter with his forearm and dumped it out on the counter.

"There should be some in here," he said, smiling.

There were all kinds of coins. It looked like a jar full of foreign coins because they were all different shapes and sizes, but they were all Canadian! The light from the window revealed the date on each one. Some were worn right down to the point I could hardly tell they were a coin, but some of them were so clear, it was hard to believe they were so old.

I started separating them into pre-1920 coins.

"I'm trying to get a feel for what it would be like to live in 1920 for a book I'm thinking of writing." I didn't really know what to say; it wasn't like I could say it was for a school project. At the same time, Uncle was such an open-minded inventor, he might just believe I'd been time travelling. I wasn't sure whether to tell him or not. *Feel him out first.*

"I didn't know you were writing a book!" he said, surprised.

Suddenly I wasn't sure which was weirder, writing a book, or time travelling. Maybe they both seemed deranged.

I held the hugest penny I'd ever seen toward the light to get a better look. "Yeah, well, I'm just thinking about it. Hey, so if you could have anything from the 1920's, what would it be, like what would be valuable today?"

"Well, I'd like a Manitoba license plate from 1911, and I think it would be a lot easier to come by in 1920 than today." He pointed up to the banner of our province's license plates encircling the room. I followed the colourful border through the sizes and uses, and realized the only year missing was 1911.

"Are they hard to find?"

He scoffed and turned his head away. "I've been searching my whole life."

"A hundred and fifty years?"

He rolled his eyes at me.

"What do these go for today?" I asked about the coins.

"Well, a good one, like this…" Uncle held up the clearest one. "…would probably go for about two bucks. They aren't expensive, they're fairly common. A fifty-cent piece like this would probably go for fifteen dollars, and a quarter for ten. It all depends on condition, and what somebody is willing to pay."

I was trying to calculate what fifty cents would be worth in 1920. "Do you have any catalogs from 1920? What would fifty cents buy me?"

"Well, let's see." He walked over to a large bookshelf and ran his finger along until he came to 1920. "Do you want spring or fall?"

"Um, spring." *Why not?*

He pulled the catalog off the shelf and wiped the dust off with his shirt. "1920 Eaton's Catalog. That should help."

I sat down on an old couch with a few springs poking through the cushions. It had an ornately carved wooden frame and overstuffed velvet cushions. Uncle whistled to himself as he did other things around the shop. I was totally mesmerized by the catalog. I started calculations on my calculator watch. Fifteen dollars for a watch in 1920, and fifteen dollars for a fifty-cent piece, in good condition, from the right time. Fifteen dollars divided by fifty cents equaled thirty. Thirty fifty-cent pieces at fifteen dollars each, would make the watch cost me four hundred and fifty dollars, if I bought old money now and took it back with me.

Not a great deal, unless of course it was worth a thousand bucks today.

"Hey Uncle, how much would this watch go for today, if you had one in mint condition?" I asked. He knew lots about antique hunting.

"Probably two hundred bucks, pretty good, eh? Fifteen dollars turns into two hundred in just over a hundred years!" He laughed and carried on digging in a big blue trunk.

Not good actually. Maybe buying old money now isn't a good idea.

"How much did people make a day in 1920? Like, say, a secretary?" I didn't really believe I could work in the fields, but maybe I could get some kind of job in the past?

"Just off the top of my head, I think it would have been around a thousand bucks a year." He started hitting something with a hammer.

One thousand dollars, divided by twelve months equaled eighty-three dollars and thirty-three cents a month, divided by twenty workdays a month (*or did they work six days a week . . . ?*) equaled four dollars and sixteen cents per day of work. So, to buy a fifteen-dollar watch I'd have had to have worked three point six days, buy the watch, then sell it for two hundred dollars. That meant I'd have made six dollars and ninety-four cents an hour, not including the time it would take to buy or sell the watch.

There has to be a better way.

If I was going to believe in time travel, it would have to be more in my favor. It seemed like even with time travel, there still wasn't an easy way to make ends meet. It was like there was never quite enough. Life always left you a little bit hungry, or a little bit lacking somewhere.

I kept looking through the catalog for ideas, things that are valuable today, but were cheap back then. There was gold jewelry, but it worked out about the same. Then I started thinking that if I had something with a name, like a Tiffany gold ring, it would probably be worth a lot more. But how would I get my hands on a piece of Tiffany jewelry in 1920 Virden?

"Have you ever seen any Tiffany jewelry from these parts?" I asked him.

"Tiffany? No, I don't think so. I couldn't tell you for sure, but I don't recall."

Blast.

Tea sets, silverware, knives, purses, instruments, they all worked out about the same. The key had to be in collectables.

I took my notebook out of my pocket to start a list and wrote: first edition books, Tiffany, research if available in Virden. This was my one chance, and I didn't want to blow it. I felt like I had my mom's spaghetti on my sweatshirt already. I added: make movies? Maybe the best thing about access to 1920 was I didn't need a cast, crew, and costumes. It was all right there, ready to be filmed. I just had to find the right slant.

Then I came across guns. I knew there were rare and valuable guns but selling them would be a real pain since I would need a license and explain where they came from. Might be more trouble than it was worth.

At thirty dollars, present day money for every one dollar in 1920 money, there were no good deals to be had.

Did they have garage sales? Probably not. They were not the generation to throw things away; they used and fixed things until they were worthless, and kept things they didn't use—just in case— they'd ever need it.

"Do you have anything really valuable from that time?" I asked. It was way too personal to ask. You really shouldn't ask questions like that if you're over five.

"I'm not going to die anytime soon, and I don't have a trunk of gold coins if that's what you're after," he said dryly, and shifted further underneath the car he was working on.

"I didn't mean . . . I just . . . I'm just trying to figure out how time travel could be lucrative." The most basic truth I could tell.

"Well, you could always invest in the stock market."

"I don't even know how to do that today; plus, wouldn't the payoff take a long time?"

"Well, if you have a time machine, you just go into the future and collect."

"What if you can only go to one time, every time?"

"That's no fun." He laughed.

"Well, nobody said it was going to be fun, it's just the way it is."

"Well, if you aren't writing it for fun, maybe you should quit."

"What if it's real?" I wanted to ask, but I was afraid he'd tell Mom, and I'd end up back in the mental hospital. "Didn't the stock market crash in 1920?"

"1929."

"What stocks were hot in the twenties? Did any take huge hikes in the summer of 1920?"

"I don't know, google it."

I went home after lunch and googled for hours about the stock market in 1920 looking for specifics, but I had a hard time finding anything helpful. I knew the information was out there, but I would probably have to go to archives on Wall Street to find them.

Were stocks even available in Virden in 1920?

Would it be wrong to play the market if I knew the results? Isn't that why Martha Stewart went to jail? I want to craft and cook and garden like her, but I don't want to go to jail—or even be guilty of something jail worthy.

I wrote off the idea of stocks. I decided to bark up the Tiffany tree. The only original prices I could find online were for candlesticks and candelabras. They actually seemed fairly reasonable, until I did the thirty-dollars-of-my-time money to one-dollar-of-1920 money. Then it was pretty bad. In fact, I would be halving my money. Candelabras were out, but lamps went for big money, and I found out that by the 1920's, they were considered old fashioned, and people were giving them away to their maids. So, I figured my best plan was to be a maid and be gifted a Tiffany lamp. *Ridiculous. Look at this apartment. I'd be the worst maid ever. I'd probably get beaten.*

I worked on the list Sam gave me. Much of the information was in the public domain and free to access, but certain sites required signing up for accounts. It was time consuming, but not difficult. I printed out everything while I ate dinner. I packed up the printouts to take to Sam. *Or spend a few hours passed out and delusional in my craft room cupboard, it's hard to know what's really happening for sure. Maybe there's some kind of gas leak in there.*

I was putting a lot of effort into something I wasn't fully convinced was real, but it felt good to think about something new.

It's been a long time since I felt anything inside.

I put on my dress clothes, rolled my eyes at myself in the mirror, and headed for the craft room.

It was still daylight outside, even though it was about five thirty. The room looked so normal. It didn't look like Doctor Who's TARDIS, with switches and levers and panels. It looked like craft heaven, not a time machine of any sort.

I closed my eyes and tried to think of reasons to not climb through the cupboard. I decided the only reason was because I feared being crazy.

If I am, I may as well have fun instead of being the sad sort of crazy. If I have early passage on a cruise ship that's really a mental institution, well, so be it. It was probably inevitable.

I pushed the back panel a little and listened for voices. I didn't hear any, so I pushed it a little more and surveyed the room. Nobody was there, but on the counter below me, there was an envelope with "Lilac" written in modern-day-guy's chicken scratch.

I climbed down the shelving as carefully as I could, but still trying to be quick, just in case someone saw me through the window. I grabbed the envelope, and ducked behind the counter, eager to read Sam's letter.

Lilac,

You don't have to worry about anyone coming into this shop anymore. I've rented the space. I'll tell you more when I see you. I just wanted you to know you're safe in there. Come to my lab. I'll be there almost night and day until I see you again. I have more research I need you to do for me. Please come as soon as possible.

Sam

It was exciting to be part of something bigger than myself. I got a flash of Sam's face in my mind and felt a little flutter in my stomach thinking of seeing him again.

Imaginary men are the best.

I exited the back door and headed for Sam's lab. As I walked, I wondered if there would be times coming through the portal when it would be raining on my side and sunny on his. It seemed obvious it would have to happen like that, but I was no expert on time travel or mental diseases. One thing was for sure: mosquitos' love was timeless.

I climbed the staircase to Sam's lab, with the smell of freshly cut wood shooting to my brain. It was different coming up the stairs by myself. Instead of ogling Sam's backside, I took in my surroundings. In my time, this office was a heritage building with years of patina on it, but in Sam's time, it was brand new. New wood, fresh paint, rough edges, and the only illumination was through the transom windows above the doors. I loved it. I was happy to be a time traveler, or a crazy person, whatever the truth was, I felt happier than I had in a while.

May as well enjoy it.

I knocked briefly on the door before opening it. I was Sam's wife after all, what would a visitor think if I waited to be let in?

And maybe he's doing chin-ups on a pipe with his shirt off.

Sam was standing at a table covered with papers, watching me walk toward him.

"Lilac. I'm happy to see you. Thank you for coming back. I thought you might not. I thought I was crazy the first few times I came through the portal." He was clearly relieved to see me.

"Thanks for renting the shop, it does makes it less stressful."

"I told them I was picking up waves in the area, and I wanted to research them for a month or so."

"What kind of waves?"

"Unspecified. It cost a fortune to get them to delay their opening, but really, what's money? I can always get more."

"Since you brought it up, how do you make money here?"

"I invent things." He looked down at his papers. "I invent small modern conveniences, like teabags for instance."

"Isn't that wrong? Won't it change the timeline or events? Won't it change the financial situation of the true first inventors?"

"Well, maybe. If so, they can find a portal and come back and invent it before me. I can't worry about everyone else. They'll have to take advantage of whatever they're presented with."

I didn't like his answer. It felt wrong, but at the same time, logical . . . in a selfish sort of way.

How do I know if the person who supposedly invented the tea bag really did? Maybe they were a time traveler too?

"How do you know you I wasn't supposed to change things?" he asked.

"Then why isn't the world a better place?"

Sam looked perplexed. "Who says whatever controls the portal is good?"

A shiver ran down my spine and made the hairs on the back of my neck stand on end.

"Is there something dark I don't know? Are you . . . suffering in some way?" I asked.

"No. I mean yes, but. . . . Please, sit." He motioned toward two plush leather chairs near the window.

"I brought the information you asked for." I handed him the envelope.

"Thank you." He set it on the table.

I sat down, taking in the smell of fresh leather, and feeling heat radiating from the sun on my face.

"Here." He handed me a glass with a few fingers of amber liquid and sat down across from me with his own.

He took a swig and started in. "My family farmed in North Dakota for over a hundred years. In fact, I've gone and met them in this time and found they work hard. It's been a struggle. They cleared the land by hand. They plant and harvest by hand, with the help of a few animals. They live in a small shack and a tent.

"By the time I was a kid they'd built up to a nice farmhouse with a proud barn and paddocks, beautiful, bountiful crops, healthy animals, and a healthy happy family. It was generations of work to build up what we had. Genetically modified seed blew onto our property, took root and grew. Come harvest, a seed corporation, which doesn't exist in your time, sued our farm for growing their seed without buying it. As if we wanted their demon seed in our land." He almost spit the last sentence out. His face was turning red in blotches.

"My father tried to fight them, but in the end, they bankrupted our heritage farm with legal battles." He paused for a long time.

I could tell he wasn't finished. There was more to the story. He took deep breaths with his eyes closed. I sat quietly and waited—my eyes focused on him. "My father had every piece of equipment paid for, no mortgage on our land, no car payments, he was wise with money, and we lived within our means. Every time he needed a new piece of equipment, he saved up for it. He didn't believe in living on credit. They took everything from us. All for seed that blew onto our property. My father, the kindest, gentlest, strongest man I knew died of a heart attack the day they came to remove us from the farm. They'd drawn out the battle for many years and on that last day, when he lost all the work of the generations before him, I lost him." He turned away and wiped his cheek.

I pulled myself to the edge of my seat so our knees were touching, and I reached out and put my hand on his hand.

"My mother hung herself in the barn three weeks later in some kind of protest." He put his glass down and stared out the window into the distance.

I felt a sharp stab to my chest.

This part I understand. I know how it feels.

Tears rolled down my face.

"All this time I thought I had fixed it because I registered the patent for the seed that blew onto our land. But when I looked it up on your laptop, it hadn't fixed anything. The same thing happened, just with another seed, another company."

I leaned forward and reached out for a hug. He put his arms around me and sobbed into my shoulder.

When he'd settled down, I said, "I can't imagine going through everything you went through. You're so strong. You took immediate action to help your family. You registered that patent and changed history. I'm impressed and amazed. How many people do that?"

"Who knows? I did, and you probably will too. Maybe history is changing all the time."

I squeezed him. "You killed that GM seed company. They don't even exist anymore. You have my full attention and respect, for sure. You fought back at the first opportunity you had. I'll do anything I can to help you. We won't give up—we'll fight until it works. Your family would be proud of you, and I am too. You make me proud to be human. You faced injustice and personal loss, and you dominated it."

He kissed my neck, pulling me closer to him.

My body was on fire. He woke something up in me. A sleeping tigress.

I was not expecting that.

I closed my eyes and pressed my chest to his, tipping my head back, and giving in to the sensation.

His passion and urgency felt asymmetrical to our conversation.

I don't know how we got here, but I'm all in.

He lifted me up and leaned me against a table. His powerful body, desperate with need, pushed the table, causing screeching noises as it slid across the floor, faster and faster until we hit the wall. He crashed his mouth to mine, leaning me back across the table, kissing me like he would die if he stopped. I was in shock, but not unappreciative.

There was a knock at the door.

Don't stop.

Don't stop.

Sam stopped kissing me, straightening himself while he pulled me to sit up on the table, and then opened the door.

"Lilac, hi." Clive took in the situation.

"Hi." I smoothed my dress back in place and pushed a wayward section of hair behind my ear.

"I wanted to see if it worked," Clive said.

"We didn't get to that yet." Sam reached behind me for the package I brought with me. "I told her everything."

Clive nodded.

They looked at the pages with interest.

"Are you going to have to register the second generation too?" Clive asked.

"It's never ending," Sam said. "I'm so glad you're here Lilac, and I'm glad we have time."

"What's going on?"

"Clive, could you show her? I need to think," Sam said.

Clive found the sheet of paper with the timeline of GM seed production in the U.S. "See, Sam's first patent was registered here and then all the patents you just brought him are registered later this year, but by the time his dad is farming, there are second generations of seed for the same crops."

"But I swear—it wasn't like this when I printed it out."

"It probably changed when you gave the patents to Sam because he intends to register them," Clive said.

"So, if we do things to affect the timeline of GM seed production, it will show up on this page?"

"That was the theory Sam came up with. . . . He's had a while to think about things."

"If I print out information about Sam's family, the decisions we make will be reflected in that, right?"

"It worked with this, so I assume it will work if we print information about Sam's family too. Hear that, Sam?" Clive yelled across the room. "The idea worked! The information is different than when she printed it. We can print your family information to help us make decisions."

The page flickered to a rearranged timeline.

"Did you see that?" I asked Clive.

"What?"

"I . . . thought it changed again."

Clive examined the page carefully. "Looks the same to me."

"Yeah, it changed back, it was just a flicker."

We both watched it. Nothing happened.

"Please do go print it," Sam said.

"Do you guys want to come back to the shop with me, maybe there's more things we should print?" I asked.

"Yes, we'll come," Sam said.

I printed three copies of news articles about his family, and two more copies of the GM seed timeline. We sat on the floor of the shop brainstorming. We started off with "what if" sentences. Nothing changed.

"Maybe we need to be more decisive. Instead of saying 'what if,' try saying 'I will,' and mean it."

"I will register every generation of patent we can get our hands on until the portal closes," Sam said.

The GM timeline changed, flickering through a few timelines. It was like changing TV channels in quick succession. It settled with a change in the GM timeline, but Sam's family history didn't change.

"See, it flickered." I said. "What do you mean 'until the portal closes'?"

"I saw that, the flickering," he said "As for the portal, what I mean is that the portal had closed on me before. One day, I went to go back, but I couldn't. The portal had closed," Sam said.

"What do you mean?"

"Obviously you didn't tell her everything." Clive looked frustrated with Sam.

"I should go." I stood up.

"It was open for eight weeks," Sam said. "Please don't go, I need you. You have time. Don't leave."

"Sam." Clive gave Sam a stern look.

"It's true," Sam said.

"They've been working on this shop for almost a month. Did you hear any noise before yesterday?" Clive asked.

"No."

"Were you in your craft room often?"

"Every day."

"Okay. I'm not pretending I understand how all this works, but it seems like, according to Sam's experience, you should have time, but please don't feel pressured in any way to be here. It's risky. You need to do what's best for you," Clive said.

Sam flashed his million-dollar grin at me. "I need you Lilac, please help me."

I haven't been anything but dead weight for a long time.

I sat back down.

I could still taste his kisses. I wanted more.

Stop being needy, that unearned passion is a red flag. Is it though? It's been a long time.

I looked at Sam, and my heart fluttered.

—◆—

"I will establish myself as a botanist, and lobby for price control on seeds," Sam stated.

The seed timeline had changed again, but his family's news remained the same.

"You are doing it. Obviously, your word means a lot," I said.

He's a man of action.

I need action in my life.

His word is his bond.

His kiss said he loves me, his mouth said he needs me, he means it.

"It's possible, so, we just need to find the right plan," Clive said.

We all shot out ideas for the next half hour, getting Sam to say them, and mean it. As words were spoken, the timeline events would randomly flicker. Nothing changed on either sheet, though.

"Why are they changing randomly?" I asked.

"Maybe time quickly plays out, then lands somewhere?" Sam said.

"But sometimes when we haven't even said something, it changes, or changes back," I said.

"Maybe it's because we're thinking something," Clive said.

"I don't like the idea that sheets of paper can read my mind." I laughed but could feel myself blushing. I looked at the floor.

"Maybe it's because, ultimately, we have free will and accidents happen. There is no fate. We're not locked in," Clive said.

"Okay, so if we go with that . . . then we just have to get the results going in the right direction, it might flicker around within a range," Sam said.

"So, maybe until the time passes that you actually register those patents, it's up in the air," I offered.

"When does time become set then? For example, these news articles and timelines—is there instantly an alternate timeline with its own history and future created, with every thought we have, every minute decision we make?" Clive asked.

"It would have to be," Sam said.

We sat there—all a bit mind blown. It was one thing to read about such a phenomenon in a book, or see it in a movie, it was another to accept it as reality.

"I feel this incredible weight of all the sad versions of myself out there, infinite sadness," I said.

The guys nodded.

"Infinite happy versions too," Clive said.

"I can't go there," Sam said. "Until proven otherwise, how about we say nothing's locked in as happened until the person who will take the action, actually does it. Up to that point there are infinite decisions, no—for the sake of sanity let's say—several decisions or circumstances that could alter an outcome. Until I actually register the patents, there is the possibility that I will do it—and there is also the possibility that I won't."

"Does that mean the world in my timeline is changing every few seconds, in millions of ways, because of decisions people are making right now?" I asked.

"If they are, you haven't noticed it until now, so you've adapted. Don't think about it," Sam said.

Do not be crippled by this. Everything is okay. Focus.

Is Lan alive in infinite timelines?

I hope she is.

I refocused on the tasks at hand. "It makes sense for now. I wouldn't say we should lock that idea in, although it sounds feasible."

But we did lock it in.

❧

We were tired and brain fried. Nobody had more ideas about how to fix Sam's family's disaster.

Time to regroup.

"Maybe we can get a fresh perspective if we go back to the basics. Sam, what's the goal here? I mean on a personal level. What are you hoping for? What does success look like?" I asked.

"It looks like genetic modification not ruining farming for the small farmer. And my family being together and happy, farming our land forever."

"Noble."

Still nothing. No fresh ideas popped up.

"Should I order us some food? Chinese?"

"Yes!" Sam said.

"I like food." Clive laughed.

"Should I bring us rum and Cokes too?"

"Shhhhhhh." Clive put his finger to his mouth. "Prohibition."

"Oh, right, of course." I looked around. "But who's going to hear us?"

"I don't know, but they always do." Clive laughed. "Isn't Coke the great national temperance beverage?"

"Not in my experience." I became moonshine-slinging Black-jack Lilac right before their eyes. "Are you in?"

"That'd be mighty fine," Clive said.

Sam nodded.

"I'll be back," I said, climbing through the portal, and placed the order.

I picked up the Chinese food for three along with forks, chopsticks and napkins. I added three cans of Coke to the bag, filled three chilled glasses full of ice and a healthy slosh of rum.

The guys had papered the windows while I was gone. It made the room dark, so I brought my Hybrid Light lantern with me. It set the perfect mood.

"Good work on the windows. It feels safer in here."

"Especially if we're drinking rum," Clive whispered.

I laughed.

"I brought cans because I feel like hearing the can open is part of it."

"Totally," Sam said.

We sat on the floor behind the counter and gave Clive a lesson in opening a pop can, and proper pouring procedure. He got a kick out of it.

"Don't you just want to show him everything?" I asked Sam.

He took a drink. "Yeah." He looked down at the floor. "Yeah, I do."

We ate and drank. We showed Clive how to use chopsticks. He picked it up pretty good, but he was slow, and hungry, so he gave them up and used the fork.

Even after we had eaten and drunk our rum and Cokes, we still didn't have any good ideas.

"I think I'm getting tired. I'm not sure I can say things and mean it anymore tonight. I gotta go to bed. I'll work on it tomorrow," Sam said.

"Maybe we should take Clive for a tour, up there."

"I'm not going through the portal," Sam said.

"It won't close for a few weeks you said."

"I don't want to risk it."

"But you don't mind if I do?" I laughed sarcastically.

"I need your help," Sam said.

Don't you care about me? I'm a person too.

Clive frowned at Sam.

"I'm afraid it was personal. Like maybe it will close on me, specifically," Sam clarified. "You guys go have fun, see if the statue looks like me."

"But won't we need a fire extinguisher?" Clive asked Sam.

"No."

"A fire extinguisher?" I asked.

"A chaperone," Sam smiled.

I turned fifty shades of red. "Oh."

Sam didn't hug me, kiss me, or even say goodbye. He just left. Clive and I packed the whole mess of our meals back into the bag.

"You know the portal might close right? It's a real risk," I said.

"I understand," Clive said, looking at the shelving. "One hour, then we call it a night and get ready for tomorrow, because Sam's work is much more important than opening aluminium cans."

Clive followed me through the portal into my apartment.

"I want to show you my car, but I don't want to drive it because I've been drinking."

"Good. One more thing, am I your brother? If we run into someone?" he asked.

Sam's kisses still lingered on my face and neck. But frankly, I thought he might be a bit moody and self-centred.

He's under an incredible amount of stress, he's focused—not selfish. Is it even selfish to put your family above yourself? I'd be moody, too, if I went through all of that. I have been moody, and I only lost one friend.

Still, I didn't want to close the door on Clive. I hadn't felt anything in years, and now I had all the feels.

I gift to broken me the agency to explore these good feelings, from wherever or whomever they may come.

"Um, no. It's okay. If anyone asks, you're my friend, but I doubt we're going to run into anyone who'll want to talk."

"Okay."

Clive's clothes were fine. He looked like a hipster. A hipster I wanted to know. I really wanted to know what his beard felt like.

I stopped at the bottom of the stairs. "Maybe we shouldn't do this, I'm being selfish. I want to show you everything, but there's work to do."

Clive gently gripped my upper arms, and electricity shot through me. I could see he felt it too.

After a beat, he said, "We have to pace ourselves. It's one hour. We are helping Sam, we're going to be successful, but we still have to live. There's nothing more we can do tonight. Who knows, something we see tonight might give us the answer."

I liked what he said—and how close he was when he said it. I hoped we would have an epiphany, but mostly I was hoping he wasn't thinking my arms were fat.

He didn't know how to open the car door but quickly figured it out. I turned on the radio. He looked so delighted I could hardly stand it. I wanted to play him all my favourite songs.

I sprayed the windshield, and the windshield wipers came on.

"Nifty! I've seen those on the streetcars in New York." He pushed the button to spray the windshield. "Never on a motorcar though, where does the water come out?"

I popped the hood, demonstrated how to open the door from the inside, then showed him how the water sprayed on the windshield. When we were done with my freaking incredible car, we walked on our way.

Everything is perspective.

He was able to pick out heritage buildings. I didn't want to go to the grocery store—the one place I always ran into people I knew—but we had a big gas station because of our location right on the Number One. I never run into locals inside the gas station. It was a bit of a walk, but I thought it would blow his mind, so we continued.

On the way he asked me about my family, and he told me about his parents and two older sisters. Clive had traveled over much of Europe during the war, so it wasn't enjoyable. He didn't want to return. He liked music, though of course, we didn't have any artists or songs in common.

From the gas station's automatic doors to the music playing over the PA system, Clive was enthralled. He kept looking at everything he saw, then looking at me, as if it was all amazing. Our totally standard gas station convenience store was unbelievable to him.

I bought far too many things I wanted him to try.

We detoured through the park on the way home, but by then the light wasn't great for seeing the statue. We stood really close, Sam looked like a great man, high above us.

"You're right, it doesn't look like him." Clive laughed.

We were getting eaten alive by mosquitos, not exactly romantic, but I wanted it to be. I wanted to feel the electricity that shot through me when he touched me earlier, but he stayed at a proper distance and spoke respectfully.

We were out exploring longer than an hour, and Clive went back through the portal with a pillowcase full of stuff for him to try. I figured it would look like a time-appropriate sack.

I went for a midnight snack and to talk to Lan.

"Is it weird that these two guys are dominating my thoughts, instead of *time travel*?"

She didn't answer me, she never did. I loved seeing her, though. Perfect skin, the soft curved lines of her face. I could imagine her laughing at me. She always thought I was frivolous and wild, but in a good way.

I'm not frivolous and wild anymore.

"I wish I could go back and fix you."

Maybe you're happy somewhere. I want you to be happy here.

I put my head down on the table crying.

If stopping GM seed corporations is hard, it's impossible to change thousands of years of cultural pressure on women.

"I tried, you know I tried to help you."

Her smiling picture didn't respond. She knew. As soon as my head touched the pillow, I was out.

———◆———

I woke up early because I forgot my eye mask, and the skylight directly over my bed let in the light of dawn. I went right to the portal and peeked through. Nobody was there, but there were stacks of things on the counter. I went down to have a look.

There was a Manitoba licence plate from 1911.

Oddly specific. He's definitely just a figment of my imagination.

An envelope with a single one-hundred-dollar bill inside.
Several dresses wrapped in paper.
A long box like roses were delivered in on TV. Inside were shoes and clothing accessories.
There was a note from Sam.

Lilac,

Here's the clothes we had made for you, I think you'll be more comfortable down here now. People will still stare because you're my mysterious wife, but at least your clothes won't stand out. If you could sell the licence plate and the one-hundred-dollar bill, I need a few things. I found, from the family history paper, a small change in my family history will happen if I establish myself as a botanist, specifically in the United States. I don't exactly know what that entails. It's not enough, but it's a move in the right direction. I'll catch up with you later, I have some things to do today. If you're not using your laptop today, could you hide it under the counter? I'd love to use it to do research.

Thank you for everything,
Sam

I took everything through the portal with me into my time, then popped back through the portal, and hid my laptop under the counter for Sam.

I laid everything out on the couch, but needed coffee and breakfast, so I got something to eat and checked for messages. There were three missed messages from the day before. One from my mom and one from my brother, just checking in. I could tell they were worried I was going off the edge.

Makes sense, I was weird with them on Saturday. They've learned to read the signs.

There was also a message from my uncle.

"Lilac. It was nice to have you out here this morning. Your mom called, she's worried about you. I told her you seemed fine to me when you were here, but she said you're sneaky. Would you come for dinner so she won't worry?"

Whoops, I should have checked that earlier.

It was still early. Even though Uncle was probably up, I didn't want to start a thing of five o'clock in the morning phone calls. With my eye mask on, I usually liked to sleep later than that. I made a mental note to call him later and maybe do lunch.

I made a plate of food, a pot of coffee, and turned on the TV. I flicked around until I found a show I could eat to. I didn't want to burst into the packages too quickly, having the mystery of them lying on my couch was sort of thrilling. I finished eating, then got to them.

Maybe I'll open the dresses first.

There wasn't any printing on the paper they were wrapped in, otherwise I would have kept it, because it would probably be worth money. Still, I tried to slide the dresses out and preserve the paper cover as best I could. I'm a paper maniac.

There was a pink dress with little blue flowers, a brown dress with little pink flowers, a white dress with blue stripes and a blue dress with white stripes. They were all surprisingly cute. They weren't *Titanic* fancy, not satin with huge bows and puffy behinds, but cute. I'd probably buy them in my own time.

I held the brown one up to myself. It looked small. I went to my bedroom to try it on. I slipped it over my head and held my breath for snags, but it was perfect. I mean it was *perfect*. I have never had an item of clothing fit me so perfectly. It had room where I needed it and was trim where I was trim. I turned around in the mirror and admired the perfection of the garment. It was comfortable. I stood like I usually do, with my back hunched and my chin protruding forward like a monkey. It still looked good, and it had pockets!

I went to the couch and gathered the others bringing them into my bedroom. They were all the same fit. It was astonishing to me what a difference a tailor made. After I'd tried on the last dress, I could hardly wait to break into the box of accessories.

There were matching ribbons, I assumed they were for my hair, though I wasn't sure. There were a couple of hair combs, the kind you put in backwards that never stay in place when you're romping around your day. There was a pair of white, crocheted lace gloves, which were beautiful and actually fit me. I kept those on for the rest of the time I was unwrapping my gifts. There was a pair of hideous looking, torture bindings for my feet which actually turned out to be quite comfortable, but still ghastly. There were also some kind of roll-on tights, which were not going to happen. I'd rolled them on both legs then stood up, and they'd promptly rolled off. I figured having bare legs would probably make me seem like a tramp, but it would be good for Sam to have a little bit of gossip to excite his life. There was a cute purse, crocheted like the gloves. I could dress like any grandmother's dream granddaughter.

I put the clothes and accessories away, admiring the beautiful sewing job. *Marvellous quality.*

The one-hundred-dollar bill was dated 1872. I couldn't find a dollar value online, so I emailed a couple of collectable currency dealers about its worth. I thought about selling the license plate online but then thought I should give my uncle the first crack at it and take whatever he offered me. I would have rather given it to him as a gift, but it wasn't mine to give, and Sam said he would have a list of things to buy, so I needed to fundraise.

It was way too early to call Mom or Kent because with the time difference, it was still technically nighttime. *If it still has a four in front of it, it's nighttime.*

I read the latest Abbi Waxman book for a couple hours, intending to distract myself from flying back through the cupboard looking for either hot-blooded man, but the book was no help; it made me want to jump on my opportunity at unconventional romance.

Have some self-control . . . and a cold shower.

Finally, it was late enough to call Uncle.

"Hey, it's Lilac, sorry I missed your call yesterday, dinner would have been nice."

"It's okay, how are you doing?"

"Good, really good actually. Will you be in town at lunchtime? I have something you might be interested in."

"Oh? What's that?"

I suddenly realized I would have to come up with a back story for the license plate, especially since we had just talked about it.

"Something we were just talking about. I bought a vintage suitcase and found it in a pouch. Odd combination. Anyway, are you curious enough to have lunch?" I was a horrible liar. I should have come up with something better.

"I'm curious. Where?"

"Gopher Creek." I said, my mouth already watering for lunch even though I was still full from breakfast. They were that good.

"Noon?"

"Yep. See you then."

"Righty-oh." He clicked off.

Feeling pretty good, I read more of my book because with the time difference it was still too early to call Mom and Kent. I read, drank coffee, peeked through the portal for any man, then repeated.

Just before it was time to head to work, I called Mom and Kent, and didn't mention anything about time travel, or falling in love with historical figures. *Maybe Clive is famous for something too? Don't snoop, ask permission first.* I was pretty sure I'd set their minds at ease, but I knew they'd still be on alert. *Just act normal for a few days, you can do it.*

I wrapped the license plate in a dishtowel, put it in my tote bag and walked across the back alley to work, wondering how I would get through the entire day. I wanted to spend the day with Clive or Sam, or both, working on solving the world's problems, not writing reports about Virden's municipal issues.

Walking through the doorway, I got right to the task of devising a way out of work tomorrow. I thought about asking for time off, but if they said no and then I said I was sick, it would look suspicious. The only option would be to burn down my office.

There was a stack of files on my desk, waiting to be processed. *That will burn nicely.*

There was a huge fabric mural on the wall from the sixties or seventies, oddly right on trend if it had been the only thing from that era. Since our entire office was from that era, it was quite a bit less than trendy, but still very flammable.

I looked around, wondering which items would survive and which would melt grotesquely.

"Good morning," Gerry, my boss, said. *Make sure the building is empty when it burns.*

"Morning." I tried to suck the life out of my eyes when I said it.

"Are you feeling okay?"

"I think I've got a stomach flu. I was up all night." I put my hand over my mouth for good measure.

"Are you sure you're okay to be here?"

"Well, I wanted to come and try, anyway. I didn't want to let you down." There wasn't much love lost between us. We'd had a rocky employee-employer relationship right from the start. To be fair to him, I'd come in broken, and he didn't know that. I was ultrasensitive and he . . . wasn't.

"You should take care of yourself." He took a few steps back. I could tell he was more concerned about taking care of himself. *It's going to work.*

"Thanks Gerry. I'm going to see how it goes. I don't want to spread it either. If I get too bad, maybe I'll just go home and rest until I'm better." I leaned forward a few degrees.

Gerry took another couple steps toward his office. "Lilac, you just take the time you need. We don't want to have the whole office sick!"

"Thanks. I'm just going to sit down now and get at my work." I took a step toward my desk and then ran dramatically to the washroom down the hall.

I turned on the fan that ran louder than a Boeing 747 lifting off and pulled a sudoku book out of my purse. I didn't come out of the washroom until I'd finished a hard puzzle.

I returned to my desk slowly, holding my stomach. I sat down, put my purse under my desk and fired up the computation beast. I took a tissue from my desk and wiped my mouth for good measure.

"Gerry said you're not feeling very good." Jane looked at me with genuine compassion.

I found it harder to lie to her. "Yeah. I'm not sure what it is. Something's going around I guess."

"Maybe you should just take the day off."

"I'd just like to get through this stack at least." I pointed to my inbox. I really did want to get through it. Actually, normally, I liked my job. It could be monotonous, but there was comfort in that. When I needed a place where I could just put one foot in front of the other, it helped me. There's no drama. It's quiet. I liked the people. "Just be a steady Eddie," my mom would always say. It was a job where I could be steady. But now, I had a pretty interesting time traveling delusion going on. I wanted to get back to it.

"I really think you should go home." I could see it was more than concern for me—she'd been told to send the zombie home.

The thing was, I knew I wasn't really sick. I wasn't really endangering anyone.

"Can I just see how far I get? It was so hard to get to my desk this morning. I'd like to make a little progress at least. Maybe once I settle in, I'll be okay." I wanted her to feel I'd be at work if it was in any way possible. It would make calling in sick for the next few days a lot easier, and the likelihood of being forced to burn the place down, so much less.

I sat at my desk and plowed through files with pained determination on my face. Every twenty minutes or so I made a quietly conspicuous sojourn to play sudoku for ten minutes in the engine room.

At noon, Jane came up to my desk. "I'm sorry Lilac, but I have to ask you to go home. We really appreciate you coming in, and you actually made it through your inbox, which is awesome, but you need to be resting at home." She was kind, but firm.

"I have to meet my uncle for lunch, how about I see how I feel afterward, maybe he'll cheer me up," I said, knowing full well I still had to go out for lunch and someone from work was likely to see me there.

"No. Please go home after lunch. Honestly Lilac, you should just go straight home. What if you get your uncle sick?" She was being so reasonable, I hated to reply so unreasonably.

"My uncle never gets sick. I'm really not that bad, I probably just need some ginger ale."

Only sick people are so unreasonable.

"Do what you have to Lilac, but you cannot come back here after lunch. Please go home and rest."

I grabbed my purse and stood up. "Really, I think I'm okay." I grabbed the corner of my desk as I stumbled. "Maybe you're right, but I'm sure he's already waiting for me." I looked at the clock on the wall.

"Feel better," Jane said.

"Thanks Jane. You're probably right, I'm probably being unreasonable. I'll sleep this afternoon. Thanks for caring. You're a good friend." I tried a little sloppy sentimentality to sell the seriousness.

———————◆◆———————

I felt thirty-five percent guilty as I walked over to Gopher Creek. I was hungry, but I didn't really want to be seen eating normally. I decided to get my food boxed to go, and I would ravish it later, in private.

"Uncle!" He was sitting at the table right by the door, drinking a coffee.

"This coffee could clean a corroded battery post!" Trying new things was hard for Uncle.

"Good, eh?" I said. "What are you going to have for lunch?"

"Don't know, can't read half the things on the menu." He said it loud with a smile. I would have been embarrassed; except, I was sure they'd heard it all the time.

"Fortunately, you have a genius with you." We went up to the counter and ordered, with only a little inter-generational humiliation.

"So, what's this thing you've got to show me?" I could tell he was about as comfortable with this futuristic Winnipeg lunch as he would be with a latex glove exam.

"You'll have to sit down. I don't want your heart to stop." I smiled.

His eyebrows arched as he sat down obediently. "Okay?"

I pulled out the royal blue metal plate. It had MAN written vertically on the left side of the plate for Manitoba, and 1911 written vertically the right side.

His eyes went as big as jawbreakers, and he reached out for it with both hands. "Where did you get it?"

I'd spent a little time thinking about my lies as I played sudoku in the washroom, and decided my first lie was the best. "In the side pouch of a suitcase I bought."

"Here in Virden?"

"No. You know what, I'm not even really sure where I bought it. I was trying to make it into a little shelf, and when I was taking it apart, I realized there was something in the side pouch." *Okay, I'm getting in a little deep.*

"Wow. What are you going to do with it?"

This is where I felt like a total jerk. If it had been mine, I would have given it to him wrapped up . . . but I actually had to ask for money for it. If I thought I could get money out of the one-hundred-dollar bill quickly, it wouldn't have been a big deal, but I figured it would be more high maintenance to get that money.

"Well, I'm going to sell it. Would you like to make an offer?" I could feel my face turning red. I was so uncomfortable. Obviously, he wouldn't buy it from anyone unless it was a great deal, but because I was his niece, he wouldn't want to dicker with me as vigorously. And yet, I wanted him to.

The silence became awkward between us.

He ran his hands along the edges, carefully. I could see the calculations in his eyes. I knew he was thinking the same things I was, but in reverse.

"Basically, what's the best price you'd pay to a total stranger for this plate?" I asked.

"Sixty dollars."

Ouch. I thought it would be worth more. Sixty dollars wouldn't go far. Disappointment showed in my face before I realized it shouldn't. It was too late, so I decided to go with it.

"You've been searching for one of these your whole life and it's only worth sixty bucks?" I went from wanting to give it to him, to demanding more money. When my imagination thought it was worth $7,000, I wanted to give it to him. Now I wanted to squeeze every last penny out of him.

I really do feel sick.

"Make it thirty and you've got a deal." I forced my eye into a cubic-zirconium twinkle.

"I'll tell you what. Let's make it a hundred, you come over for dinner tonight, and we'll hang it up together." He smiled back, but with a five carat, non-blood-diamond twinkle in his eye. He's the real deal.

"I can't do dinner tonight, but I want to be there when you hang it up. I've got some things on the go—can I call you when I have time?" I asked.

"It will be hard for me to wait to put it up there. Don't put me off too long. I'm old, I could die you know."

Our lunch arrived and we ate. I hadn't planned on it, but it felt disrespectful not to eat with him. We chatted about other things, but his fingers kept grazing the porcelain finish on the Manitoba plate. He was happy, and I was happy he was happy. In fact, he was so happy with the license plate, he didn't once mention the barbaric food torture he was experiencing.

He gave me a hundred dollars from his wallet as we said good-bye. *Who carries around that kind of money?* I'll tell you who: old guys who feel time slipping away and still have space on their hundred hectares for more rusted-out junk. *Gotta love them.*

I went straight home, trying to look sick on the way for the sake of keeping my job.

I'm free.

I put on the brown dress and the shoes, put my hair in a ponytail with a real hair elastic, and then tied a ribbon around it. I peeked through the portal, nobody was there. I crawled down and went to Sam's.

He was there, fully clothed.

"Where do you sleep?" I asked. *That was forward.*

"Back there." He laughed and pointed to the back of the room.

I went to check it out. Behind a waist high bookshelf was a small cot, single pillow, cotton or linen sheets (I'm no expert) and a wool-looking blanket.

"Are you comfortable?" I asked.

"I never thought about it. I guess so."

"I could bring you fitted sheets."

"Or I could invent them." He laughed.

I nodded, only half disappointed. "Or you could invent them."

"I have so many things for you to print for me. Did you see the notes in the laptop?"

"No, I didn't think to look! Hey, what was with the license plate?"

"It's the first year of license plates in Manitoba. I figured most collectors would love to have one, plus it'll fit through the portal." He smiled, not looking like any invention of my subconscious.

My subconscious never gets it this right.

"Are you a university student?" he asked.

I realized that was the first personal question he asked me.

"No."

Inadequate.

"Most of things I'll need from you is research. I'm not sure how you'll get it."

"I'm quite resourceful." I was hoping I'd be rewarded with

more kissing, if I was being honest. *You can't just introduce hot, passionate kissing, then act like nothing happened.*

"Let's go to the laptop. I'll walk you through what I need."

I kinda just wanna stay here though.

"Should we be holding hands when we walk places?"

"We could. We are supposed to be newlyweds, after all." He took my hand.

I felt hot. "I mean, just to sell it."

Sam laughed.

"Should we kiss?"

"In the street, no."

"Here?" I asked.

"Who are we selling it to here?"

I knew my face flushed beet red. I turned back toward the bed.

"Do you need a bigger bed? Like if someone came in here, would it be weird you only have one small bed?"

"We have work to do. We can figure out decorating later." He softened his words with a laugh and pulled me out the door.

At the shop he opened the laptop and pulled out a handwritten list. *I guess I was a little too eager to see him, I didn't even look at the laptop.*

"I need all of the latest papers you can find on these topics." He handed me a list of words that meant nothing to me.

"No problem." I'd find a way or make one.

He handed me another list. "Also, if you could find me textbooks on these topics, anything you can find, I'll take it all. Can I leave that with you?"

"Yes."

"You're the best."

So, no kissing then?

This is serious Lilac, get to it.

I got right to it. The information was hard to find for free. I was able to find textbooks, but with shipping they were between a hundred and three hundred bucks each.

The $100 from Uncle would barely buy one textbook, and I wasn't sure which one to bet on. Eventually, I just went down the list, and if I didn't get something useful on the first page of search results, I moved on to the next word to search. I was getting nowhere. After a couple hours of searching, I only had twelve pages of information that probably weren't useful.

I got an email reply from one of the currency dealers.

Lilac,

The 1872 one-hundred-dollar bill would be worth about $250K today. It's believed they were all redeemed. Are you positive what you have isn't a forgery? How did you come by it?

Tanner

Not a quick way to get money. It isn't like anyone would hand over that kind of money without rigorous testing. I would also have to come up with a great story about how I got it, which could prove difficult.

I replied to Tanner using the big lie of the day.

Tanner,

The hundred-dollar bill was in the lining of a small trunk. I was upcycling it into a footstool. I have no idea if it's a forgery, but the trunk is from around the right time period. How can I tell if it's real?

Lilac

I began hoping nobody would ask to see this suitcase or trunk.

I also wondered about the aging process, if the things would look "aged" enough under a microscope or whatever tool they use to identify aging.

I printed out the probably useless twelve pages, put them in an envelope and threw them on the counter in 1920.

I need to take a new tack here.

Who would have information like this, besides universities who are paid to share it?

Think outside the box.

What about an activist group?

The first hit was an activist/lobbyist group called Gabler Consulting.

Can't be a coincidence.

I received an email reply from Tanner, the currency dealer.

Lilac,

Bring it in, I'll have a look.

Tanner

I'll do that.

I went back to investigating the Gabler Consulting lead. Under "Our Story," there was a brief write up about Sam Gabler. Pretty much just his legacy letter I'd seen in my school textbook, and a few details about being an inventor in Virden, Manitoba. I emailed asking for a meeting, citing my specific interest in Sam Gabler.

These are interesting developments. For sure worth a kiss or ten.

I rushed back to Sam's with the twelve useless pages.

I burst through the door. "You're never going to believe this!"

Both Sam and Clive looked startled.

"First, the one-hundred-dollar bill is worth $250,000! Second, there's a GM activist group called Gabler Consulting named after you! They have a whole write up and everything." I was out of breath from running, the stairs, and passionate excitement.

They both looked happy, but neither moved in to kiss me.

I should have saved some of that information for a private moment.

"How about the information on the list?" Sam asked.

Inadequate.

"Here, I wasn't able to get much. Textbooks are available, but I can't afford any until I can sell that one-hundred-dollar bill." I handed him the envelope with the twelve pages.

"When will that be?" Sam smiled, but it looked like a smile you plaster on.

Inadequate.

"I don't know. The currency dealer said I can bring it in, and he'll have a look. He's in Winnipeg."

"What are you waiting for?" Sam smiled.

Inadequate.

"Oh. It's a three-hour drive, by the time I get there he'll be closed." Truthfully, I hadn't even thought about going today. For me, Winnipeg was a day trip.

"We really appreciate everything you're doing Lilac. You're doing a great job!" Clive said. "So much good news!"

I don't feel like I'm doing a great job.

"Yes, thank you Lilac. It feels like there's so much to do. I'm not a scientist. It's hard to know where to start. I feel like a fraud," Sam said.

"Well, you are a fraud." I laughed. "The thing is, you're doing it for a good cause and you're succeeding, so, just keep going. What you've done already worked, to a certain extent, you just have to do more of the same. By the end of this you'll really be a botanist. Just like a plumbing student performs plumbing work as an apprentice, but they're not a *plumber* until they're licensed. Every student is a fraud in that sense."

"Interesting take," Sam said.

"It's going to be fine. We'll get you set up with everything you need. If you want to watch YouTube videos tomorrow about genetic modification while I'm gone to Winnipeg, it might give you a big head start."

"Don't you have to work?" Sam asked.

"I faked being sick. I'm a fraud too, if it makes you feel better."

"What do you do?" Clive asked.

"I work as a clerk at the Virden town office. With computers."

A nerdy way to impress him, but it worked.

"Bees knees," Clive said.

"Thank you for what you've done today. I better study these notes you've brought me. I know you have a big day tomorrow. We should probably call it a night." Sam invited me to leave.

"Yeah, it's a big day, hopefully a smashing success."

They both just stood, looking at me.

"Okay, goodbye."

"Goodbye," they said.

Halfway down the stairs I heard a sharp shout of anger. I couldn't make much out, but I heard Clive say something like, "one day you're ravishing her, the next … manipulating … selfish." I heard Sam say, "understand." I figured I should be on my way before one of them stormed out of the door.

My laptop pinged as I entered my apartment. There was an email from Ben at Gabler Consulting. He'd agreed to a telephone meeting.

CHAPTER 4

Zeta

♫ **"Long Time Running"** ♫
by The Tragically Hip

Not being married to Sam will be worse than being married to Phillip. Go tell him, now. Take action now or regret it forever.

Immediately after I sold the last packed-up supper I went to Sam's. I saw Clive leaving, so I waited until he turned the corner before I went up to Sam's.

Be brave, get it out before you become too fearful.

He opened the door.

"Sam—I love you—Phillip divorced me six years ago." *There, I said it.*

Sam looked bowled over. He searched my face for meaning.

"What?"

"I . . ."

"Come in." He opened the door wider, then closed it behind me.

I kissed him like I'd wanted to probably, if I was honest, since the first day we met. He kissed me back, taking over the kiss. He backed me to the wall, kissing me hard. I kissed him, urging him toward the table. He kissed me back, pushing me against the wall. I tried to adjust my gun, but realized it wasn't my gun.

I pushed him back. "Stop, stop. Wait," I said breathless. *It can't go like this. I want to do things right.*

"Phillip might have been shooting caps, but I'm sure you aren't." I tried to cool us both off. I held him at arm's length. "Do you have coffee? I need to sit down."

Sam made us coffee while I tried to pull myself together. Watching him didn't help. He was everything Phillip wasn't. He was strong like Phillip, but kind. When I told him to stop, he did. I watched his forearms and muscular hands as he prepared the coffee. Strong hands, used for good. *I've been so foolish.*

Sam put my cup in front of me and sat down. "I know it's not as good as you make it, but I've tried to follow your instructions."

"My instructions?" He couldn't possibly remember.

"It was many years ago, I'm sure you don't remember. Before you made suppers, briefly, you sold coffee in the mornings. I asked why yours was so much better than mine. You gave me some tips, and I've been using them ever since."

"I do remember, I'm surprised you do."

"I remember . . . please tell me about Phillip."

A scrapbook of memories came to mind, landing on watching him walk away, exhausted from beating me to death, or so he thought. To me, that was our defining moment. I'm sure when Phillip thought of me, he thought about staring down the barrel of my gun hundreds of times in a relentless, year's long fight to regain his dominance.

"What do you want to know?" I asked.

"You're divorced?"

"Yes."

"Why didn't you tell me?"

"I wasn't a good wife in the end, to Phillip."

"Phillip wasn't a good person, I can't imagine he was a good husband," Sam said.

"No matter who Phillip was, I became a bad wife. I carry this."
I pulled my gun from within my skirt.

"Bad wife, or practical woman?" He didn't flinch.

"I wanted my family here; I needed to make money to bring them here. I didn't think I'd be able to keep my job if I was divorced. Then the war started, and it was easier to say he was gone to war. It's terrible, but people were more willing to buy my suppers and give me their laundry to do, because they thought Phillip was at war. Phillip owed me." It sounded awful, but I always thought of all people, Sam would understand, because his family had been murdered.

"When were you going to tell everyone?" he asked.

"I was trying to come up with something. It's been over a year now since the war ended, and it's getting hard to explain why he's taking so long to get home. But I'm so close to finishing the house. I have rooms for my brother and parents. All I need is money to get them here."

"But you're definitely divorced?"

"Yes."

"Marry me."

"What about your wife?" I asked.

"Oh. Right. Lilac isn't my wife . . . yet. Lilac . . . I said she was my wife, but actually we're not married yet, and you change everything." He hung his head down. "I'm a horrible person. I've been hoping every day we'd hear Phillip was killed in battle."

A slow, low laugh came from deep inside me. "Me too."

He took my hand. "Zeta, marry me. Forget about Lilac. We're not married and we're not ever going to be. I loved you from the moment you first pointed your gun at me." He laughed.

"What?" *I never.* "I never pointed my gun at you."

"Yes, you did. In the park."

"No. When?" *Can't be. Why would I? How could I forget?*

"Years ago, when I first came to Virden. At night. I was in the park. I didn't see you, and evidently, I startled you. I didn't see your face but heard the click of your gun and saw a glint off its barrel. I don't remember your exact words, but you told me to back off. I recognized your voice, your accent. I didn't blame you at all. I could have been up to anything."

"That was you? I thought that was Phillip." I remembered the panic pulsing through my veins.

"If you hadn't pulled your gun on me, I would have never asked you for help with my documentation papers. I figured you had the ability to make them, because of all the signs you'd made around town. But after our encounter, I figured if you carried a gun without a permit, for your protection, you'd probably help me with my documents, for my protection."

"How do you know I don't have a permit?" I asked.

"Because I went to get a gun the next day, thinking everyone was carrying one, and they told me Virden doesn't approve permits for handguns, only hunting rifles."

"Oh." *Caught.*

"The documents have served me well, by the way, never had an issue."

"Thank my father when he arrives, he taught me everything I know. He's an artist and a printmaker." I felt a stab to my heart just thinking about him. "What will Lilac do, won't you break her heart?"

"All Lilac could ever be to me is a stand in for an unattainable you. That's not fair to her."

"You're absolutely not married yet?"

"No, and you're absolutely divorced?"

"Yes."

"So will you marry me?"

"Yes!"

CHAPTER 5

Lilac

♫ **"Miss Sarajevo"** ♫
by Passengers and Luciano Pavarotti

I had a morning telephone meeting with Ben from Gabler Consulting, and then I was off to Winnipeg; hopefully, to sell the one-hundred-dollar bill. Before my tasks started, I popped my head through the portal to see if anyone was around. Sam was waiting for me.

"Lilac, I need to talk to you."

I climbed down the shelving.

"I shouldn't have kissed you, and I should be kinder to you . . . I should have thought this out better . . . I'm in love with Zeta, from the post office. I thought she was married so I just kept pushing thoughts of her away. I kissed you because . . . I'm so sorry. I kissed you because I was thinking of her. Something you said made me think of her and I just, I don't know. I just snapped. There's been a lot going on. I've been holed up here, obsessing on revenge for eight years, imagining that I'd destroyed the people who destroyed my family. Finding out it didn't work was crushing, but then to have your help, I appreciated it so much. I'm not around women, I mean I see them, but you were hugging me, and I was talking about my family, and you reminded me of Zeta. I'm just so sorry. Then, I felt guilty, maybe. . . . The bottom line is, you're getting information so quickly. You're a force. You did not deserve me messing with you. I didn't mean to, but I did, and I wish I could take it back. As fast as I can think of something to help my family, you're doing it. This attempt will be a million times stronger than before, I almost can't believe you're real."

Well, isn't this ironic.

I started laughing. "I don't know if you're real either!"

We were both laughing. There were tears, there was snot, it was bonding.

"For the record, it did feel off. You kissing me like that. It didn't feel like we'd earned that kind of passion, but I'm not going to lie to you. I liked it, and I wanted more, until you just said it was for Zeta. Now, not so much, but I haven't felt that . . . alive . . . in a long time. No regrets on my end." I laughed. "Wait, go back, you thought she was married, but she isn't?"

"Uh, I have to get back to you on that. Pretend I never said that for now, okay?"

"If you feel about her the way you kissed me, and she isn't married . . . what are you doing here, go!"

"I will, I just needed to do this, too. It's all important, and besides, she's working right now."

"Okay, but I want details later. Back to business . . . I got a hundred bucks for the license plate."

"Oh, not bad. I thought it would have been worth more."

"Yeah, me too."

"Don't worry about it—money is my problem, not yours. Whatever you can get for the hundred-dollar bill will help, and if not, I'll figure something else out. Those were just my first ideas." He smiled.

Okay, I know Zeta is on the scene, but a little tiny bit in me still wants to kiss that gorgeous smile. No. No.

I got back to my apartment, and on the phone with Ben from Gabler Consulting.

"So, what exactly is your interest in the information you've requested?" Ben asked.

"I'm writing a book." *That came easy.*

I waited. I always found it better not to babble explanations, especially when they were lies. Not that I lie often, it's a terribly low thing to do, but also, my memory was too awful.

"What kind of book?" he asked.

"A novel. It's fiction, but I like to dive deep when I research. I found some documents about Sam in our local archives, and I find his story compelling. I have a lead on a cache of his notes and work. I'm trying to do as much research as I can now, to understand whatever is in there, if I can get it." *Phew, stop talking.*

"Interesting. We would be interested in having a look at them too, if you can get them. It could be helpful. Mostly what we do is fight for farmer's rights. We lobby to ban dangerous GMOs, and defend small farms being sued by big companies, but that's treating symptoms, putting out fires. I've always had this . . ." He trailed off.

"What?"

"It's . . . well, I've always had a secret wish that Sam Gabler did more. I'd love to find a huge stash of misfiled patents that would nullify the patents wreaking havoc today. He's so mysterious. So little is known about his scientific life. I wish he'd shown more of his work. Anyway, I'm interested in anything you find. If nothing else, we can post it on our website, he is our namesake after all."

"What do you mean by show his work?" I asked.

"Well, most botanists . . ." Ben talked, and I rigorously took notes.

When he seemed pretty much tapped out on that subject I asked, "Do you think there's a point where seeds will be good enough, and designer seeds won't be lucrative anymore?"

"Yes. I think we're maybe even there, but there's still fifteen years left on most of these patents," he said. "I'm not sure that the remaining independent, non-GM seed farms can survive fifteen more years."

"Yeah, that's a long time to fight. I hope my source does pan out. I'll share everything I find with you."

"Thanks."

"I need a lot of information for my book. Do you have textbooks I can borrow?" I asked, knowing the value of what I was asking for, and worrying a little about not being able to return them.

"I do, but do you really need that?"

"I want this book to be my manifesto." *I really hope I'm using that word right.* "I want to research it thoroughly, and really understand what I'm talking about, it may take me a few years," I said, as if it were a totally normal request.

"I'm not sure what value most of it will be to you. Pretty much all of it is well after Sam's time or work. I don't see how you'll weave complicated formulas into fiction. Unless your intended audience is scientists in the field of genetic modification . . ." He laughed, but not mockingly, it was a warm laugh.

Own it, Lilac.

"Actually, that's exactly what I was thinking. Draw them in with a biography about the father of their field, then sell them Sam's beliefs on the moral obligations of wielding the power they do. It'll be subtle, but maybe some will come around?"

We were fighting the same battle. I wanted him to know his books and papers would go toward fighting the same cause. Everyone allows writers to be procrastinators, especially writers without publishers. Except maybe writers' families, but in this case, that was not applicable.

He was quiet for a good thirty seconds. "You never know." I could see he didn't have a lot of confidence in the idea, but he was willing to let me have a go. "I can give you access to our database."

Ohhhh, even better than I imagined.

He secured me an ID and gave me a brief rundown of how to access each paper or textbook, and its associated documentation.

"It looks like I have my work cut out for me!" I said, just as enthusiastically as I felt. "I can't wait to dig in! Thank you so much for your time, I can't tell you how excited I am to get access to this kind of information. Thank you. I'm ready to immerse myself in Sam's world." It felt good to say one totally true thing.

"You're welcome, please keep me posted about that cache," Ben said.

"I will absolutely be in touch the instant I have something."

━━━━◆◆━━━━

I was excited to tell Sam about the database and pushed open the back of the cupboard to peek into the shop.

"Hello?"

"Hi!" Clive popped up right in my face.

I banged my head on the top of the cupboard in surprise. "I got the information. I got access to a database of information." I said it as calmly as possible, even though I was screaming inside.

"Great. What's a database?" Clive asked.

"It's a library inside a computer, in this case probably with hundreds or thousands of textbooks and papers in it," Sam said.

"Yes, everything you could imagine!" I said.

Clive climbed down and I followed.

"That was really quick. I thought you were going to Winnipeg?" Sam said.

"I am, but I had that call first, and I wanted to tell you about it. If things go well today, should I get another laptop for down here?"

"There's an idea," Sam said.

"Tech items become obsolete so quickly." I hated to think of how short the lifetime of the computer would be.

"Well, for however long it works, I will use it, that's all we can ask for right?"

"Yeah, if I can get $250,000 today, why not get one?"

"What if, when the portal closed for me, it didn't close all the way. Like, what if a very small hole was actually still there. What if a Wi-Fi signal could still get through, even if the bigger hole closes? Something obviously connects these parallel times and these two locations, maybe it's always a little bit open?" Sam said.

"Interesting theory. Absolutely worth a shot. If the portal closes, I'll keep my internet running, maybe even get a signal booster for the cupboard, hopefully we'll be able to continue communicating." I didn't want to think about the portal closing, but better to prepare for its inevitability. "I'll get you a few super surge-protector power bars too."

"We're slated to get electricity from Winnipeg next year, the lines are already being run," Sam said.

I hadn't thought of that.

"Should I try to find a little generator? Something that would fit through the portal?"

"I'm not sure it would be compatible with the fuel we have now. Also, I couldn't run it inside, and getting spotted with it outside somewhere would be detrimental. It would be loud and attract attention. I think it's safer just to wait until next year. Maybe look into power converters? Something that would convert unstable electricity into electricity to run a laptop," Sam said.

"Boy, I sure wish I could be more helpful. I have no idea what you guys are talking about," Clive said.

"Don't feel bad, I really don't know either, but I'm going to get help," I said.

I took a few notes, and added books on computers, and discs to reinstall. It was like packing for a lifetime trip. There were so many things he was likely to need.

What if this doesn't work? What if I wake up in the middle of the night three months from now, closed off on the other side, and I think of something that might have made the difference. Something that could have made this plan work?

Sam was navigating through the information on the database, taking in the magnitude of what was there. It was daunting. I just had to keep reminding myself we, or at least he, had decades to get through it. The patents should be registered immediately, but showing his work could take time.

"I'm going to print out everything, just in case the portal ever closes," I said.

"Good idea. This is valuable Lilac, thank you." Sam nodded his head but kept scrolling.

The portal can never close, but it will.

I remembered my notes. I ripped out the pertinent pages from my notebook and handed them to Sam. "This is the stuff Ben, from Gabler Consulting, needs to make his battle easier."

He scanned them quickly and then started at the beginning again, this time getting all the details. At first, he leaned against the counter, riveted by what he read.

I stayed quiet, only speaking to translate the occasional illegible word.

After quite some time passed, he started nodding his head and pacing slowly. He looked up at me, humming from somewhere deep inside.

"Okay. I think I can see where he's going with this. Some of these are going to be hard, but I get why it's important," Sam said.

I'd been impressed too, it was nice to see the case come together, but I was still a bit overwhelmed at how much work it was going to be. "I thought it was cool how he even mentioned the specific steps that needed to be in the documents. I'm sure Ben has no idea what we're up to, but he was detailed."

"Yeah, how did you get him to give you this?" Sam asked, with an eyebrow raised.

"I told him I had a lead on a cache of documents from Sam and asked him if there was anything he wanted me to look for."

"Good idea," Sam said.

"Thanks for not being disappointed."

"Why would I be disappointed?"

"Because I've been lying."

"You must have me confused with somebody else. I lie all the time. I'm a time traveler living in 1920, everything about me is a lie. I've gotten so good at it, even I believe my lies."

We all laughed, like a freeze frame at the end of *Murder, She Wrote.*

Back at Sam's lab, we picked the easiest thing on the list, and Sam wrote a draft. It hit all the beats, but Sam didn't have old-fashioned handwriting that would peg him as being from this era. It was too casual, too flashy, and not meticulous enough. We asked Clive to write a few sentences, but still no match. Who wrote the original documents? Technically, when I was in Sam's time, they hadn't been written yet, so there was nobody to ask.

"Maybe you are going to have to learn to write like this," I said.

"Zeta can do it, I'm sure," Sam said.

I elbowed him and raised both eyebrows. "Maybe you can

find out. I should get going. I'll see if I can find textbooks to buy for you to keep. The database is amazing, but it's probably easier to read from a bound book, in the long run, than loose printed pages. Setting you up with everything you need is my number one priority right now, just in case the portal closes."

"Thanks, Lilac," Sam said. "I'm going to use the laptop while you're gone today."

They walked me back to the shop.

I went to climb through the portal.

"Wait, I brought you a ladder." Clive wedged a ladder from the base of the counter to the cupboard, holding it steady with one hand.

"Thank you. That was thoughtful." I started climbing.

"Lilac!" Sam called.

I turned to look at him.

"Printer ink!" he said.

"I'll get it." I climbed the next step without looking and accidentally put my hand where Clive's hand was.

That same bolt of electricity ran through me. My heart skipped a beat.

Reckless behavior while climbing a ladder, Lilac . . .

Just in case Clive was looking up my skirt, which I was sure he was too much of a gentleman to do, I bent at the waist as much as possible to stretch out all the cellulite.

"See you tonight!" I yelled back through the cupboard.

"Be safe!" Clive said.

Next up, call in sick to work.

Beep.

"Hi Jane, it's Lilac. I'm going to Winnipeg today to get an herbal treatment. The doctor here said there isn't much he can do for me.

Anyway, have a good day. Hopefully I'll be back tomorrow." *Lies, lies, lies! Now I'm going to have to make up some herbal treatment procedure. I'll have to make sure I say it was a gong show and just made me sicker, or else she might want a recommendation!*

I dressed in the best, but not my trying-too-hard, outfit I could muster, put on a little makeup, and some real, but not extravagant jewelry. I wanted to give the impression of middle class, educated, don't-rip-me-off, this-isn't-a-forgery persona. I looked in the mirror and was satisfied. *If I was good at forgery, I would've forged good hair.*

I grabbed the hundred-dollar bill, some snackies for the road, and headed off, making sure to look sick until the highway separated widely enough that nobody would be able to recognize me on their way to work.

The three-hour drive to Winnipeg gave me a lot of time to think about things. I thought about what it would be like to give up the present and live in the past. I thought about the work we had to do to save Sam's farm and family. I tried to think of a way to save Lan. I couldn't think of anything. She'd had a mountain of expectation on her, relentless criticism, and a life plan set out for her from before birth. I hadn't been able to help her with any of it, and I was right there with her. What could I do to help her from the past?

Stop. Don't think about it today. For one thing, you're driving. Just focus on today's task. One step at a time.

I arrived at the currency dealer, I felt like I was sneaking across the German border in an air balloon. Probably too much coffee.

"Hi, I emailed about the one-hundred-dollar bill." I stood tall with my chest out like I was on a war poster.

"Hello." The guy smirked, as if I was going to pull out Monopoly money.

"Here it is." I carefully removed it from the envelope.

I was paranoid he would turn his back to me and exchange my bill with one that was fake. Just like I would be with a jeweler if I needed a diamond put back in a ring. I get that from old people.

He pulled a small magnifying glass out of his pocket and put it right up to the bill. Then he laid it on the counter over a white glass rectangle and turned on a light underneath. He pulled a larger magnifying glass on a swivel overtop of it, making all kinds of noises. He shut off the light underneath, turned on a light within the magnifying glass itself, and carefully viewed the bill from side to side. He flipped the bill over and viewed it the same way. Then he picked it up and smelled it. Now I knew he was an expert.

"I have to make a phone call," he said. "Will you put that back in the envelope and just wait here for a few minutes?" He smiled at me with a lot more respect now.

See, my hair wasn't lying.

I half expected ninjas to come through the door and take the envelope. I felt like I should hide it, but I didn't know where, and for all I knew I was under surveillance.

"Where did you say you found this again?" he asked, coming back into the shop from his office.

Suitcase or trunk? Oh man, lying is not my deal.

I felt a cold chill go through my body. I tried to look normal and not open my eyes too wide.

"In the lining of a traveling case." *That should cover my bases. Seriously have to write these lies down.* "I had it for years, it wasn't until I was taking it apart for a craft project that I found this!" *Think, was that the story for Uncle Jack? I don't have the nerves for this, just stop talking!*

He nodded like he was buying it. I hoped he would buy it. I was willing to sell it cheap--$100,000 should do nicely, I decided. *Ha!*

"I called some of my colleagues over to get a few more opinions. We don't see finds like this often, I'm sure they'll be here quickly."

Colleagues? Like bikers with chains?

"So, you think it's real?" I felt free to show my excitement, because who wouldn't, really?

"I think so, but I've never seen an authentic bill before. It has all the markings to be authentic from that time frame. One of the men who's coming has seen one, so hopefully he can shed some light."

I really wanted to ask when I could get my money, but I was pretty sure this wouldn't be a quick sale item. They would probably want it to go to auction or something, or maybe they would buy it and take their chances.

"Are you interested in buying it?" *I mean really, let's just cut to the chase.*

"I'm interested. That's part of the reason I want the other guys here. Between us, we can get an offer together. I think we'll be able to work out something good for all of us, so you're interested in selling?" I suddenly realized he was an honest guy, and I was holding all the cards. It felt good but was also a lot of pressure.

"Yeah, I'm interested in selling. I'm certainly not going to frame it and put it on the wall. I'm going to go live in Hawaii!" *A few days ago, I would have said Paris . . .*

I started thinking—it would obviously be in my best interest to sell it quietly, especially since it wasn't mine to profit from. The last thing I wanted was to be in the media because of it. Even if I received drastically less than it was worth, Sam would be able to buy every last thing he needed to do his research and accomplish his mission.

It wasn't long before the posse arrived. I was expecting a bunch of pawn kings, but instead they were a bunch of literary geeks. I was right at home. They came in with their glasses, and pockets full of pens, and notes.

Nobody tried to take the bill out of my sight, and they all waited patiently for their turn. There was excitement, and calculations transpiring all around. Dollar signs and rarity were most likely on their minds, plus potentially other random thoughts sprouting underneath their sparsely covered noggins.

After twenty minutes of public deliberations, they decided to take it to the back room, sans me. The door shut behind them. I placed the bill back in the envelope, and wandered around the store, realizing I could probably have anything in the shop thrown into the price of the bill. I could have any rusty, ripped, fusty old thing I wanted! The truth was, of course, I wanted them all. *It's in my blood.*

I thought about lab equipment, books, microscopes, or whatever else Sam would need. Suddenly $100,000 didn't seem like enough. *I wish Sam was here, I have no idea what I'm doing.*

I saw a box of old skeleton keys. They were priced at ten bucks each. I have a weakness for keys. I made a mental note to get that box thrown in as a memento of this whole adventure, it would probably be all I would end up with.

Finally, they came out of the back room.

"Okay," said the alpha geek. "We have an offer for you."

"Great. Lay it on me."

"Fifty thousand dollars."

"Cash?" It was important to me to have no paper trail all of a sudden.

"Oh . . ." He turned around to nodding heads. "Yes, we can do cash."

Fifty seemed low to me. "Do you think you'll get two fifty for it?" Strait shot from the hip.

"Well, that's just the thing, you see, we don't know what we'll get for it. You could take it to auction, but it all depends on who's buying, and then there's the auction house cut. Everything costs money." He was clearly as nervous as I was.

"You don't know any private collectors you could sell it to, directly?" I felt I could push a little more.

"Well, we may, but there are no guarantees."

"Could you contact them?" I asked.

He smiled and took a breath. "What price seems fair to you?"

"Well, like you said, everything costs money. This is your business, not mine, so this bill is more valuable to you than it is to me, because I don't have your connections. I would be happy to take seventy thousand in cash. And this box of keys." *Don't show weakness. Pretty sure asking for the box of keys is showing weakness.*

He turned around to look at his colleagues. They went into the back room again, and I browsed for more items to use for negotiation. My price was going up by the minute, like a terrorist.

I had no idea how much Sam needed, really. We had a lot of textbooks in the database, I just had to print them, but obviously a proper book would be better. Maybe there were more things Sam needed that he didn't want to ask for until the money was there.

They came back out. They were sweating. I felt stupid. How did I get into these things? The last thing I wanted to do was hold a gaggle of geeks over a barrel.

"Sixty-six thousand cash," he said.

That's a lot of money. I wondered how hard Sam had worked for that bill. I wondered if he worked harder than sixty-six thousand dollars' worth. Either way, we needed to expedite cash flow, because that portal would close.

"Do any of you guys have historic books on genetics?" I asked.

Crestfallen, the negotiator looked at me like I was giving them the runaround.

"Part of what I want to spend the money on is an elaborate gift for my father who loves genetics. I would be happy to accept the equivalent of the remaining four thousand in goods from your various businesses." I tried to say it with a perfectly serious face, even though I felt ridiculous.

Brown tweed bowtie spoke up. "I have a sizeable collection of antique scientific volumes." He turned to the others and said, "Of course we would have to work out some arrangement for the value of whatever she acquires from me." There were hearty nods and grunts of approval.

"Great. You guys get your cash together, and put these keys with it, and I'll check out your science section." I said to the man with the stash.

He gave me the address and directions and said to ask for Sue. They went their way, and I went mine.

I was feeling quite flush, so I went for sushi before heading over to the book shop. I savoured every morsel. It was a good day after all. I was feeling much less stressed and much less exhausted.

Sue took me right to the section. There many more books than I was expecting. There were three sections of floor to ceiling shelving full of various books on different sciences. I inspected each one carefully. I figured even one chapter inside a book could be valuable, and since I had $4,000 to work with, I really didn't want to leave anything behind. After a couple of hours, I had a stack of books reaching mid thigh that included trace elements of plant genetics. It was hard for me to figure out what would be of most use to Sam, so I just took them all. I also took three atlases because I loved and wanted them.

Sue made a record of my pickings and snagged one of the young guys to help me to my car with the two large boxes of books. I wasn't sure I could have done much better on eBay.

I drove back to the original shop, locked up the car and went in.

"You're back!" Tanner said.

"I'm back. How did things go?"

"Good, we got the money."

"You have it here?" I said, feeling like I should be wearing a ski mask or something.

"Yes. You have the bill?"

"Yes. Here." I handed him the envelope.

He had a good close look at it again with the same tools he used the first time. "It isn't that I don't trust you, it's just good business practice to be careful."

"I totally agree." I kept my mouth shut so he could do his work, and I could get my money.

"Looks good. Congratulations, that was quite the find." He reached out and shook my hand. "Now don't blow this all in one place. Go to Hawaii, but remember—money goes quickly if you aren't careful. Don't miss your big chance to really change your life. This is it. Don't fritter it away." He handed me a box of fifty- and one-hundred-dollar bills. It was truly shocking to see $66,000 all in one place. It was a lot of money! I pulled out a few bills, not that I would be able to tell if they were fake or not, but they looked good to me.

"Can I get your expert opinion on something?" I asked.

"Sure."

"Are these real?" I said with a smile.

We laughed and it was done. I felt shaky going back to my car. I'd never handled so much money even digitally, never mind in person. Suddenly everyone on the street was a thief.

I went to the University bookshop and bought used textbooks. It was worth the money to have a hard copy. I picked up a laptop, a serious business surge protector, a laser printer with a high-capacity paper tray, and ten toner cartridges. I bought ten boxes of printer paper because I had no idea how big the database was. I figured I would be printing all day and night, every day and night. I loaded up a prepaid Visa, with a $25,000 limit, for buying things online anonymously, and grabbed some Mexican takeout, eating in the car in a posh neighborhood. Then, I drove home cautiously. Of all the times not to get in an accident, this was it.

I thought about stopping in at Uncle's on the way home, but I knew the secrets of the day would be written all over my face, so I pushed on home, and scooted my derriere through the portal as quickly as possible. I left the money in my time but brought the books through to 1920. I left them in the empty shop for Sam to carry back to his lab. I was a lady after all. Besides, I'd already lugged them up the stairs to my apartment, and through the portal.

Sam and Clive were at the lab.

"Lilac! How did it go?" Sam was excited.

"Guess how much I got for it?"

"A hundred thousand?" Big smile, eyebrows up, Sam guessed wrong.

"Wow, I should not have asked you to guess." It hurt my immense pride in myself a bit, but I carried on.

"Let me guess!" Clive said.

"Okay."

"Let's see. A one-hundred-dollar bill from 1872 . . . it's gotta be worth five times that much in your time . . . $500!"

I laughed.

"Sixty-six thousand cash and a whole bunch of science textbooks starting in the 1800s. Say I done good." I put my hand up for a high-five.

"You done good." Sam high-fived me.

Clive looked interested, but didn't follow suit.

"Do you have high-fives in 1920?" I asked.

"No." Sam laughed.

"It's like an informal congratulatory handshake, in the air." I said to Clive.

"It looks like a spank," Clive said.

"Spank me!"

Clive looked a bit concerned but did it.

I hadn't felt so silly, happy, or giddy in a long time. I could hardly remember the last time. "Thank you. I'm glad you're happy; there were so many moments of uncertainty today. I'm glad you're happy with the results."

"I'm glad you just sold it. Obviously, at auction it might have gone for much more, but the process would be too long. Thank you for being decisive," Sam said.

"Come see the books, they're in the shop."

We went back to the shop and brought the books to Sam's lab. I helped because I'm not really a lady, I just say I am sometimes for kicks.

We sat in the leather chairs beside the windows and looked through each book carefully. We put page markers at the pertinent spots and chitchatted about excerpts we found interesting. Sam had already put effort into learning about the process, so he had a better grasp of the types of things we were looking for.

"You did really good Lilac," Sam said, a couple pots of tea later. "I wanted to be there with you, but you did really good. I am grateful you're so capable."

That felt nice.

"You'll have to find a really good hiding place for all this. I should probably bring you a fire-proof safe or something, just in case."

"Good thinking," Clive said.

"I put twenty-five hundred on a prepaid Visa for any online purchases. I need you to make me a list of equipment you want, because I should get on that right away. Oh, and I bought a laptop, but I haven't set it up yet."

"Thank you." Sam took a deep breath, reached for paper and a pen, and started a shopping list. "Part of the problem is, I can't have futuristic science equipment in here. It would be very suspicious. I'll have to buy some of the equipment in this time, but I still want to have basic modern pieces of equipment I could keep hidden, to make learning easier for me.

Later, I set up the laptop, got the printer going, and began printing out the database. Every time I heard it stop, I loaded another ream of paper and continued printing. I placed an elastic band around each book printed and stacked them in the boxes for the reams of paper. I worked, watching *Columbo*, until I couldn't keep my eyes open.

CHAPTER 6

Zeta

♫ **"She Belongs to Me"** ♫
by Bob Dylan

I watched Sam enter the papered-up shop across from the post office. When I got a break, I went over to see him, but I heard Lilac's voice inside. *I knew it, he is marrying her. Why is he hiding her in this papered-up shop? Maybe he's holding her captive?*

I gripped the cool gun in my skirts and peeked through a seam in the paper. I couldn't see anything, so I walked along until I found a sliver of space I could see through. Sam and Lilac were talking, looking into a glowing book. Clive was there too. All three of them. Their faces were shining in the dark room. I took a walk around the block both to clear my head, and to go around into the back alley. I wanted a better look inside without drawing attention to myself, like I would have in the middle of the street. The alley was empty. I found a spot to peek through where I could see the book better. There absolutely was light coming from it. No mistaking that.

Lilac didn't seem to be in any trouble, and Sam didn't seem the least bit romantically interested in her.

What is that thing?

"Mrs. Barker?" Mr. Grover called out to me.

I didn't want anyone inside to hear me reply, so I walked closer to him. "Yes?"

"Just checking that you weren't caught in the bushes there. They look unruly."

"Yes, they are—no, I'm fine." I looked at the bushes. *Lilacs.* "They're lilacs. I want some for my property. They're so nice in the springtime. I thought maybe I could buy them from the owner, since they seem unwanted here." *What am I babbling on about?*

"Oh. Yes, they have a nice scent in the spring. I always mark the changing season by the lilacs."

"I have some, but I wanted to see if these had any differences in their blooms. I couldn't tell, they're shriveled and dried. No matter though, I'll be happy to buy them anyway if the owner will sell. It would make a lovely hedge don't you think?"

"Yes. Lovely. Well, good day." He lifted his hat to me and left.

I went back to the post office because my break was surely over.

⬤

As soon as I finished my shift at the post office, I went to confront Sam.

I pounded on his door.

"Zeta. I'm so happy to see you."

"I'm happy to see you too, but I need transparency Sam."

"Okay." He looked nervous. "About what?"

"Lilac. Is she leaving or is she staying?"

"I'm not marrying her, but she isn't leaving right away."

"I saw you, Lilac, and Clive looking at a glowing book. What was it?"

"I don't know what you're talking about." I'd observed Sam for enough years to know he knew exactly what I was talking about.

"You were at the papered-up shop. I saw you through a gap in the paper."

"You were spying on me?" he asked.

"Yes. Why shouldn't I? If you're to be my husband."

"Of course. Of course. You're right, of course. We were just reading a book. Lilac had a business proposition for Clive, and I was helping them sort through some of the numbers."

"It was metal and glowing."

"I don't know what you're talking about. It must have been a trick of the light from the window."

"The windows are papered up, Sam."

"I don't know what to tell you. We don't have a metal glowing book." He laughed at me.

"Don't you think I know you well enough to know when you're lying?"

"I didn't know you were lying about Phillip."

"But I can tell when you're lying," I said.

"I didn't tell you the whole truth about my family."

"So, you're telling me you lied about your family to prove I can't tell when you're lying, so that I'll believe you don't have a metal glowing book in the shop?" I was furious.

"When you put it like that, no. I guess you're just crazy."

I turned on my heel and left before I could shoot him between his eyes.

He followed me.

"Sam Gabler, if you take one more step in my direction, you'll regret it. I don't want to see your face right now. Get away from me." I pointed for him to go home.

When I got home, Holly, the girl I had hired from next door, was there weeding the garden. Thankfully the walk home helped me cool off a bit.

"Mr. Rose and his crew finished up today. He told me to tell you he had an idea for a porch," Holly said.

"Thank you. I'm sure he does, and I know he'd do good work,

but that will have to wait a little while. Did you have a look at what they've done?" I asked.

"No ma'am."

"Well, come in, let's go see." I was happy to have someone to share it with.

The main house was a small one-bedroom home with a kitchen, dining room, living room, bedroom, and indoor bath. Mr. Rose and his team built two additional bedrooms and a utility room off the kitchen. I wanted extra room for laundry and canning.

I'd been following their progress carefully, I trusted Mr. Rose, but sometimes men don't think of the comforts that make life nice. I didn't want any drafts, and I wanted choices for furniture placement. Having every wall with a door, window or closet in the middle left little choice for where a bed could be placed.

We took a tour. All the finishing touches were done. Baseboards, fresh paint, picture rails with hooks, and the curtain fixtures.

"It's hard to believe it's done," I said.

"Your family will be so happy. When do they arrive?"

"I'm working on it."

"And Mr. Barker? Any word?"

"Not yet, do you have time to help me prepare suppers today?" I didn't want to think about the Phillip mess. Or Sam.

"Yes ma'am."

We made the pasta and added fresh ingredients to a base sauce I had canned last year. *Everything will be easier when my family arrives.* Topped with fresh herbs and a little aged cheese, *buonissimo!*

"Thank you for your help, Holly. The garden looks lovely, and I was grateful to have your help with suppers. I was in a bad mood when I arrived. The food would not have been made with love if you hadn't been here to cheer me up." I paid her for her work and sent her home with some rhubarb.

"Thank you, Mrs. Barker, I'm sure Mother will send you back a slice of rhubarb pie!" She yelled as she ran across the field toward her home.

I packed the jars of pasta sauce and noodles into the padded crate in the wagon, covered them with a blanket, and headed back to town making sure my beautiful Palomino, Zizzo, kept a gentle pace so the jars wouldn't break.

As I sold the suppers, I replaced the full jars from the crate with returned empty jars. It was a slow way to make money, but every little bit helped. *Tonight's money is the first of the savings toward my family's passage from Italy.*

I'd used the last of my savings to pay Mr. Rose to finish the house. Before the war, I hadn't had enough money to bring my family to live with me, and besides, I had nothing to bring them to. Phillip and I lived in a battle zone, with no extra private space for my family. Toward the end of Phillip's tenure, I had the bedroom, which I kept locked at all times, and Phillip was camped in the living room. Once he was gone, saving money was easier because he wasn't building up debts all over town. But then the war started and passage for my family wasn't possible. I used the time to build bedrooms, plant an orchard, designate garden areas, and collect furnishings to welcome them to a better, secure, more comfortable life.

CHAPTER 7

Lilac

♫ ***Jurassic Park* Theme** ♫
by Thomas Oliver

As soon as I woke up, I resumed the printing process.

I didn't have time to go to work, but I was running out of days for a believable stomach flu excuse. I needed the possibility of something much more serious, like Ebola. That seemed a little too serious, plus I would be quarantined at the hospital, and then there would be no helping Sam. Maternity leave would be great, but even if I could fake a pregnancy, I would have to be far enough along to make it work.

Well, I am on the pudgy side.

I googled "faking a pregnancy." There was a surprising amount of information on the internet about how to fake a pregnancy. Six months paid leave from work was appealing, but the next step was faking a miscarriage. I didn't want to be the callused, peeling, dirty, summer heel in a pretty white sling back who would dredge up emotions in people who had actually experienced something so terrible. I dropped the idea.

Mono was next on my list. I did a little research and found out mono is hard to test for, and doctors often give a diagnosis based on symptoms. Faking lymph node inflammation would be hard, but not impossible. I knew my lymph nodes swelled up when I ate gluten. That did present a bit of a problem since there could be other, much more severe, consequences.

I researched faking other illnesses, but none had the same bang for the buck that mono did.

"Virden Medical Clinic," the receptionist cheerily answered the phone.

"Hi, this is Lilac Clemens, I'd like to make an appointment with my doctor."

"Okay, can you hold for a minute?"

"Sure."

I started to feel genuinely sick and exhausted. Mono exhausted.

"He's booked pretty solid for the next couple weeks, but I just had a cancellation for tomorrow afternoon at two if that works for you?"

"Sounds great. See you then."

"See you then."

So, I had just over twenty-four hours to fake mono. I had to get my lymph nodes up and my lying liar lies down pat. I decided to research first and leave the poisoning until later in the day. I wouldn't be much use researching after that for a few days.

I wrote a sticky note of mono's symptoms and stuck it to the front of my notebook.

Beep.

"Hi Jane, I'm still not feeling well. I'm going to the doctor tomorrow hopefully he can get to the bottom of this. Sorry to let you down, I hope things aren't getting too out of control over there without me." I was kind of sarcastic, but really, without me there would be a lot of extra work on her desk, and I didn't like dumping it on her.

Next on the agenda was online shopping with Sam. I selected and dressed in a time-appropriate costume. The initial printing was finished, so I set it up again, and split up the printed documents into books and papers, then added them to a box, and peeked through the portal.

Sam was there.

I pushed the box through to him.

"Wow, you've been busy."

"Yeah, I bought a high-volume laser printer, ten toner cartridges, and ten boxes of paper. I'm not sure how it will work out on the paper to toner ratio, it might be a hot dog to hot dog bun scenario, but I'm hoping I'll be able to print the whole database before we find out." I laughed.

"Awesome."

Sam had a pot of tea and two chairs set up at one of the tables.

"This is nice. Perfect for a day of online shopping," I said.

"We have a problem. Zeta saw us using the laptop."

"How?" I looked to the papered windows.

"She was looking through a little sliver of an opening in the paper."

I noticed there were new strips of paper hung over all of the seams.

"What did you say to her?"

"I told her she was crazy."

"You what? Sam—never tell a woman she's crazy, unless you want to see true crazy like you can't handle."

"I could have used that information yesterday."

"I feel like that's pretty basic. You should have learned it on Sesame Street."

"Anyway, what am I supposed to do now? She's furious."

"Do you trust her?"

"Yes. I asked her to marry me. That's a secret. Do. Not. Tell. Anyone. Also, I think her writing matches the documents.

"If you trust her enough to marry her, just tell her. Bring her over, I'll take her on the tour."

"You're right. I will. When she's finished working."

"It's good timing really. If you told her after the portal was closed, you'd risk her thinking you're crazy."

"Oh, so it's okay if for her to think I'm crazy, but not for me to think she's crazy?" He was incredulous.

"You evoked the word crazy to lie to her. Big difference."

"I don't see it."

"Yes, you do. Stop defending yourself. You did something wrong, don't die on this hill. Admit it, apologize, and move on. We'll both have more respect for you if you do."

He tried to reply, but I shooshed him for his own good.

We filled our Amazon cart with purchases for the cause, and a few things that would make Sam's life easier.

Clive burst through the back door. "Dr. Harver, a famous botanist, is speaking!" He could hardly get the words out fast enough.

"Here?" Sam was excited too.

"Well, no, not here, in New York, but at least you won't have to travel to England to meet him." Clive's excitement diminished, losing steam as he looked at Sam's face.

"New York." Sam said it like it was impossible. "When?"

"Next Tuesday." Clive handed Sam a folded page from the newspaper.

Sam looked totally overwhelmed.

"Don't worry about a thing," Clive said. "I've been to New York a few times, I know exactly which trains to take, and I've even been to this venue before. All you need to do is pack. We'll have to leave by tomorrow evening."

Sam's eyebrows knotted and he held his head with both hands like he had a massive migraine.

"I just need to think about this," Sam said.

"Check the timeline and family history pages," I said.

Sam nodded. "Yes, do you have yours here?"

I went to the counter and pulled my timelines from a folder.

"I will go to New York and meet Dr. Harver," Sam said.

There were a few flickering changes on both pages, but not enough on the family page.

"I will go to New York and make a solid connection with Dr. Harver."

Again, a few flickering changes, but not enough on the family page.

"Will you come with me?" he asked Clive.

"Yes," Clive answered.

The pages changed a little more.

"Will you come?" Sam asked me.

"Yes." I said it and without thinking, but I meant it.

The family page changed drastically.

There was a picture of Sam with his parents and a little league team. Everyone was wearing red jerseys. The caption noted Sam was the coach. Everyone was smiling, happy, and safe.

We were stunned.

Sam's eyes started tearing up, staring at the picture.

"How long is the trip?" I asked.

"Five days there, five days back," Clive said.

The family page started to flicker back.

"What if the portal closes while we're gone? My family will never know what happened to me. It will destroy my mom." The weight of the ramifications of the trip came down on me.

The picture changed completely. A school photo of Sam with the caption, *North Dakota graduate feared missing in Manitoba.* The article went on to sum up the terrible history of his family.

We were speechless.

"I wish we could create a page like this to see what my family will go through if I go to New York," I said. "But I can't look at future history."

"Please come, I need you Lilac, this is everything to me." Sam took my hands in his and looked into my eyes.

"I . . . I . . ." I didn't know what to say.

Sam hugged me, his body shaking. "Please, I need you," he whispered in my ear.

I was tearing up too. I wanted to help him, but I thought of my mom spending the rest of her life searching for me, wondering if I was okay. I couldn't do that to her.

"Maybe there's another way, maybe Lilac isn't the only key. What could Lilac offer on the trip? Maybe someone else can do it," Clive offered.

Sam loosened from the hug but held me in his warmth. "We don't have time; this will fix everything. Lilac, I need you, please." He traced his finger along my face and behind my ear, clearing my hair out of my eyes. He took a hanky from his pocket and wiped the tears from my face.

I felt my brain cracking open.

Clive stood up. "Sam, stop. Lilac has family too. You can't ask this of her. She's already done far more for you than the last woman, but this is too far—you can't ask her to do this."

Whiplash.

"What?" I asked. "What do you mean, the last woman?"

"The other woman who came through the portal," Clive said.

"What are you talking about?"

"Sam, I thought you told her everything." Clive stared Sam down.

Sam didn't say anything.

"Stop touching her." He pushed Sam's hand down, releasing

mine. "Don't look at her like that, this isn't something you should charm someone into doing."

I felt as used, and stupid, and dirty as was possible.

I felt a blackness coming and my heart was hurting.

"I told you the other night, you don't understand. I kissed her because I was thinking of Zeta. That's the truth. I told Lilac that," Sam said.

Clive looked at me for confirmation. I nodded.

"That's despicable and inappropriate, but it doesn't change what you're trying to do right now. You have this power over people, Sam. I won't let you use it on Lilac for your gain. I didn't see any harm in your thinking—charming her into doing what she was willing to do. But now, you're forcing her. She isn't doing this willingly."

Sam looked at me. "There was another woman who came through the portal. It was while Clive was away at war. I didn't tell you about her because it hurt. I didn't know you, and I didn't want you to think about your options. I'm selfish, I know. I just need your help. I'm sorry, Lilac. She wouldn't help me, but I did get something valuable from her—data. She's the reason I have total confidence you won't be stuck in 1920. The portal was open for me for exactly eight weeks, and it was open for her for exactly eight weeks. So, I know you're safe to go back and forth for eight weeks. We have plenty of time."

"Why wouldn't she help you?" I asked.

"She had her own problems, she couldn't even hear mine. She was hiding in the apartment, squatting there. She never had the ability you do. She wouldn't have been able to accomplish half of what you have. She was looking for quick ways to score financially, she didn't give a rip about mankind, that's for sure."

"Eight weeks, for sure?"

"Yes, I promise. I'm sorry I didn't tell you about her, I could see right away you were so much more competent and capable, and I knew I needed your help. You could have done a thousand things to help yourself since you've been here. I selfishly needed you to focus on me."

"Why didn't you go through the portal when she opened it and correct the problem yourself, Sam?"

"I didn't know then that it would close on me."

"So why won't you go through it now, if you know it will be open eight weeks?" I asked.

"It was traumatizing when it closed. And I'm not totally sure it won't close on me. I'm scared it might have a conscious and hate me."

"I want to say that's not logical, but really, who knows? I don't know anything about the portal, except that it's open. Maybe it's a good idea you stay away from it." I sighed. "I'm going to go upstairs and not be here."

"Wait." Sam took my hand.

"No. You wait. I'm angry and need to cool off." I went back to my apartment and dove into the ice cream.

⸻

"Lilac?" Clive called from my craft room.

"Yeah, come on in." I was laying on the couch eating.

"Are you okay?"

"No."

"May I?" He motioned to sit on the couch.

I moved my legs so he had room.

"I hate that I'm that girl," I said.

"Well, you are a girl. Sam's just a charmer all the time. You're inherently kind and helpful. You weren't tricked into helping him, you would have helped him anyway."

"Do you think he kissed me because he was thinking of Zeta, or just to manipulate me? In that exact moment I thought he was falling for me."

"That's the logical conclusion, because you are lovable."

I laughed.

I thought about Sam carrying me across the street, the winks, the smiles, the unnecessary touches. *Yeah, he's a big flirt.* "He's a player, and I got played."

"Mostly he's harmless. He makes people feel good about themselves. Yes, he can be manipulating. He's broken a few hearts. I excused his behavior as Sam being Sam. His love life is his business. For most women, a heartbreak is part of growing up. One of his cast-off's read me a passage that's stuck with me: 'Next to being married, a girl likes to be crossed in love a little now and then. It is something to think of, and gives her a sort of distinction among her companions.' I've been justifying Sam's way with those words ever since."

I laughed. "*Pride and Prejudice*, Mr. Bennet. It's true I guess, but how do you know that book?"

"Mandatory reading with sisters. Have you been crossed a little in love? I'm sorry, I shouldn't have asked that."

"It's okay. Yeah, I have, a little, now a little more. I feel stupid. I don't want to go around with my guard up all the time. It would be nice if people had good intentions toward each other. I hate having to put on body armor."

"When I got home from the war, I was broken. I couldn't even look anyone in the eye. Sam smoothed everything over for me. He took the attention off me and helped me find my place again. I was grateful for his personality then."

"Hopefully Zeta can fix his wagon." I laughed.

"It's interesting he mentioned Zeta. I always thought there was a little something between them. It's hard to tell because of his way, but I felt like he looked at her a little longer than others."

"I'm sure there's more to the story. He wouldn't tell me. When you called him out, I worried he just made up the story about Zeta, but I couldn't think of why."

"I do think there's something between him and Zeta, but still, when he saw that you coming to New York fixed the timelines, he turned on every manipulation tool in his vast repertoire. I couldn't let Sam do that to you."

"Thanks."

"I didn't know he hadn't told you about the other woman, I assumed he did. Sorry about that, it might have changed things."

"Probably not, I would have wondered why on earth she wouldn't help and work even harder for him. I mean, I care about the world; I care about farmers. I'm sorry about his family, and if I can help, I want to."

"What do you think about going to New York?"

"I have time, if it's safe and it will help, why wouldn't I? I only came up here because I felt like screaming at him. Even though he's a jerk, he's been through a lot. I wanted to cool off before I responded."

"You're a good woman, Lilac."

"Do you think Sam's lying about the eight-week window?"

"He has reason to, and he's a good liar, but I believe he was telling the truth. What did you think?"

"I don't feel like I'm a great judge of information right now. Can you think of any way we could confirm it?"

We sat thinking for a while. Neither of us had any ideas.

"Want some?" I offered him my spoon to eat some ice cream.

He took it and ate a spoonful. "This is amazing."

"Right?"

We kept thinking and eating.

"All we have is his word. You know him better than anyone,

could you ask him and see what you think? I trust your judgment. You saw right through his love bombing, and I think you could see through false intentions."

"Love bombing?" Clive chuckled. "Good words, fitting. Dangerous, relentless, devastating." He rose from the couch. "I'll do it."

———◆———

I didn't listen right next to the portal, but I did go into the craft room to compile the printed pages and reset the printer and was able to hear the tone of their conversation. Jerk or not, I wanted to help Sam because, in the end, he might just be a good man grieving. Clive was firm, Sam's replies were subdued. There wasn't any crying. They talked for about forty minutes. When I heard Clive coming back across the room, I returned to the couch.

"Lilac?" Clive called.

"Come in!"

He sat beside me. "I think he's telling the truth. I wouldn't risk your family for his. I asked him every way I could think of and looked for his tells. I believe him, and I believe you have eight weeks total before the portal will close."

I felt a wave of relief. "Thank you, Clive." I hugged him and felt full body electricity. I could hardly let him go it felt so good.

"You are more than welcome," he said, and hugged me harder.

There was only so long a hug felt friendly, and we had surpassed that time by a long shot. I pulled back. "Why do you think I need to go, what possible difference could I make?"

"I don't know. Maybe we should go look at that newspaper article again."

Just before we went back through the portal, I hugged Clive again. I was addicted to how he made me feel. *He is not the rebound, maybe he's been the first shot all along.* "Thank you for . . . helping me feel better. It's more than just today, I've been having a hard time in my life, and I feel better than I've felt in a long time."

"Me too." Clive lifted me off the ground with his hug, then we crossed the portal to set ground rules with Sam.

***

"I'll go with you to New York, but no more lies, and no more flirting with me to get your way." I wagged my finger at Sam with my hand on my hip.

"I swear it. I'm sorry," Sam said.

"If we're going to do this thing, I have a lot of preparations. I need a bag or suitcase."

"I have one you can use," Sam said.

I reached out my hand to shake his. "We're going to save your family, together."

He shook it. "Thank you and I'm sorry. No excuses, I'm just very sorry."

"I accept. Please get my luggage."

Sam left and Clive and I examined the article announcing Dr. Harver's presentation, word by word, for any clues as to why my attendance would change the timelines. At the bottom it mentioned a list of other botanists who would be in attendance. Dr. Wang was mentioned among them.

"Perhaps Dr. Wang is Chinese. I speak Mandarin—maybe that's why?"

"You speak Chinese?"

"Yeah, my friend Lan was Chinese, I took Mandarin in school and practiced it with her and her family, I'm not so bad."

"You're full of surprises."

"You don't know the half of it."

"I'm interested to find out," he said, running his finger down my arm.

I felt my face turning red.

Sam returned holding what looked like a carpeted satchel. "Here's a bag you can use. The handle is a little bit broken, but it works fine if you just hold it like this." He pulled the leather strap tight and back over itself.

"Thank you."

"When do we leave and for how long will we be gone?" I asked Clive. "I have to get out of work and tell my family something."

"I'll go purchase our tickets. I think two weeks would be on the conservative side. Five days there and five back, plus a couple of days there."

"I think we should only spend as much time in New York as necessary," Sam said. "I want to get back to the work we have to do here. I'll need to prepare all of the patents for registration quickly."

"If you can get two weeks, Lilac, I know we can be back within that window," Clive said.

"Okay, I'll get right on it."

Back in my apartment, I collated printed pages and set the printer up for the next round.

I decided mono would get me out of working, but I didn't think my doctor would be able to make a diagnosis quickly. Skipping out of work for two weeks without any notice would be impossible without a very contagious illness. Actually, contracting a contagious illness would make the trip pointless because I would be sick the whole time and miss out on everything. The other real possibility of taking a modern-day superbug plague to New York, and wiping out the future as I knew it, was also unpleasant. Concocting an excuse for my family was no picnic either. I talked to one family member or another every day. After two or three days I would have the Royal Canadian Mounted Police looking for me.

Better to get it over with.

"Hi, Mom."

"Lilac, my sweet girl, you sound happy."

"Yeah, I wanted to let you know I'm going camping off grid for two and a half weeks. I didn't want you to worry, since you won't be hearing from me." I hated lying to her.

"Oh, sounds exciting."

"Yeah, I'm super stoked. I'm going with a group, there's a doctor and a hunter and a parks naturalist with us, so I feel like I'm going to be looked after no matter what comes up. I don't know what I contribute to the group, but I was happy to be invited." My lies were flowing so easily. *I'm a horrible person. If I die in a train crash, they'll never know what happened to me.*

"You have your sterling personality. You'll make them all laugh."

"Thanks Mom, I love you. I've got to pack, but I'll call you when I get back." Hearing her voice was killing me, lying to her was killing me.

"I think it will be healing for you to be outside in the wild and the sunshine. Happy trails, my dear, I love you."

"Love you too, bye."

Ending the call, I still felt unsettled. I wrote a long letter to my family telling them how I loved them, and the absolute truth about what was going on: time travel, the portal, lying, everything. I thought if something unforeseen happened on the trip, at least they would have my explanation, however unbelievable it was. *If I really was going on an off-the-grid camping trip, there'd be a good chance they'd never find my body if something happened to me. Every day on this planet, no matter what time we live in, there's a chance we could die.*

I heard the printer stop, so I collated the pages and put them in the box. That box was full, so I set it by the portal, and racked up the next round of printing before heading to Brandon. I had to buy things for the trip, and I didn't want to run into anyone from work.

Uncle!

I called Uncle and arranged to stop by to hang the license plate on my way to Brandon. I knew he wouldn't be able to wait two and a half weeks; he'd be suspicious of my story if I delayed him hanging the plate. I repeated the story I told Mom while we were hanging it, and he was so happy and distracted—he just wished me happy camping. *Sheesh, and I'm mad a Sam for manipulating me?*

In Brandon, pizza was the first stop on my list. Next up, I hit the bakery. I wasn't sure how much gluten it would take for my glands to mimic fake mono, but I needed to make sure I had enough on hand. I bought a pepperoni pizza, a soft pretzel as big as my head, a chocolate cupcake, a baguette, a sausage roll, a cinnamon bun, a lemon poppy seed muffin, an herb scone, and a piece of New York cheesecake—in honor of the trip. *That ought to do it.*

Looking at the boxes and bags on my passenger seat, I wondered how much food I could physically consume. Even without gluten, this much food would make me sick.

Once back at home, I made a final phone call before I started in on the gluten. I didn't want to be loopy when I called Kent.

"Howdy," Kent said.

"Hey. I'm going camping. I'll be off the grid for a while."

"I'm glad to hear it. You need a break and some exercise. Nothing beats running-from-bears boot camp."

"Very funny. I just wanted to let you know so you wouldn't worry. Apparently, it's a non-issue."

"No, have fun camping. I'm glad you're going. Just remember— bears only view pepper spray as seasoning."

"That's such an old man joke, Kent. You really gotta watch some TV or something."

"I'll get right on that."

"I'll be gone for two weeks or so . . . Depends if I hate it and want to come home." I thought I sounded normal. *Am I trying too hard to sound normal?*

"Wow, must be nice to have two weeks off!"

"Yeah, the perks of working for the town, I guess."

"Well good for you, have fun."

"I will, I'll draw you a picture or something."

"I look forward to it."

Suddenly, I felt like if I died of tuberculosis on the trip, this would be our last conversation. My throat closed up and I felt like bawling.

"I love you, Kent."

"You're not going to get eaten by a bear." He knew exactly what I was thinking, just not the full circumstances.

"But you know I love you, right?"

"Believe me, I know. I know you do your best anyway." I could see his bratty smile right through the phone. "I should probably get going, apparently I have some TV to watch."

I didn't want to let him go, but I didn't want to be weird, either.

"Okay. Well, have fun and I'll talk to you in a couple weeks."

"Later," he said and clicked off.

I had a little meltdown.

I resisted the urge to call into work until I had the doctor's note in hand.

I couldn't pack much, so I just packed all the clothes Sam gave me in the carpet bag and carried it to the portal. I thought of one more thing to do while I still had brain power. I googled the names of the other scientists listed in the ad with Dr. Harver and printed out my research.

Now, down to the eating of the gluten. Maybe I should warn Clive and Sam.

———————◆———————

I picked up my research and went through the portal. No one was in the shop. I walked to Sam's lab. Both Sam and Clive were there.

"First, here's some research about who else is going to be in New York. Second, I need you guys to know something."

I could see Sam was holding his breath.

"I'm in, don't worry" I said.

He let it go. "Thank you."

"Do we know when we're leaving yet?" I asked.

"I paid for the tickets already, we leave at five o'clock tomorrow evening," Clive said.

"Thank you. That works. By the way, we have a disease in my time called mononucleosis, I don't know if you have it now, or what it may be called. Anyway, I think I can fake its symptoms, and it will qualify for sick days from work without any questions for the next few weeks."

"Okay," Clive said.

"The thing is . . . to fake it, I have to eat something I'm allergic to. I won't die, but it's going to make me feel really sick."

Clive looked concerned. "Is there some other way, this doesn't sound like a good plan."

"I need to keep my job, because in seven-ish weeks I'm going to wish I did, you know?" The thought of leaving Clive stabbed me in the heart.

"Yes, of course, but could you take a vacation from work?"

"I've already used my vacation days. I've been trying to think of another way, but we're getting down to crunch time, and I need to make some kind of plan. This was all I could come up with."

Clive glanced at Sam. I could practically read Clive's mind. *What do you think, Sam? You're the expert liar here.*

"Mono is a good excuse, it's super contagious, long lasting, hard to diagnose, and will meet the threshold for sick leave, for sure," Sam said.

I shrugged at Clive.

"How sick will it make you?" Clive asked.

"Here's the thing. It makes me tired, but the main thing is it gives me hallucinations." I waited for the thunder.

Sam laughed. "What do you mean?"

Clive looked worried.

"I mean, I'm going to think I see things that aren't there," I said.

"Like what?" Sam asked.

"I usually see raptors, like from *Jurassic Park*."

Sam burst out laughing like it was the craziest thing he ever heard.

"What's that?" Clive asked.

"A dinosaur," Sam said.

Clive looked to me for confirmation.

"Yeah."

"That sounds terrifying."

"It is, that's why I don't ever eat it," I said.

"What exactly are you allergic to?" Sam asked.

"Gluten."

"Bread, wheat, flour ..." Sam explained to Clive.

"Because of genetic modification?" Clive asked.

"It's a theory," I said.

"So, this mission is important to you too," Clive said.

"In a way. Although I'm very used to not eating gluten, obviously, it would be nice to confirm if genetic modification was the culprit."

"So, if you're doing this, what do you need from us? How can we help?" Clive asked.

"Actually, I came to tell you because I want you to understand what state I'll be in tomorrow, and probably for the first couple days of our trip. It will wear off, but even a couple days later I still might have brief, scary flashes of things."

"Should I be with you?" Clive asked.

I wasn't expecting that. I planned on pigging out alone. "It's a lot to ask. I truly just came to warn you."

"Really, I want to. I was a field medic. I would feel better if I could monitor you," Clive said.

Having him with me would make me feel better. *Let the good wash over you.* "Okay, that's very kind. I would appreciate it."

"Thank you," Sam said to Clive.

———◆———

We climbed through the portal back to my apartment. It felt nice to be cared about.

"I have enough food for both of us. Do you want to try some more food from my time?"

"Yes, I loved the things you got me from the fuel station."

"What if you get sick from my time gluten too?"

"Well then it's going to be an interesting night, isn't it?" He laughed.

Very.

I set the temperature to preheat the oven.

"I think we should start with pizza because you're going to love it." My mouth watered as I said it.

"Okay, whatever you think, I'm here to help."

"Should we watch a movie while we eat?"

"Yes, I would like that."

"We could watch *Jurassic Park*, it's about dinosaurs."

"Do you think that's wise, Lilac, considering your halluc-inations?"

"They're already burned into my mind. At least then—you'll know what I'm seeing."

"Sound reasoning. Let's do it."

I queued up the movie on the TV, all ready to go. The oven chimed, so I put the pizza in and selected plates and napkins. I poured our drinks and brought blankets over to the couch for the full, movie watching experience. As soon as the cheese bubbled, I brought the pizza to the coffee table and turned off all the lights so we could eat by the blue light of the TV screen, like normal people.

Just before we got to the scene where the lawyer is eaten by the T-rex, our pizza was finished, and Clive was fully engrossed. I paused the movie.

"What do you think so far?"

"I can see how this would become burned into your mind," he said.

"I need to keep eating gluten, I want to make sure I'm good and sick tomorrow."

"I understand. I'm full, but do what you must."

"Yeah, I'm full too. Maybe I should pace myself. I don't want to make myself sick."

He laughed. "Isn't that the point?"

"Right, right. See? It's already affecting my mind. I'll eat one more thing." I ripped the oversized soft pretzel in two, leaving half for Clive.

I sat back down.

Clive moved closer to me. "Since I'm here to monitor you, I should probably be closer to you so I can do that properly. I'm clearly not coming closer to you because I'm terrified of what we're watching."

"You'll hear no protest from me. The first time I watched this in the movie theatre, I screamed."

"Did you?" He laughed.

"I did."

We carried on, getting closer and closer with every scary scene until I woke up to the sound of scratching on the skylight above my bed. I was too scared to reach for my glasses, but I tried to see by barely opening my eyes.

I saw a huge shadow—my worst fear.

I always knew this day would come.

Scared out of my wits, I shut my eyes, my breathing accelerated causing my blanket to move up and down with every breath. I panicked, certain the vile creature could hear me breathing and see the blanket moving.

Tap. Tap. Tap.

It's not real. It's not real. It's not real.

I opened my eyes—just teeny tiny slits. There it was! Nine feet straight above me. I stared into the raptor's illuminated eyeball as it cocked its repulsive head to the side, eyeing its next meal—me!

Where's Clive, wasn't Clive here?

I squeezed my eyes shut and prayed for it to go away. I prayed to wake up. I prayed for the hallucination to stop.

Tap. Tap. Tap.

If time travel is real, maybe a raptor came through a portal to stop us from using the oil from its fossil? I don't think that's how it works.

I couldn't control my erratic breathing. Each gasp for air was never enough.

Turn on the lights, just turn on the lights and it will disappear.

If it disappears when I turn on the lights, that means it isn't real right now, just go back to sleep.

My face and ears were burning.

I quickly hit my touch lamp and the light went on. I looked at the skylight and all I could see was the reflection of the lamp. I put on my glasses and looked up again. I thought I saw the flicker of a blinking eye. I shut the lamp off, and the raptor screamed into the glass.

I covered my ears trying not to hear its obnoxious screeching. I was still wearing my jeans and T-shirt, but I wrapped my blanket around me and ran from my room, pillow in hand. I was going to crash on my couch, but a raptor was curled up on it.

This isn't real, this isn't real, this isn't real.

I didn't have curtains on my living room or kitchen windows. Soon I heard the tapping. Even without looking I could imagine raptors scaling the heritage building, bricks falling to the ground as they climbed. I hoped they wouldn't wake the sleeping raptor on my couch.

I wanted to call Mom or Kent, but it was the middle of the night and they would want to know what was going on. I didn't want to tell them. Besides, what could they do?

This is probably a hallucination. They can wake me out of it!

I grabbed the phone and went into the corner of the kitchen.

"Howdy," Kent answered.

"Kent?"

"Um, yes, Lilac. Bears won't eat you." I could tell he was trying to minimize how much sleep this was going to cost him.

"I ate gluten."

"How much?" I could hear him sitting up in bed.

"I'm seeing raptors."

"Let me make some coffee."

Tap. Tap. Tap.

"Wow, you're good at that," Kent said.

"At what?!" Now I was double terrified—Kent had heard the raptor too.

"At making raptor noises."

"What?!" I pulled the blanket down and looked at the creature's razor-sharp, demented smile just outside my kitchen window. I yanked the blanket back over my head, and smooshed myself further into the corner, because, for sure that would help. I put my head down, shaking and fighting tears.

"Lilac, I'm kidding. I heard you jump. I deduced, I commented."

"You're a bad brother and I hate you."

"It's 3:00 a.m. on a work night. I'm not a bad person if I have a little fun with you."

"Fair enough." I said it, but didn't mean it, and looked at the raptor again. It was trying to figure out the lock mechanism on the window, a gnarled talon poking at it.

A real raptor would just break the window.

"It's trying to open the window lock!" I whisper yelled, and then realized I was talking to my brother *through the remote control.* I flung it to the floor.

Carefully, I felt my lymph nodes, and they were up, but not solid.

I need a solid diagnosis. I want the gluten out of me, but I need to do this, for Sam's family, and all humanity.

"Lilac? Are you okay?" *A raptor ate Clive's voice box!*

The raptor crept toward me. I screamed and curled into a ball.

"Lilac, it's me, Clive."

I tried to fight it off through my blanket, but it managed to rip it away from me. *Like unwrapping a burrito.*

"Lilac!"

Clive grabbed my wrists and lifted me to my feet. "Lilac, look at me. It's Clive." He hugged me, and wow, his arms felt nice. And there was that familiar electric zap.

"Clive?" I saw him, it was Clive, and then I started bawling.

He hugged me tighter. "It's me, you're safe. I've got you. Everything's okay. I'm right here."

He kept holding me and I kept crying. It'd gone from terror to confusion to tears of relief.

I felt my lymph nodes. *Hard as rocks.*

"Feel, it worked." I guided his hands to my neck.

"I could have told you that without feeling your neck." He laughed.

The raptor outside the window snapped its jaw at me. I jumped.

"Where do we go from here?" Clive asked.

"I should probably try to go back to sleep. Eat more in the morning. I see the doctor tomorrow afternoon."

"Okay." He followed me into the bedroom, watching me closely.

"I'm going to put some pajamas on."

"Okay, don't forget who I am," he said as he left the room.

"K," I said.

I quickly changed into my PJ's because the raptor was up on the skylight watching me.

Clive came back into the bedroom, and sat in the chair, looking perfectly normal.

"Can I tell you something?" I asked.

"At this point, anything." He grinned.

"When you touch me, it feels like electricity's running through me."

He chuckled. "For me too."

"Do you think you could just have your hand on me while I'm sleeping? I want to for sure know it's you when I wake up."

"I can do that." He lay on top of the blankets, next to me. "Get comfortable."

I did. He moved closer and held my hand.

When I woke up, we were still like that, and I knew who he was right away. He was looking at me. I felt silly.

"Good morning," I said.

"Good afternoon." He laughed.

"What time is it?"

"One."

"I can't believe I slept so late." I yawned.

"I was a little worried, but your color, pulse, and breathing were fine, so I figured you needed it." He swept the hair from in front of my eyes behind my ear.

"Thank you for looking after me, sorry about last night."

"It's beautiful that you'd make this kind of sacrifice for Sam's family, Lilac, even after everything."

"In the grand scheme, it's a small thing," I said. "A few days of gluten hallucinations in exchange for two people's lives—worth it."

"Sadly, I think there are lots of people in this world who wouldn't think it was worth it."

"None of them are in this room though." I desperately wanted to kiss him, but I didn't. "I should probably call work."

* * *

I put on a pot of coffee and called in to the office.

"Virden Town Hall," Jane said.

"Hi Jane. It's Lilac. I'm sorry I didn't call earlier. I just got up. I'm still sick. I'm going to the doctor this afternoon. I'll let you know more when I know more," I said, sounding exactly how I felt—exhausted.

"It's okay Lilac, I know you're going to the doctor, you called yesterday. You just rest," she said, soothingly.

I forgot I called yesterday, so much has happened since then.

"Thank you, Jane. I sure wish I could be there." I kinda did wish I could be there. I wished I could be everywhere I wanted, and do everything I wanted, and never let anyone down. Unfortunately, life wasn't like that, you had to prioritize.

"Feel better and we'll see you soon," Jane said, just before she clicked off.

I closed my eyes to think, and I heard tapping.

Leave me alone.

More tapping.

"Leave me alone!" I yelled.

"Lilac?"

It was Clive. Well, Clive's head on a raptor's body. "Coffee." He handed me a cup, cream stirred in already.

"Touch me," I said.

He touched my arm and turned back into Clive, head to toe.

"You're very cooperative."

"Only with things I want to do anyway." He laughed. "While you were sleeping, Zeta came up. Sam told her about the portal. She came to see for herself. I showed her a few of the things in here that you showed me. I'm not an expert, but I tried. And, she had news. She's coming to New York with us."

"Good, maybe she'll make Sam behave himself." I laughed.

"Agreed."

"Do you have things to do before we go?" I asked.

"A few, but do you want me to come to the doctor with you?"

"I'll be okay. I mean, I won't be, but that's the point. It's better if I go it alone."

He hugged me, and yes, I experienced a full body jolt of electricity. "Please be careful, Lilac. I'll be waiting for you in the shop, so we can go to the train together."

"Thank you, Clive, for everything, this has been the least bad hallucination I've had."

I watched him leave through the portal, then I ate quite a bit more of the bakery items to solidify my medical situation. I dressed and felt my lymph nodes. *Brass balls.*

I'd never had so much gluten in such a short time before, so I wasn't totally sure what would happen.

I grabbed my purse and the list of mono symptoms, so I could review them while I waited.

"Lilac? You can go into room four," the receptionist said after I'd been waiting only a few minutes.

I walked down the hall looking for room four, which sounded close, but turned out to be down a long hallway, and around the corner. I looked into an open door and spotted a little girl. She smiled at me and then stuck out her two-foot forked tongue.

I moved along a little faster, found my room and shut the door. *Anything you see that's weird isn't real.*

I had to wait quite a while until the doctor came, which was good because I was there for mono, not anxiety attacks. By the time he got there, I'd memorized my symptoms and was calmed down.

"What can I do for you today, Lilac?" he asked.

"Well, I've been so . . . tired," I said, feeling tired as I said it.

His head flickered just for a second into a raptor head. "Oh?"

"I've had a sore throat, though it doesn't feel too bad today, mostly I just feel tired. I had a fever last night; I was sweating and then cold." I tried to ignore the shape of his head changing. I closed my eyes both to look tired and to stop seeing the transformation.

"Hmmmmm." he said.

"I went to Winnipeg with some friends for the weekend last month and my girlfriend just called to tell me she has mono. I've only been feeling sick for about a week or thereabouts, so it probably isn't that, but I thought I should mention it."

"Well, actually, mono can take a while to show up." He reached toward me to feel my lymph nodes. His arms were scaly, and his fingernails turned into claws.

I took a deep breath and closed my eyes as he felt around gently.

"You've certainly got some kind of infection," he said. "How are you for strength?"

"I've been weak, sometimes I'm too tired even to eat. I can hardly lift a glass of water."

"Are you sleeping okay?"

"I feel tired and I'm sleeping, even sleeping in late, but I just wake up tired, I'm not sure if I'm not sleeping deeply or what."

"Let me have a look at your throat."

I always gag when they put that wooden thing in my mouth, so I have learned to open my mouth wide the first time.

He shone his little light in there. I knew it wasn't red, but I hoped the other symptoms would be enough.

"Good."

I slumped back down in my chair.

"Headaches?"

"Off and on. Not migraines, just the kind that make you want to sleep for relief."

"Let's just take your temperature."

I couldn't fake this one either. He put the thermometer in my ear.

"Not too bad, but you've got a low-grade fever."

Must be the gluten.

"Well, I'll send you for a blood test, but don't be surprised if it comes back negative, mono is a hard one to pin down, the tests aren't always accurate. I would suggest treating it like mono for now."

I could hardly believe my ears. It was a full win.

His face was also now fully reptilian.

"What about work?" I asked.

"I'll write you a note." He rolled his chair back to his computer and started typing.

"How long do you think I'll be off for?"

"I'm sorry to say it could be a while. How about you come and see me again in a week?"

"Okay." I didn't want to fight him on it, but I knew I would be gone for two weeks at least.

He hit print and then looked at me as the printer prepared and then printed my magic note.

"You'll need to get lots of rest. Drink lots of fluids, no active sports, no strenuous activities. Gargle with salt water when your throat hurts, take Tylenol for headaches or fever. Mostly, sleeping is going to get you through this." He gave me a pity smile.

The printer beeped. He turned around, grabbed the note and handed it to me.

"Thank you," I said to the lizard doctor.

I walked out the door as calmly as possible, though once I had my back to him, I was fairly certain he was going to pull me back into the room and eat me.

I tried to act normal walking down the hall, but I was walking too fast and tripped on my flip flop. I couldn't go down gracefully either, I had to take a janitorial cart with me. Twenty raptor heads popped out of doors all along the hallway, and I started crying.

Way to fly under the radar.

One of the lab lizards brought a wheelchair over and a couple of other raptors helped me into it. I'd scraped up my knee a bit, and my head was fogging over, I could feel my grip on reality getting harder and harder to hold on to.

"I'm sorry, I just need a minute." I held up my hand. I needed to refocus. "Thank you all so much for your help." It wasn't that I wasn't grateful, I just had so much gluten in me it was unbelievable. With the pain distracting me I was losing all mental control.

"Lilac?" asked a scary clown.

I just stared at her. *That's new.*

"Sorry, are you Lilac?" she asked again.

"Sorry, yes, I am." My crazy cover hadn't been blown quite yet.

"I'm supposed to take you for your blood work. Is that okay?"

"Sure."

Before I could get my bearings, she was pushing me in the chair.

Well, this is nice.

We arrived at the lab, and the scary clown pulled a huge needle from the drawer. I couldn't react, so I just smiled and turned my head. She did her thing while I imagined blood pumping from my arm all over the room.

"There you go." She put the most normal looking Band-Aid in the world on my arm.

After that I went straight home. I waved at the raptors that waved to me, nodded at the ones who nodded at me. I was home inside eight minutes. I set my clock for a one-hour nap and tried to sleep off some of the crazy.

I woke up to the sound of my alarm ringing, instead of raptor tapping, which was refreshing.

I looked at my list of things to do and called work.

"Virden Town Hall," Jane said.

"Hi, Jane. It's Lilac. The doctor says I have mono. I have a note, should I bring it in?" I asked.

"Well, if you have mono, you probably shouldn't come in, not that we don't love you, but really, it's one of those things nobody wants to get."

As she said it, I could already tell she was feeling bad for saying it and would probably drop off flowers with an apology.

"How about this? I'll take a picture of it and text it to you."

"Sounds good."

"I think I'm going to go stay with family until I feel better."

"Oh, okay . . . I wanted to send you flowers."

I know her so well, what a sweetie.

"Awww, that's very thoughtful Jane, but to tell you the truth, I'm too tired to enjoy them, but it's very kind."

"Okay. Well, you rest and drink lots of fluids and hopefully we'll see you real soon."

"Thanks Jane."

I hung up before she could ask me if I'd have email access or a phone number where she could reach me.

I took a picture of the note and texted it to her with the comment, "I don't have roaming on this phone number, but I'll let you know when I'm back in town."

She texted back, "Thanks. Feel better. Hugs."

Almost ready to go.

I emptied my fridge of things that would go bad and left a note on my table for Buck and Jan if they came into the suite for some emergency reason and wondered where I was. I cleaned my bathroom and made my bed. There were raptors lurking, but they kept their distance, and I focused on the tasks at hand.

Finally, I put on my period-specific clothing and crawled through the portal.

CHAPTER 8

Zeta

♫ **"Bad Romance"** ♫
by Scott Bradlee's Postmodern Jukebox

Sam came to buy supper from me.

"I'm sorry," Sam said.

"For what?" I took his money and empty jar, then handed him a full one.

"I have a lot to tell you. I'm sorry I wasn't honest with you. You deserve better."

"Explain."

"I need to talk to you, privately."

There was a time the thought of being with Sam privately sent fire through my blood. Not today. Today it opened the gates of hell.

"I'm busy." I still had eight suppers to sell.

"I'll wait, or I'll buy the rest of your jars, whichever you prefer."

"Wait." I didn't want my beautiful food going to waste, he wouldn't be able to eat eight jars before they spoiled. Also, I wanted him to wait. I was furious.

I made sure to make extra conversation with each customer. He waited and didn't even look irritated.

"I've sold my last supper. What do you want to say?" I asked.

"I'd like to show you the book we were looking at." He motioned for me to follow.

I left Zizzo tied up and followed him.

Inside the papered-up shop there was a smidgeon of light coming from the top of the shelving on the side wall.

"First, I want to say I'm sorry I lied to you. More than that, I'm sorry I covered my lie by saying you're crazy." Sam winced like a slap was coming.

"Get to your explanation." *I'll hear him out, but I can't imagine what he could say that would redeem him.*

He pulled the metallic book from under the counter. "I'm from the future." He opened the book. There was a very flat typewriter and an incandescent picture page. "Lilac is from the future."

"What do you mean?" I asked.

"I came here from about a hundred years in the future. That is a portal into the future." He pointed to the top of the wall where the light came through.

"What are you saying?" I could not understand.

"I mean I didn't grow up in this time. I grew up a little over a hundred years from now. I came through the portal. To you it seemed like I just moved to Virden, but I actually already lived in Virden, albeit very briefly, just in the future."

"I don't believe you." *This is worse than calling me crazy.*

Sam climbed the ladder and called Lilac. Several seconds later Clive's head popped out.

"Sam?" Clive said. "Oh. Zeta. Hello."

"I told Zeta, but obviously it's hard to believe, I wonder if you'd mind showing her?" Sam asked.

"Absolutely. Lilac isn't well right now, she's sleeping. Come, but please be quiet." Clive disappeared.

I felt like a fool being taken in by Sam who is probably a confidence man, he certainly has the skills. I gripped my gun in my skirts.

"You go first, Sam."

"I can't."

"I'm not climbing into a cupboard, you go first."

"Really, I can't but look through before you go. It's not a cupboard. It's an apartment in the future."

I climbed to the top of the ladder and looked through. It was very bright, it was daytime. It was clearly a large room, not just a cupboard. Still, I didn't want to be trapped in a concealed room. "I'm not going in there."

"Look." Sam changed the incandescent picture to a moving picture with a person talking. "This is impossible, right? I am from the future, and this machine is also from the future."

"I remember you showed us moving pictures with sound like this when you first came. I thought you were a traveling showman."

"Yes, it wasn't this machine, but something like it. I had a projector."

"I remember the big box."

"I put it in a big box, but it was something, not exactly like this, but this size. I wanted to disguise it, because machines like this haven't been invented yet."

"Even worse. I'm not going into some future trap," I said. "I don't understand why you won't go first, if it's safe."

He took my hand. "Zeta, I would never do anything to hurt you, I love you, please just see for yourself."

"Don't you use your charm on me Sam Gabler! I know all your tricks!" I felt angry he would try.

He backed off. "Zeta, I told you my family was murdered because that's how it felt . . ."

He told me a terrible story of his family history, and what he was trying to accomplish.

"Zeta, I don't mean to rush you." Clive popped his head back through the opening. "Lilac isn't well, I should really be monitoring her. I know it's scary to come in here, you can take all the time you need, I'm just going to go back to her, feel free to come in when you're ready, just be quiet and come find me."

"Yes. I'm coming." I felt satisfied. I still needed more explanation from Sam, but honestly, I knew Clive was incapable of selfishness. If I was trapped, he was too, and between the two of us, we'd find a way out. Sadly, I didn't have as much confidence in Sam. I climbed the ladder and went through the opening.

The room itself was normal, but there were very bright lights coming from the ceiling and more machines like the book in the shop. There were dozens of large paint tubes, not made of metal, but of something shiny. A completely black chair with half a dozen levers sat in the middle of the floor.

"Come, you're going to love this," Clive said.

He took me to the kitchen and showed me a refrigerator. "I haven't seen this model before, but I've seen ones like it."

"Yes, but we don't have electricity in Virden yet." He opened the door.

Cool air blanketed me, the refrigerator was lit up inside, and there were giant grapes and shiny packages I'd never seen before. I had to admit, if this was an extremely elaborate ruse, to what end? Just so I wouldn't be mad at Sam for calling me crazy?

Next to the sink, Clive pulled a metal door downward. "This machine washes dishes."

I thought about all my canning jars. Even though customers brought them back clean, I still washed them once more before I filled them with fresh food. This would make it a lot easier.

Clive turned a knob on a strange model of stove. A black spiral slowly started to glow dark orange then red. "It's electric."

There was a flash at the window.

"Come, look." Clive pointed outside.

There were motorcars, but small, enclosed. Dozens of them. Obviously, this was impossible to fabricate.

I looked at Clive. "Really? We're in the future right now?"

"Yes, we really are." He looked so excited.

"Okay, I'll listen to what Sam has to say. What's wrong with Lilac?" I didn't even believe Lilac was up here until this moment.

"It's a long story. Sam can tell you. I really should get back to her."

"Take care of her, thank you for . . . the tour."

Climbing back through cupboard, through the portal, I approached Sam.

"So?" he asked.

"Why didn't you tell me earlier?"

"So many reasons, but all of them don't matter anymore. I hope you'll still be my wife, I hope I didn't mess that up. You're free to marry, Phillip isn't in the picture anymore. You are in my closest confidence now." He looked unsure of himself, a rare occurrence.

"Sam, I didn't trust you. I genuinely thought you were tricking me, to trap me. What does that say about our relationship?" I asked.

"Okay, it's not good, but I'd just lied to you, and this whole situation seemed impossible. Everything we know about life says portals through time are impossible. Maybe..." He held his open hands in front of him and slowly moved them toward the ground in a calm down motion. "Maybe your feelings of mistrust toward me weren't about me, but about the situation. How could you believe even your own father if he told you about a portal into the future, you'd think he was drunk or lying, even though you trust him."

It's true. Even from my father this would seem impossible. "But my first instinct was to not trust you, even before you told me about the future."

"Of course, because you're smart, and on some level, you must have known I'd been lying to you for years. But not because

I wanted to. I've loved you all this time, I hated lying to you, but what choice did I have? Put yourself in my shoes and ask yourself what you would have done. You were married to Phillip, who was clearly not reliable to keep a secret. Yet, the marriage bond is strong, and I would expect you'd tell him. How could you keep a secret like that from your partner in life? Even after Phillip went to fight in the war, I knew he'd come home one day."

Sam had a point, though Phillip was only a decent person for about a month, he hadn't held that charade for long.

<hr>

I had a million thoughts running through my head. I let them run.

"In fairness, I've been lying about Phillip too. I did it to rescue my family in Italy. Life is hard for them. They've been taxed to poverty, lost their land, and corruption in our region is so bad, there's no hope to get it back. But my family's still alive. If they'd died like yours had, and I could change that, I'm not sure if there's a lie I wouldn't tell. I understand desperation Sam."

"Thank you. I feel like we can help each other. I want to help you get your family's land back, will money get it back?"

"No." I thought about their status.

"Lots of money?" Sam smiled.

I laughed. "Do you have lots of money?"

"Zeta, whatever you need, we're going to make it happen."

"I wanted to have a nice place for them to come to, here in America. I built bedrooms for them, planted an orchard, and a garden. I'm trying to earn money for their passage. I hope to have them here for late harvest next year."

"You've been busy."

"It's my dream to have them come here and start a new, comfortable, happy life." I thought about Italy and wished it could still be the home it was when I was a girl, but that seemed impossible now. Virden had harsh winters, it was true, but we would learn new ways. The big, open sky and plentiful, fertile land more than made up for its drawbacks.

"How about if we get them here for harvest this year?" Sam asked.

"I don't know how that's possible." It would be a dream.

"I need to go to New York. Clive and Lilac are coming too. I need to meet a Dr. Harver there . . ." He explained the situation and showed me two pieces of paper that flickered with alternate futures as we spoke back and forth.

"Will you come? We can purchase passage for your family and arrange for their travel to Virden."

I could hardly believe everything he was telling me. I couldn't believe it was possible I could have my family, here, with me in a couple months. "But it's so much money."

"Zeta, I need your help, I have work for you to do, I intend to pay you handsomely for it. Beyond that, my money is your money, I hope your family will be my family." He put out his arms for a hug. "I don't want to presume I'm allowed to touch you now."

I laughed and hugged him. "Are you rich? I know you're an inventor, but I didn't know you were rich. You don't even have land."

"I'm trying not to attract attention. Many of my inventions I have manufactured by different companies in Winnipeg and Regina. I don't want anyone digging too deeply into my life or history, so I spread my inventions among them, and put each under a different business name to keep my anonymity. On that note, I need to tell you something. This made Lilac angry. It might make you angry." He let go of me and stood back again. "I don't actually invent things myself. I take ideas from objects we have in the future." He winced again like a slap was coming.

"Do you imagine I'm going to hit you?"

"Honestly Zeta, I'm a little afraid of you, in a good way, but yeah, you have that Italian passion." His face blotched with red starting from his neck.

"That's fair, my temperament might be . . . unbridled at times." Though I tried to keep it restrained. *Sam is a man who needs someone he's afraid of, otherwise he could get quite unruly.* "Why was Lilac angry?"

"She said I was stealing ideas and fortunes from their rightful owners, changing the timeline and financial situation of the true inventors."

"Do you know Leonardo da Vinci?" I asked.

"Not personally." He laughed. "I know who you're talking about, of course."

"So, Leonardo is a great Italian. He is a true inventor. He invented thousands of things in his life. The mind of an inventor is constantly going. How many times have you thought of an idea and then discovered it already exists?" I asked.

"A few times I guess."

"For an inventive mind this happens, they make discoveries, only to find someone else has already discovered this thing. Instead of stopping them, this creativity only spurs them on to go faster. I think by inventing things earlier than originally occurring, you will only inspire more creativity. You will spark further invention. This doesn't make me angry."

"There is one more thing. Is this writing yours?" He showed me a document that looked very old.

"I don't remember writing this, but yes, it looks like my writing." I had to admit.

"It's from 1936."

"I don't understand."

"Lilac brought it from the future. It seems like we were going to be partners all along." Patches of red climbed up his neck again.

There were fragments of soulmates, or destiny, sparking in my mind. I thought of *Great Expectations*. "'You are part of my existence, part of myself. You have been in every line I have ever read.'" I felt heat climbing up my body.

He kissed me and I kissed him right back. He pushed me against the counter with his kisses, and I pushed him back against the wall with mine. Back to the counter, against the papered window, against the wall again. We tumbled to the floor, rolling with him on top of me, and then me on top of him. Our bodies couldn't be close enough. I wanted to feel his skin on mine. I pulled his shirt from his pants and felt the heat of his body. When I unbuttoned the last button on his shirt, something brought me to my senses— it wasn't his body, his body made me senseless.

"We aren't married. Phillip had limited capabilities, but I already feel your vitality, and the women in my family are known for their fertility. I won't do this until you marry me!" I yelled it as much at him as a stern warning to myself.

We were both panting as we got to our feet and pulled away.

"Get ready for New York, we'll be gone two weeks, we leave tomorrow. I'll marry you at the first chance we get." He stood away from me, shirt hanging open, majestic body beneath, breathing heavily.

"Stay over there, if you come any closer, I won't be able to stop myself." I panted.

I didn't trust myself to go anywhere near his orbit, so I climbed over the counter and left. I woke Zizzo and drove him with the madness of Jehu all the way home for fear if I didn't, I'd turn around and ruin myself.

I didn't bother cleaning my jars. I thought Lilac might let me wash them in her contraption when we got back. I packed my most professional looking clothing, fit for meeting with the scientific community. I fretted and stewed, then finally made a list, and went to bed.

In the morning, I arranged for Holly to look after Zizzo and keep the garden going while I was away. Most surprising, I asked my boss for two weeks off from work at the post office, and my boss said no.

"Sir, it's a family emergency." Sam would be family soon and it was his family's emergency.

"You can't expect to tell me today that starting tomorrow you need two weeks off," he said.

"Actually, it's starting today, I have many things to prepare."

"You need to request, in advance, for time off. I need to consider the situation and decide. You don't demand accommodation from me."

"Sir, the very definition of an emergency is an unexpected situation that requires immediate action. The fact that it involves my family should make it even more understandable."

"You can't just expect everyone to jump because you need something."

"Sir, I've worked here, loyally, for nine years. I need you to return that loyalty by giving me the time I need to help my family."

"I'll give you my decision by the end of the week. Attend to your duties."

If Sam and I were to be partners in botany, eventually, I'd have to give up this job. I preferred not to cause an upset in the community. In Italy, friction and outbursts were normal. I'd found in Canada, people were reserved with their feelings. Quitting my job would cause future problems and reflect poorly on Sam as well.

"Sir. I know you took a chance on me when you hired me. You

even kept me on during the time Phillip has been away. You have kept my household going, and without this job I would have been in a dire situation. I beg you to reconsider." It's the best I could do.

He almost looked like he was going to reconsider.

"By the end of the week, Mrs. Barker."

"I'm afraid that won't do. I formally resign my position." I didn't give him a chance to respond because if he did, I felt I might shout at him.

"I quit. My boss wouldn't give me time off. I hope you really meant what you said about marrying me, and about being rich."

"What?" Sam looked ready to take action. "Oh! I did and I am. I'm not the richest, but I'm richer than we'll ever need in Virden."

"So, it's okay that I quit the post office?"

"It's okay with me, but you've worked there a long time, you might miss it. I know you enjoyed it."

"I did enjoy it, but that document you showed me yesterday, the one I wrote, suggests I have another job ahead of me. I think working next to you will be equally, if not more . . . stimulating." I winked but kept my distance.

"Agreed!" He smiled and winked back. "About that, you've been married before, what will I need as far as documentation to get married?"

He laid a few documents in front of me.

"Bring them all. Things might have changed since Phillip and I got married. I'd rather be over prepared than under." *Thank goodness he reminded me. I need to pack my identification and divorce documents too.*

"We leave at five, Clive already purchased our tickets."

"When will we marry?" *I want your body.*

"We could get married here, in Virden, but I think it's better if we get married along the way somewhere. The less details our neighbors know, the better. It will cause enough of a stir already."

"Agreed. What's the plan in New York? I know you need to meet with Dr. Harver, but do you have a plan?"

"No. Everything has happened so fast, I don't have a plan yet, but we'll have time on the train to think about it."

"Sam, I wanted to ask you, did the portal open on the same date this time as the last two times?"

"Not exactly, but in the same time range."

"So you were expecting it."

"Not really, I was conscious of it, but maybe also dreading it. Last time went so badly. But when I heard there was a woman in her underwear walking the streets, I suspected. Obviously, when I saw her clothes, I knew right away where she'd come from."

"This time is going better, and you have me now, and I have you. Together, we're going to save both our families. And make one of our own." *When exactly are we getting married? What time, precisely?*

He laughed. "A month ago, I couldn't have imagined the roller coaster these past few days have been. It's hard to believe you're standing in front of me, about to be my wife. I'll never see my saved family, I can never go back to them, it will never be exactly as it was. All I can do is save them in this timeline. But you're offering me the next step forward. Love, sex with you—sorry for being so blunt but it's all I can think about in this moment, family, children. Before, I didn't let myself think about these things. I was so set on my past I didn't imagine a future. I mean, I did think about you though. I shouldn't have, but I did. I figured one day Phillip's reckless behaviour would catch up with him, and I could swoop in." He laughed.

"On that note, I better finish preparing for the trip. Promise me you'll arrange for us to be married at the earliest possible opportunity." I needed some cool air.

"I promise!" He stretched as tall as he could and saluted me, his clothing pulled tight to his body, suggesting outlines of features yet unexplored. "Do you need help with anything? May I carry your luggage?" he asked.

"I do need help, but I'll manage. It's best we're not alone." I laughed and left.

I made the rest of my preparations, impossibly excited about all the welcome events that lay before me, but especially securing passage for my family. No—especially marrying Sam.

CHAPTER 9

Lilac

♫ **"No Sleep Till Brooklyn"** ♫
by Beastie Boys

Clive, sporting a raptor tail, waited for me in the shop. He was packed and ready to go.

"May I take your bag?" he asked.

"I'd better keep it because I know the exact knack of it." I smiled to myself.

"As you wish, but if you change your mind, I would be happy to carry it."

"Here's money." He handed me a wad of cash. "Just in case we get separated or something goes wrong, I want you to be able to get yourself back to Virden and home."

"Thank you, Clive—can you just hug me so your tail will go away?"

"My pleasure, truly." Clive hugged me close to him, his tail disappeared, and I never wanted to let him go.

We arrived at the train station in plenty of time. Zeta and I had to sit in the ladies' waiting room, which I thought was silly, but it was the way it was. I didn't know how much she knew, so I didn't know how to make conversation with her. It was awkward. Also, I kept seeing raptors on patrol outside the station which was unnerving, and I didn't want her to know.

"I think we should wait until we're in our cabby shack on the train to talk," Zeta said.

"Probably. You're very wise."

Normally I would read a book or play a game on my iPad, but that was obviously not an option.

Must buy books.

I couldn't even make a list in a notebook. I really needed to go shopping. I need a notebook and pen or pencil from this time.

"Do you know if there's a gift shop in this station?"

"No. There isn't," she said. "Would you like to read a book? I brought a few."

"I'd love to. Thank you."

She opened her bag to show me a pristine, first edition *Anne of Green Gables.* I started sweating. *Start the car …*

I couldn't say anything to her right then, I'd have to wait until we were on the train.

I picked up *Anne of Green Gables,* and became so focused on the book, the raptors left me alone.

The building began vibrating. *Here we go.* Nobody else seemed bothered. *I'm just hallucinating an earthquake. They don't even get earthquakes here. This isn't real.* Zeta put her book away.

"Do you want me to keep it for you until we get on the train?" she asked.

I must have looked confused.

"The train—it's coming." She pointed outside, though we couldn't see it yet.

"Oh. Yes, please." I handed her book back.

We walked over to and stood by the door. There was a shadowy dust cloud in the distance. As the train came closer, I could make out the details of the engine. It almost looked like it was trying to outrun a dust storm. The building shook violently. I was in awe it was still standing and going strong in my time.

They don't build them like they used to.

We were so close to the door that when the train, and its dust cloud, came to a stop, a blast of dust blew under the door and covered our shoes.

"Looks like it got you," the raptor attendant said, looking at our shoes as he unlocked the door.

"I'll remember that for next time." I smiled back at him, trying not to look as scared as I felt.

He opened the door, and we went into the dusty air and found Clive and Sam.

We waited, as a few people departed the train, then we surrendered our tickets and boarded.

As we walked down the open-seating aisles, people stared at us. Not, I'm sure, because we were particularly interesting, but just because we were something new to look at. Sam led with Zeta in tow. Clive followed next, and I followed his tailless behind.

"6B, this is us." Sam opened the compartment door, and we filed in.

"I didn't know they had train compartments in 1920," I said.

"They didn't, and they're called cabby shacks." Sam smiled and winked at me.

"Oh boy." *Rascal.*

The cabby shack was beautiful, shiny-polished dark wood, and brass. I flopped down on the seat to get my bearings. The curtains were open, and I could see old Virden outside. It wasn't normal to me yet. I felt like I was dreaming.

"There's four, fold-down bunks here," Clive said.

We were no sooner settled than the train whistle blew.

"All aboard!"

I thought that was only in the movies.

I hoped Sam would take the lead on telling us what Zeta knew, because I wasn't in any shape to chair a conversation. He didn't. I felt stupid for our first in-depth conversation since the day she nursed me from my car crash to be about hallucinating dinosaurs, so I just sat quietly. Nobody made a move at conversation.

A few minutes later, the train creaked and groaned, and ever so slowly started moving. As soon as it started moving, I realized I was so distracted with everything else, I'd forgotten something very important—motion sickness medication. I was good for about eight minutes. Then, I started feeling very nauseous. At twelve minutes, I opened the window just in time to for the dust to enter the compartment, which made a real mess of our cabby shack, and my face.

I barely made it through the next ten hours to Winnipeg. Every time we stopped, I would get out for fresh air and tell myself I didn't have to get back on, but I kept getting back on, for Sam's family, and humanity. Clive held my hair back when I threw up, and he kept insisting we go home.

But I insisted we stay. "This is important for Sam."

"Yes. Sam and Zeta can handle it. I can take you home."

"We both know this trip doesn't work without me," I said.

"You're already suffering an allergic reaction to gluten, now you're train sick. Your body will only tolerate so much, Lilac. Maybe we can come up with another plan," he pleaded.

"All aboard!" The T-Rex conductor roared.

I took the first step up the train car's steps.

Clive stood his ground, on the ground, and held my hand. "Please, let's go home."

"Sometimes ginger helps," I said. "Could you try to track some down?"

He shook his head. "I'm worried about you." He helped me back to our cabby shack.

He said to Sam, "Find ginger root."

Sam and Zeta left.

"Lilac, this might be more than you can give. It's true, this New York trip, with you is a great opportunity, but not the last chance or anything," Clive said. "We'll find another way. The portal opened twice before, surely it will open again. We can try again next time."

I felt so sick I could hardly talk. I wanted to die; it was that bad.

"It's fine. I'll get through it. I've been carsick a million times. I can't believe I forgot Gravol."

"You're stubborn as a mule!" he shouted.

Oh no you didn't.

"Clive, I want Sam's family to be okay without you as part of his plan! I want to fix his family on this trip! . . . Because I want you to come home with me! . . . To the future!" I shouted right back at him then barfed in the bowl I had for that purpose.

"You do?" He rubbed my back and gave me something to wipe my mouth.

"I know this is all so fast, but it's intense and that portal will close in seven weeks, and if I had to choose right now between roughing it through this sickness, or possibly never being able to see you again after seven weeks, I choose being sick for a few days." I wasn't shouting anymore. "I've never met anyone like you, and I want the chance to know you better. I don't even want to wait until the portal opens again. If you don't want to come to the future, it's okay, but I want you to have the option. I don't ever want to say goodbye."

"You've only known me a few days."

"I know, and for part of that time, I thought I was interested in Sam." I barfed again. He rubbed my back, and I felt my eyes tearing. "But the truth is, I felt a connection to you right away. When we took our adventure trip to the gas station, I hadn't felt that happy in a long time. You stood up to Sam for me, you looked after me last night, you're looking after me right now. I'm just saying, I don't know what this is, but I don't want to close the door on finding out. If I go home now, I don't think you'll leave Sam behind and come with me."

"You might be surprised." Clive laughed.

I laughed too, then barfed again.

"I know you have your family, but maybe they'd come. They sound adventurous. Maybe we could find a way to get all of you papers in the future. I think we could work it out. I know my mom won't come to the past, she won't even live in Manitoba in the future anymore, she needs certain comforts."

"Sounds like my mom too."

"See?" I heaved, but nothing came up. "They'd be great friends. Your mom would love the future."

"I'm not ready to say goodbye to you either, and if you weren't covered with vomit, I'd be more tempted to kiss you right now," Clive said.

I laughed the best I could. "Okay, so just let me get through this, not fighting with you will take some of the stress off my plate."

"I won't fight you—I'll help."

Sam and Zeta came back with ginger. I pretty much grabbed it and took a big bite letting it burn my mouth as I chewed.

I talked big, and it was nice to have Clive on my side, but I wasn't sure if I could physically survive five days of throwing up, the dehydration alone would kill me.

At the next stop, I got off the train and lay on the grass until it was time to go. Just the thought of getting back on the train had me second guessing myself. I tried to remain calm, because I didn't want Clive to insist we turn around. I held my ground, and he carried me back to our cabby shack.

"See if you can find a doctor," Clive told Sam.

Clive pulled down a bed. "Do you think laying down would help?"

"I don't know."

The train started up again with its creaking and groaning, and I moaned along with it.

Looking out the window made it worse, thinking of something else made it worse, lying still made it worse, and rocking made it worse.

There was a knock at the door.

"We found the doctor. We're going to be in the dining car," Sam said.

I sat up, dry heaving into one of my dresses I'd balled up for just that purpose. Not much was coming out anyway.

"The doctor is here, Lilac." Clive rubbed my back.

I couldn't look up; I was contorting too severely.

"Hold her still." I heard him say to Clive.

"I have some medicine for you Miss, but I'm going to need you to hold still. Can you do that for me?"

I took a deep breath and tried to calm down and be still. "Yes."

"Do you think you can lie down?"

Clive was holding me tightly, and it was calming.

"I think I can," I said.

Clive helped me to lie down on the bed.

The room was churning. I closed my eyes and felt myself spinning out of control. I felt such a strong urge to sit up and puke, but I knew there was nothing there anyway. My head was burning.

The doctor held my arm, and then there was a pinch. It was distracting. It felt good to feel something other than erratic movement. A few seconds later, he let go of my arm and wrapped it with a cloth dressing.

"There, that should help you very soon. I've given you some

cocaine," the doctor said without any shame or embarrassment.

I was shocked, but I felt better. I felt like I could do this. I could make it to New York and back.

"Thank you, Doctor," Clive said. "May I come and find you, if we need you again?"

"Certainly. I do have some other options that might help her if that doesn't work."

He left. We sat quietly for a few minutes. I felt a change coming on.

"How are you feeling?" Clive asked me.

"Good, I feel like I could pull the train." I sat up. "And you're handsome." I kissed him.

"Sorry, I'm sure that tasted like barf."

"No, it was gingery . . . nice." He laughed.

I had no more motion sickness, and I felt like I never would again.

Tap. Tap. Tap.

I looked to the window just in time to see a raptor tail swish as its owner jumped up onto the roof with a loud thud.

I looked to Clive. "Did you see that?"

"What?"

Violent scratching noises started coming from the roof.

"Do you hear that?" I pointed up.

"What?"

I closed my eyes and hid in his chest.

"Nothing."

"Well, obviously it's not nothing."

"The raptors are back." I blurted out, one inch from his very handsome face.

"Is that better or worse than train sickness?"

"Better. Just protect me."

"I can do that. Fighting imaginary dinosaurs is well within my ability."

The scraping sounded like digging, I could picture the roof of the wooden train car splintered thin and about to give. I wanted to close my eyes and cover my ears, but logically I knew I would just be giving in to my mind. And like crying, if I got hysterical, there would be a much longer recovery time. I focused on the idea that there were no raptors, but my mind continued deceiving me. I would not let it win.

That's when Clive pulled off his handsome face, and revealed he was a raptor.

"Touch me!"

Clive/raptor complied immediately and pounced, turning back into Clive. He sat on the bunk with me, wrapping his arms tight around me. I felt safe.

"I have to tell you something," Clive said.

"Please don't tell me you're a raptor, or love bombing me because you have a fetish about vomiting women."

"Interesting hypothesis, but no."

We were sitting on my bunk, I was sitting in front of him, my back to his chest, with his arms and legs and arms wrapped protectively around me.

"Sorry, what is it?" I closed my eyes to focus on his words instead of the insanity around me.

"It's a long story."

"We've got time."

"It would take me days to tell the whole story, so I'll tell you the shorter version for now."

"I accept."

"I started the war as a pilot. I hated the war. I didn't want to be there. They pump you full of all kinds of propaganda, but I knew the people we were bombing were just as scared as the people on our side being bombed." He took a deep breath. "My plane was shot down, the navigator in my plane died. Most of the guys in my squadron died. I was injured but not captured. I hurt this arm." He lifted his left arm. "I was hurt it so badly, I couldn't fly anymore, but the truth is: I didn't want to shoot enemy fighter pilots down, or drop bombs anymore, so I was glad I couldn't go back." He stopped again, rested his head on my head and was quiet for a while.

I rubbed his arm.

"I wasn't right, in my head. I mean, I wasn't seeing raptors, but I kept seeing our plane going down, and I kept hearing my navigator behind me, screaming. Every time I closed my eyes, I heard him screaming." I could feel him crying behind me.

I couldn't hug him, because he was behind me, but I put my hands on the outside of his arms and squeezed him in closer to me.

He took a deep breath. "They trained me to be a field medic. The things I saw as a medic . . . war is a gruesome, disgusting beast. It wasn't just what the enemy was doing, I saw our own men kill prisoners who could have been patched up, just to expedite things. I saw the worst in men, and my nightmares got worse. I had them during the day. I had them with my eyes closed, and with my eyes open. My mental state worsened, until I couldn't do my job anymore. I ended up being shipped to New York with a bunch of American soldiers like me, mentally sick. They wanted to patch us up and send us back. That's why I know New York."

"Were they able to help you? You seem good now."

"I'm better than I was, and I'm fine with you, but I'm not good. Most people in Virden avoid me because I'm not right. I want you to know that. I'm not right in my head sometimes."

"I'm not either, as you know."

"This isn't about something I eat. Just sometimes, if I get sick, or too tired, I'm not right."

"I understand what you're saying. In my time it's common with soldiers. We call it post traumatic stress syndrome. PTSD. You can't go through all that and not be affected. There are treatment programs. There's help for you, Clive. It may not be easy, and I don't think it really ever goes away, but there is help."

"Really?"

"Yeah. You're not weak or crazy, or whatever you imagined yourself, and you're not alone. It's common. I don't think we're meant to see things like that."

"I don't think so either."

"Was it hard when you first got home?"

I could feel him crying again.

"When they released me, I got a letter informing me my family died in a boating accident three months prior. My parents, my sisters, all dead." He put his head on my shoulder and cried for a long time.

I cried too.

We sat like that, grieving together.

"My friend Lan is dead. She killed herself."

"I'm so sorry."

"Me too."

<hr>

Sam and Zeta knocked and the door and came in.

Once the door was closed, Clive said to Sam, "Train sick is gone, but the cocaine made the raptor hallucinations worse."

"Okay. Well, I'm not sure what to do with all that information, but we brought food."

Clive ate like a normal human. With all the excitement, the raptors came back, so I ate in hyper-diaper abject fear.

Everyone else was ready for bed, but I was wired for sound, so there was no sleeping. We were trapped on a train, with no way to burn off all my energy. Plus, I had raptors all around me, so there was no peace.

Clive was in the bunk across from me.

"I'm right here if you need anything, okay? Please wake me up if you need to leave the cabby shack or if you're not well. I'll try to get some sleep so I can be there for you tomorrow."

I twitched and jumped at random reptilian attacks in my bunk while everyone else slept soundly.

When we arrived in Winnipeg we had to change trains. Clive loaded our luggage onto the next train. We had an hour until it left, as they were doing scheduled maintenance. I promised to stay in the cabby shack while everyone else went for supplies, but after a while, I thought of a solution to my problem that didn't involve cocaine.

The station was incredibly dirty, not like New York-subway-dirty, but like dirt-floors-dirty. Mud puddles, dust, the smell of industrial oils hit my nostrils, and every person I saw was grimy. Even nicely dressed women were coated with a thin layer of dust, me included. Raptors bobbed their heads in and out of the crowds and climbed the stone pillars, screeching. I tried not to let it bother me, but it was a concern. Nobody else seemed to be reacting to them, so I was pretty sure they weren't really there. I felt confident in my own insanity.

There were clear signs of abject poverty, as well as disgusting wealth. I wanted to slap them all and tell them they're all dead in my time, to stop being fools, and enjoy life. To the poor I'd say, ride the rails until you get to the West Coast, at least you'll be poor by the sea and avoid Winnipeg's winter. To the rich I'd say, don't just take what you can get, think about the people and environment you're hurting, money isn't important, live your life and fill it with love! I guess I would say the same things to people in my time.

I should say the same thing to myself and Clive and take our white butts to Hawaii for a tanning.

I looked around for a Shopper's Drug Mart, but of course, there wasn't one. There wasn't even a hot dog stand. There was a saloon though. I figured if I couldn't find medicine at least I could numb my sickness. I briefly wished Clive was with me. *Just hurry up or everything will be ruined.*

The saloon didn't have a swinging door like in the Wild West. I guess the weather in Winnipeg isn't exactly conducive to that. Everything else was as I expected, which made me suspicious it was all my imagination. There was a long wooden bar with bar stools of wood and brass, bums on each one. A questionable lady played the piano with another, even more questionable lady, singing. Card games were ongoing. I imagined everyone was gun slinging, though I couldn't actually see any guns. There was a second floor with doors which no doubt hid unsavory people. All I wanted was a drink.

Everyone was staring at me. I could see how I would be a little out of place, so I just got right to the point.

"I need a whisky."

Rowdy laughter filled the cavern.

"You and me both, sister," said a prospector-looking man at a table near me. I was quite sure there was no gold rush in Manitoba, it must have been his hat.

"Don't you stir up no trouble, we don't have no drinks here ma'am on account of your prohibition," the barkeep said, clearly mistaking me for a protester or something.

"Oh. Right. I forgot."

The laughter started again.

"Well, do you have some ginger ale?" I asked. "I'm quite sick from riding the train and I'm going all the way to New York. I don't know how I'm going to make it, I feel like I'm going to die on that train." I knew the cocaine would wear off and I'd be back in that nauseous situation soon. Although the cocaine worked, I was afraid of getting addicted. *Can you get addicted in five days? I'm addicted to Clive in about the same time. Probably best I don't find out.*

"We don't serve women in here," was the bartender's curt reply.

"They're in here." I pointed to the musicians.

"They serve us, we don't serve them," he said. Hooting and hollering followed.

"That's fine. I've got ten dollars for anyone who will serve me." I walked out the door. I was mad and I was also worried someone would pee in a cup and bring it to me.

Right on my heels was a middle-aged man with a salt-and-pepper comb-over/beard combo.

"Young lady, I'm a doctor. I could give you a cocaine treatment if you like."

"Thank you, but it doesn't seem to work for me." There was no sense in saying I didn't want to try what he was prescribing; doctors hate that. "I'm at the end of what I can take with this trip, and I have so much farther to go."

"I suffer from the train sickness myself. I understand your feeling. I don't go anywhere I can't walk or ride a horse. You think whisky will help you?" he asked.

"Well, it doesn't exactly help me feel better, but I have found it settles me, so I can bear it and fall asleep. I have a cabby shack on the train."

"When does your train leave?" he asked.

"Any moment, I have to make my way back now."

"Wait here."

He went back into the saloon. Within minutes, he came back out with two white paper bags.

"This one is the ginger ale, mix it with this one. It's whisky, not good whisky, but it will do the trick."

I was so grateful I felt like crying my head off. Also, I was excited to try genuine prohibition moonshine. I handed him the ten dollars. I thought he might refuse it, but he didn't.

"Thank you. I hope your journey is a pleasant one," he said, bowing.

"I'm sure this will help, thank you."

He went back into the saloon, whipping his raptor tail behind him.

Clearly the gluten still wasn't out of my system, and I'd added cocaine, and now I would be adding moonshine. I wasn't sure how my brain would take it.

CHAPTER 10

Zeta

♫ "Dance with Me Tonight" ♫
by Olly Murs

Sam and I tried to get married in Winnipeg. He was able to find out where we needed to go, but getting there was an ordeal. Once we found the place, he tried to expedite the procedure with money, but ultimately, we had to run back for our train unsuccessful. We'd transferred onto a train going into the United States.

"At our next big stopover, we can try again," Sam said.

"Do you think getting married in the United States will be a problem? Will it cause us trouble in the future as far as documents go?" I wanted to get married at the next possible opportunity, but not if it would cause a lifetime of hassle.

"I don't know. Likely it would be smoother if we married in Canada, but I don't know anything about it."

"We're mature adults. We can wait ten days." *I absolutely cannot.*

"Can we?" Sam smiled and wrapped me in his arms in a full body hug.

I pushed him away while I still could. "Not like that we can't. Breathing space, sir." I locked my arm out, my hand on his chest.

His pupils were dilated, his arms reached out and his hips drew closer.

I ran to our chaperoned cabby shack laughing. Sam chased after me at a pace that suggested he accepted the situation.

CHAPTER 11

Lilac

♫ **"This Is the Time"** ♫
by Billy Joel

Fortunately, I boarded the train before the others did. I was well into the moonshine when Clive arrived.

"Oh good, you're here," he said. "I brought you whisky . . . oh I see you've already got some."

I smiled at him and took another swig, trying to see Clive instead of a reptile.

"Where have your sideburns gone? Where are your teeth I love? Where is your chest hair? Where are your revealing pants? Where are your arms of a statue? Where is your soft beard that I love?" I could hear myself saying the words but couldn't stop.

"Am I just a piece of meat to you?"

"Meat I'd like to sink my teeth into," I said, too quietly to be joking.

I could feel my head sliding down the seat but couldn't stop it.

When I woke up Clive was sitting on the opposite side of the cabby shack reading the paper. I was laying in my bunk, feeling like barfing again.

"Good morning sunshine."

"I need a—barf coming *now!*"

He handed me his empty coffee cup.

I filled it, my eyes watering from frustration. He gave me his hanky and rubbed my back.

Why did I forget to bring Gravol . . . of all the things to forget . . . why . . .

The next four days on the train were pretty much the same. Drink, sleep, barf, then repeat. Slowly, Clive morphed back into himself, and all the raptors disappeared. It was touching how he stayed by my side; I couldn't have been a worse traveling companion. When the train would stop, he'd wake me up to go to the bathroom, then ply me with drink to go back to sleep before we started up again. He carried my bag when we had to change trains and was always there when I woke up in the night. As I fell asleep for the fiftieth time, I thought to myself what a loyal husband Clive would make. Granted, the cabby shack was his assigned seating, but he could have joined Sam and Zeta in the dining or observatory cars, or joined a gentleman's poker game, but instead he sat at my side, even though I was at my absolute worst. I was far past falling in love, I was there and built a house.

When we arrived in New York, I was exhausted. Clive was too. It was a long time to be on the train in the best of circumstances. We arrived at five in the morning. I was so dizzy, I was useless. I went straight to bed napped until ten o'clock. My body was tired, but I didn't feel motion sick, so I got out of bed. The guys were eating breakfast by the window in the living room of the suite.

"Well, look who's up. You must be starving," Clive said.

"I am!" Whisky and ginger ale for five days doesn't offer the body much.

"Sit here." Clive pulled out a chair and lifted a silver lid to reveal a steaming hot breakfast.

This man is a keeper. You can't tell me this isn't love.

"So, we meet Dr. Harver at two. He's speaking at three, but I figure if we get down there early, we'll have a chance to meet him and maybe make an impression. Zeta and I came up with a plan," Sam said.

"Do tell," I said.

"Do you remember the Roxanne number from Moulin Rouge?" Sam asked.

I furrowed my brow. "One of these things is not like the other."

Sam laughed. "I'll tell you how it goes."

"Please do. I'm intrigued."

CHAPTER 12

Zeta

♫ "Electroqtango" ♫
by Electrocutango

Although Lilac was the key to the trip's success, she was absolutely out of commission. She couldn't help plan anything for the remainder of the trip. Clive was loyally by her side, so he was of no use either. It was up to Sam and me to strategize.

"I think we need to do something unforgettable, so you stand out to these scientists for the rest of their lives. So that when you write to them, or when they see your published scientific papers, your face comes to their mind right away." I spoke quietly to Sam.

"Makes sense."

"I think we should show them a moving picture from your machine."

"What should the subject be?"

"What moving pictures do you have?"

"We can make anything we want, we could make a movie of you talking. Personally, I think there's nothing more unforgettable."

I felt a tingle down my spine and warmth in my chest.

"You can make your own movie?"

"Yeah, no problem. We could build a box like I did before, put a piece of glass as a screen with some white fabric inside to obscure the device. It would have sound—I have lots of music we could use in the background. It would be easy. The hard part would be keeping the secret of how it works."

"Everyone would want to know, true. Is that why you stopped with the moving pictures when you first came, because everyone wanted to know how it worked?"

"No, it required electricity, and when the portal closed, I couldn't charge the devices anymore."

"Do you have electricity now?"

"Yes, everything is fully charged, and I have power banks with me. When we get to New York, we can recharge."

"This is excellent, what movie should we make?"

Sam's neck blotched with red going up his face. He took a drink of water. "I think people love hearing about themselves. We know lots of the people who are going to be there. We've done research on them. Why don't we make a short movie and call it, *Scientific Achievements in Recent History*, and basically just have you go through a timeline of their discoveries and inventions. We can get Clive to do a drawing of each one. If we can make them laugh a few times, even better. Then they'll never forget."

"I love this idea. Let's do it."

Sam completely took the lead because I didn't know how to work any of the machinery. I put together a play script. Clive penciled the drawings while he sat watching Lilac sleep. We waited to record the film when Lilac was fully asleep. Having her vomiting in the background wouldn't work. The movie wasn't exactly funny, until Sam used the times I said my lines wrong in quick succession at the end. Even though I felt somewhat embarrassed, it was funny, and it would help us to be unforgettable.

"I think they're going to remember my face, but we need to make them remember your face," I said after he showed me the final product.

"But yours is so much prettier."

I felt warm tingles where I was trying not to. *Don't start this again.*

"What if my lines were answers to questions you asked? Could we insert you asking the questions?"

"We could do that." Sam spent several hours editing himself in. It turned out well.

Sam was able to add the sound of film flapping and a bit of graininess to the overall look. Even though our movie was of high quality, and was sure to dazzle the scientists, I believed it was within the range of possibility.

At one of the stops, Sam rushed off the train to find supplies to build the box. I purchased a newspaper. It had updated information about Dr. Harver's visit. There was a gala in the evening. It gave me an idea.

Sam came back beaming. "I thought I'd have to build a box, but I was able to buy this display case, it's perfect!"

"It's full of pocket watches."

"Yes, but the box is already perfect, it saves so much . . . time." Sam snorted in a way that made not having sex with him immediately easier.

I laughed because his joke reminded me of my father. *They'll get along perfectly.*

"They were cheap anyway. I thought about giving them as gifts to scientists, but I don't think that's the kind of impression we want to make. They'll remember us as Ingersoll sales reps."

"Valid point. Can I help transform it?"

"Do you have a white scarf?"

"Not plain white."

"Any fabric in plain white?"

I felt my face turn red. "Underthings." It didn't feel right to have any of those items on display in front of a bunch of men, and

I wasn't ready to surrender them to Sam either. "What about a piece of paper?"

"Yes, perfect, of course!" He was satisfied with that, thankfully.

None of the paper we had was large enough, but Sam was able to acquire several large, thin sheets from a drafting office at one of our stops. I was able to cut one down and letter in: *Samso Gabler - Botany & Biology*. It wasn't to my standard of perfection because vibrations of the train made it a challenge, but I knew it still looked professional.

"I love it, but should it just say Sam? I think it might be more acceptable, or Samuel?" Sam asked.

"Samuel isn't your name—besides, I love your Basque name."

"Gabler isn't my name either. I just don't want it to detract from what we're doing."

"I can do another one with Sam. Best foot forward, whatever you think that is, I trust you."

"I know we're not married yet, but could you put Sam and Zetarica Gabler?" He cocked his head to the side and smiled.

"I think it might detract."

"We're a team. Your name belongs there as much as mine." He nodded encouragement.

"You're that confident we'll marry?" It felt like it would never happen.

He looked over at Lilac and Clive who were sleeping after the last big round of throwing up.

He cleared my hair away from my neck with the lightest touch and kissed my neck. "If you'll let me, nothing in the world could stop me."

I felt tingling and moved my head to the side because I didn't want him to stop.

"Oh no!" Lilac sat up, Clive sat up and put the bowl under her mouth just in time.

Poor things.

At the next stop I lettered a new piece of paper: *Sam & Zetarica Gabler - Botany & Biology.*

Sam affixed it inside the box and ran through a rehearsal viewing. It was perfect, sure to dazzle.

With that project out of the way, I had another one brewing.

———◆———

"There's a gala the same night as the presentation. If we can get invited, I think I have the perfect way to make us memorable," I said.

"Even more than the movie?"

"I think, if we can get in, this will seal the deal. Have you heard of the tango?"

"Yes ...."

"My cousin, who lives in Argentina, taught me. I think if we danced the tango well, it could really help us stand out."

"Yes. I am one hundred percent for this idea." Sam's neck blotched in red that eventually overtook his face. "I can dance, but I don't know how to tango. I mean, I've seen *Take the Lead,* but I've never done it."

"I don't know what *Take the Lead* is, but you have the personality for it, and I can teach you the steps."

"I'll learn and perfect any moves you want to teach me." He ran his eyes down my body. "I think you need a different dress."

"Obviously." *I doubt New York has exactly what I need, but I know just the alterations I can make.* "Do you have any tango music? The music is important."

He searched his machine.

He laughed. "I only have one. From *Moulin Rouge,* called 'El Tango De Roxanne.'" He held device to my ear.

The music started. I gasped, but Sam was laughing. I closed my eyes to listen. By the end of the song, I could hardly breathe. "It's perfect."

"I agree. They'll never forget us. Ever."

I mentally went through the catalog of tango steps my cousin had taught me. I'd tried to teach Phillip when we first married. Although he had the anger, he didn't have the passion or intensity to make it believable. With Sam, it would be different.

"When do we start?" he asked.

"Now. I need to know how strong you are. Stand."

He stood. "Play it again for me." He did, then put the wired ear attachments in both of my ears. I studied his body with new context. "Hands up." *Caspita.* Sam pulled me right up against his chest and look down at me. Heat filled my body. "Turn." The music and his glorious body pushed me past all sense.

Lilac moaned. *Agreed.* I looked at her, she was green. Our movement wouldn't help with her motion sickness.

"I need to assess your strength, somewhere else."

"We can't take this with us." Sam took the music from me.

I didn't need it, I would never forget what I'd just heard.

As soon as he closed the door to our cabby shack, I whispered in his ear. "We start this tango now." The hallway was empty. Countryside sped past us. I ran my fingertips over his neck, and his skin tightened under my touch. We locked eyes. *Biceps, defined and hard.* I felt a pull toward him I didn't want to resist. "Sleeves, up." I forced myself back, to watch. He folded from the cuff once, twice, a third, then pushed the sleeve up past his elbow. By the second forearm I was in trouble. I swallowed hard at the sight. *He knows exactly what he has.* He unbuttoned one more button at the neck of his shirt, snapped his hands to his hips, turned his face to the side, and thrust toward me, two beats. *Caspita.* I'd stopped breathing. I filled my lungs, hooked my fingers in his belt and pulled myself toward him. *Abdomen, lower back, strong.* My fingers went to his remaining buttons. *Stop.* I turned to walk away but he grabbed my hand and pulled me back.

"Endure," he growled.

I wanted to smile at his perfection for the role, but my cousin taught me never to smile while tangoing. His chest felt as good as a medium-rare steak—I tried to take a healthy bite. He laughed, and I put my fingers against his lips. "No." I pointed my toe and pushed one leg straight behind me until I couldn't go any lower. I felt my skirt rise up my leg to my upper thigh, my hands dragging down his body.

I heard people speaking, entering our car. Sam pulled me to my feet, put his hand to my lower back, and aimed me toward the dining car. At the end of our car there was a small alcove Sam pulled me into just before I could exit the car.

"I think it's only fair I also know how strong you are." His voice was in a tone I'd never heard from him before.

"I'm not done with you." I matched his tone back.

He put his arms up, elbows resting on each side of the alcove. Legs shoulder width apart. "Explore." He smiled.

"Tango is not this easy." I turned, but he pulled me back.

"Hard is what you're looking for?" He pushed me to the wall with the full force of his body. His very. Hard. Body.

Glutes, hard. Back, strong. And yes, one other part of his body hard as steel.

"I'm satisfied." I was pinned and the only place to go from here was straight to hell.

"I doubt that. I know I'm not."

A gentleman opened the door beside the alcove. Sam turned, greeted the man, then pulled me through the door. He spun me in the gangway and dipped me so low I felt his cheek on my breasts, my hair touching the floor. He stood us up slowly, holding me tightly. I wrapped my leg around him, like I should not have. He lifted me to do the same with my other leg, but I dropped back to the floor, leaving the gangway. He followed. As we made our way through the next three cars, he assessed as much of my musculoskeletal system as I'd let him. Finally, we entered the dining car. It was empty.

"We'd like to dance, could we move these tables?" Sam asked a nearby attendant.

The attendant agreed.

"Now, we need an audience. To test your nerve," I said.

"My nerve is fine, how's yours?" He kissed me right in front of the attendant. A long, hungry kiss.

I moved his hands to my hips, turned around, and writhed seductively to the floor and back up again, facing the attendant. His jaw dropped along with my caboose.

"It's coming back," I said. "We don't want to choke at the gala."

I taught every move I knew, and we practiced, dancing through the open-seating section. All eyes were on us, except for the children's, whose mothers' hands covered them. *With that music, this will, most certainly, be unforgettable.*

Sam adapted moves as he saw fit, if I approved, I continued on. If not, he found out immediately. I didn't think we had time to learn a lift together, but we practiced dragging and lifting from the floor. Every open seating car got two shows, one on our way to the end of the train, and one on our way back to our cabby shack. Gangway shows were private, just for Sam and me. Eighteen cars of eyes on us, interactions with passengers. I imagined they were the scientists I needed to press upon. Press upon them we did.

If we can do this with these clothes, and no music, the gala guests will be flabbergasted.

"I don't want to go back in there," Sam said when we had danced back to our cabby shack, sweating and approaching his zenith.

"What do you have in mind?" I was afraid to ask, lest it was the same thing I had in mind.

He growled my exact thoughts back to me.

"We're going in here and staying in here." We stayed in the safety of Lilac's sickness for the rest of the trip. Sam stayed on his bunk, and I stayed on mine. It didn't stop us from looking or imagining, but at least it stopped us from doing. *Our tango will be the better for it.*

Upon our arrival in New York, the only room available in the hotel Clive thought would be best, was a suite. Lilac and I took the bed, Sam and Clive took the couches. We all slept for a while. When I got up, the men had ordered breakfast. Lilac was up soon after. Sam and I ate across from each other, our feet touching under the table.

CHAPTER 13

Lilac

**♫ "I Gotta Feeling" ♫
by Black Eyed Peas**

Clive and I wandered around hipster New York for a couple of hours. I wanted to pull out my phone and take pictures of people. Moustaches, beards, tight vests, trim pants—hipster New York.

Typewriters were everywhere! We stopped for lemonade when we became thirsty. We walked through Central Park. It was just as charming as I remembered, except it was filled with sharp dressed characters and no joggers. The dresses were phenomenal.

I have to buy at least one dress while I'm here.

Soon it was two o'clock. We met up with Sam and Zeta at the campus and looked for the auditorium. A notice was attached to the poster outside the door that Dr. Wang would not be in attendance.

"If it's not to talk to Dr. Wang, I wonder why I'm here?" I really thought speaking Mandarin was going to be my contribution.

"I'm sure it will become clear." Zeta smiled at me.

We sat in the empty hallway, waiting for Dr. Harver.

An usher came along and opened the doors. We selected seats in the back by the door. Clive and I saved the seats while Sam and Zeta watched for Dr. Harver in the hallway. Soon, the room was full of accomplished-looking gentlemen. I felt somewhat intimidated. To be fair though, I had more scientific education than anyone else in the building, except Sam. We grew up on Bill Nye, *Mythbusters*, Ted Talks and YouTube channels like *Veritasium*. That's more of a scientific education than any student in 1920 received. A hundred years changes a lot. My annual pass to Science World growing up was money well spent.

Dr. Harver didn't show up until ten minutes past scheduled starting time. She was a woman.

No wonder she never gained fame for her discoveries. Some women managed it, but most probably never saw recognition for their work.

Sam and Zeta couldn't even introduce themselves because she was genuinely late.

She was charismatic. Her presentation was entertaining and interesting. She asked for a volunteer from the audience. Sam put his hand up with all the other willing volunteers.

"Stand up and say something." I elbowed him.

He stood up. In a booming voice he said, "I would like to volunteer."

All heads whipped around.

"Bold confidence and a strapping body, two of my favourite things. Please join me on the stage."

Sam adeptly assisted Dr. Harver's demonstration, and she kept him on stage, throwing questions at him which he either answered correctly or with a witty retort. She played off him for the rest of the hour. Whatever skills she had in charming a crowd, Sam was her match or better.

Afterward, she came over to meet our group. Sam introduced Zeta as his assistant. She invited the two of them to join her for the evening.

Clive and I walked with them to a fancy black car with suicide doors. Clive recognized the other passengers, some of New York's elite. They drove off for an evening of making all the right connections in New York.

"Good thing you told him to stand up," Clive said.

"Doesn't really make up for a week of train ride misery for everyone."

"Lilac, him standing up might have just saved his family's life. Maybe that's why you came? Don't sell yourself short all the time, it stabs me." He feigned a stab wound to the heart.

I hugged him, resting my head on his chest, taking in the scent of Clive. "Thank you." I never wanted to leave. I wanted to bury myself in his chest forever.

"What are we going to do tonight?" I asked.

"It's a surprise." He raised his eyebrows at me, challenging me to accept.

"Should I buy a new dress?"

"Definitely." He offered me his arm, and off we went into the warm summer afternoon.

I wanted a Coco Chanel dress, but 1920 was a little too early. I did find a glamorous sleeveless red dress with a skirt of a dozen chiffon layers and a ruffly V neckline. It was perfect. I chose red patent heels to match. Clive found a barber shop for a haircut, beard shaping, and a shoeshine. Right nearby was a beauty salon. The owner buzzed around me, styling my hair and applying dramatic makeup. We were ready for a night on the town. We stopped at the hotel to drop off my old clothes. I caught a glimpse of myself in the mirror. I was an exotic pinup stranger. In that second, I decided to be free, free from myself, from guilt, and from worry.

Just go be the beautiful girl in the red dress!

Clive took me for drinks to a secret, password-only basement bar where we met up with some of his New York friends. They were all wonderfully hipster, but down to earth, funny, smart, interesting people. I liked them right away. They were the lower-class wonderful nobodies that time forgot. They weren't the ambitious sort who gave their life to business or inventing or politics or exploitation. They gave their lives to friends, enjoying the moment, love, ideas, music, and family. I respected that.

We stayed there, eating pasta and drinking moonshine until men with tommy guns showed up, and the whole place cleared out fast. From there we went to a private penthouse party. Music played on a gramophone, and the balcony doors were open to the greatness of New York. A cool breeze made it feel good to be alive. The dancers were serious. It must have been an early form of swing. The girls were dancing on the ceiling! Their partners would fling them around wildly, like Jackie Chan choreographed the dance. I wanted to do it, but I just couldn't see how. It was like a foreign language—if you don't speak it, it's hard to tell where the breaks between the words were. I couldn't break down their dance moves.

"Do you want to dance?" Clive asked.

"I'd love to, but I don't know these dances. It looks fun though."

"I know how." He took my hand and spun it over my head, my skirt lifting like a ballerina twirling on stage. From there it's a blur. I was in his arms, then flying toward the open balcony doors, then back in his arms. It was so much fun—I couldn't stop laughing. It almost felt like I was either exercising or having a massage. When the song was over, I was exhausted but wanted more.

"Pffft, and you said you couldn't dance."

"I can't." I was heaving each breath and laughing. "I don't think I can do anymore."

"You can." For the next hour he danced with me nonstop, until we were both breathless. I felt like a starlet. I loved him, and I loved who I was with him in that dress. As quickly as we'd come in and danced, Clive twirled me out of the room—on to the next adventure.

Out in the cool air of the night, I looked down the gas-lamp lit street. I could hear clopping hooves and putting engines. What a marvellous time. Sort of like my time. There's my car, a model made before I was born, sounding like an airplane and smoking like a chimney, driving on the same roads as sleek Teslas, gliding silently to their destinations.

I hope I live to see hover cars.

"There's a bunch of people enjoying the beach, what say you?" Clive asked. The beach sounded heavenly, but it seemed like I was having too much fun, guilt making me concerned about the mission.

"What if that wasn't what I was supposed to do here? What if there's something else I should be doing right now?" I asked. "Maybe we should see if Sam and Zeta are back yet."

"There's no chance. That crowd parties until dawn," he said. "Besides, how do you know what you're supposed to do isn't at the beach?"

He had a point. So, to the beach we went. We took off our shoes and walked in our bare feet, my toes squished into the warm sand. The nice thing about a beach in 1920 was, you didn't have to worry about stepping on a needle in the dark.

Phosphorescence glowed around the people playing in the ocean. *Amazing.* I wouldn't have thought anything so beautiful could be living in those waters.

"This is crazy. We're right by all these factories, but still the water is clean and full of life," I said.

"The earth is amazing—it can take whatever we dish out," Clive said.

"It won't be able to do it forever."

"I disagree. The earth is more powerful than you understand. It will always be stronger than we are."

I wanted to argue with him because he was wrong.

I guess in a way he's right, when we finally destroy the ecosystems so badly that we can't survive, the earth will get rid of us and go on. It doesn't need us to survive, only we need it.

"Maybe, but I can tell you for sure, New York water doesn't look like this in my time," I said.

"Right. You're the expert on long-term effects. I forgot myself for a moment, I apologize. What's it like in your time?"

"You know what, it's a nice night, let's not talk about that right now. We'll get time, don't worry, I'll tell you."

"That's fair. I'm sorry, this timing is bad, but nature calls, I'm just going to go to the washroom." He pointed over at a wood shack down the beach.

I put my feet in the water while I waited, but soon I couldn't resist. I slipped my dress over my head and ran into the water in just my super modest, 1920's underwear. I got hoots and hollers. It was funny to me because in my time, what I was wearing was essentially a tank top and shorts, but in this time, I was being scandalous. I liked it. I splashed around in the glowing water like the pinup girl I'd become until I started to wonder if it was phosphorescence or nuclear waste I was frolicking in. Just then I heard a whole lot of yelling and shouting coming from down the beach. When people started running into the water around us, I tried to find Clive. Because I don't see that well in the dark, I had no idea if there was going to be trouble. I was sorry then that I was tramping around in my wet underwear. I didn't want to yell out his name because I didn't want to look scared to whomever the rowdies were. I just huddled closer to a group who weren't yelling, and hoped they'd protect me.

"Who are those guys?" I asked one of the girls.

"Just a bunch of rich guys. They're trouble. Fun to play with, but don't get your heart involved." She whispered the last part quickly.

"Hello ladies!" One of the guys yelled out to us.

"The sparks are flying tonight. It looks like all three of us are meant to be," he said, reaching for me first.

"Sorry, this one's meant for me," Clive said.

"That's fine chap, there's plenty to go around," the guy said.

I hugged Clive. "I'm so happy to see you—I was panicking a little because I don't see great in the dark."

"So, you took off your clothes and jumped in the water?"

"Yes."

He laughed and hugged me tightly. "If I'd have known you were providing a wet-underthings display, I would have stayed here and peed in the water."

"Gross!" I playfully slapped his muscular chest and laughed while he twirled me around in the waves.

"Looking good!" He whistled.

"Will you help me find my dress?"

"Do you really want to get out? I mean, look at this?"

The water glowed everywhere there was movement.

He took my hand, and we dove into the phosphorescence. I forced my eyes open, and even though I was afraid of toxic waste, I was more afraid not to experience the moment. It was like flying through space, hand in hand, stars zooming by. Maybe I'd get X-ray vision as a side effect. When he stood up, I wrapped my legs around him and gave him a hug. I never wanted to let him go.

"Hey, do you folks want to go to a party at the Waldorf-Astoria?" a young woman asked us.

"What do you think?" Clive asked.

"Why not? Sounds fun. Should I go over to the washroom and get changed?"

"I'm not letting you out of my sight. You don't have much more you can take off and I want to be there when you do."

I felt myself getting warm all over despite the cool water.

I grabbed my dress from the shore and slipped it over my head, even though I was soaking wet. I stealthily pulled my underclothes out from under the dress.

"You're naked under that dress now?" Clive couldn't take his eyes off me.

"Clive, we're always naked under our clothes. You're naked under your clothes." I blushed.

"See, it's different when you think about it, right?"

He was right. It's different when you think about it.

The night was warm, so by the time we got to the hotel, I was mostly dry, and absolutely all the way in love. Clive held my hand tightly the whole way.

The Waldorf-Astoria was much swankier than the last hotel, but the dancing wasn't as wild.

I was overtired and the moonshine was strong. Clive ran into some friends, and went on an errand with one of them, leaving me in the care of his friend Mario, who was studying chemistry. We were lounging on a velvet settee, and he was telling me how hard his studies were since he's not a great reader, how he shouldn't be up so late because he had class in the morning, and how he had papers to work on, but he didn't want to miss this fancy party.

"What do you love about chemistry, Mario? Why do you do this to yourself?" I thought about how much easier it is in my present day, because there were videos to watch, so many other ways to take in information.

"I love the unknown. I love to be on the edge of new discoveries."

"What discoveries do you want to see happen in your lifetime?"

"I want space travel. I want a flying machine of my own. I want a time machine."

I sat up a little. "Do you think chemistry will get you there?"

"It's all part of it. Many pieces come together to make a whole. Fuel for instance."

"Okay, but if you could have a time machine today would you get in it?"

"Yes," he said decidedly.

"What if you could never come back to this time?"

"Could I take my family?"

"Would they go?"

"No." He laughed.

"So, if you could go forward a hundred years, but you could never come back, and you could only take family who wanted to go, would you?"

He didn't seem weirded out, it was a normal three o'clock in the morning sort of a question. I thought it would be fun to take him with us through the portal. It would make me feel a lot better about where all the missing persons end up.

"Nah, none of the good ones would come." He laughed it off.

It made me think about my friend Naomi, who always used to ask me if I'd eat a spoonful of poop for a million dollars. If she ever asked me again, I'd say yes.

Clive came back and we danced until dawn. I've never been so tired in my entire life. We went back to the hotel—I was ready to zonk out. Sam and Zeta still weren't back. As we dragged ourselves through the door, I collapsed on the first couch I saw.

CHAPTER 14

Zeta

♫ "El Tango De Roxanne" ♫
by Jose Feliciano, Ewan McGragor, Jacek Koman

Right after breakfast, Sam and I went shopping. The movie machine was tested, and ready with plenty of power for several dozen showings, if necessary, though I imagined some of the same people would gather around for each showing. We needed the right clothing to stand out. Sam knew exactly what looked good on him, and I could trust him to pick the right clothing for the day, so I planned on going my own way to conserve time, but watching Sam model clothing had too strong of a pull. For the initial part of the day, any dapper outfit would do, but for the gala, he had to be devastatingly handsome. *I want to watch him try several sumptuous options.* Love him, or hate him with jealousy, the goal was that he was never forgotten. Rivalry could be a good source of publicity as anything else. Sam didn't actually have to invent anything—he just had to make a bigger mark on the world. Tonight was the night.

"Let's do your clothing first, let me watch."

"Do I get to watch you with your clothing?" he asked.

I wanted to take his breath away at the gala, so he could absolutely not know what I was planning to wear.

"It's bad luck for the groom to see the bride before the wedding."

"This isn't our wedding."

"You'll wish it was."

We parted ways, agreeing to meet back at the hotel, then walk to the campus together.

I needed two dresses with gloves, a sequinned shawl in black, and a long, black, silk wrap-around skirt. It wasn't easy, most shops were overtaken with flapper clothing. I was not interested in looking like a dripping, drooping rectangle. I didn't have time to get something custom made. Gloves were easy, a shawl was easy, so I purchased those. The one thing the flapper girls did have going for them was underwear. I couldn't move how I wanted to with a corset on. I was able to find quite a selection, and bought much more than I would probably ever need. *It's Sam's money, he'd approve.* I couldn't find the wrap-around skirt, so I bought two large, fine shawls for the purpose. I found a shop with dresses in stunning colors and waistlines. I bought two. Next, my hair was styled with my specific parameters, and my nails—fingers and toes—painted.

I hired a driver who loaded my packages, took me to a perfumery, and waited while I decided on a sultry scent from House of Guerlain. The driver, then the porter carried my packages to the suite.

Sam was ready, freshly shaven, hair coiffed, looking robust.

"I'll be ready in twenty minutes." I kissed Sam on the cheek while the porter laid my packages out on the bed. Sam smelled like musk, forest and sea. *"This is why you should never be alone with a man,"* I heard my mother's adamant warning.

I saw Sam sitting to read the newspaper as I slid the bedroom doors shut. I hung my clothing for the gala and dressed for Dr. Harver's presentation. Professional, but low-key alluring.

Dr. Harver showed up for *her* presentation completely alluring. She invited Sam to the stage, and they flirted through the entire program. I knew he was playing a role, and it was part of the plan, but I had to leave the auditorium twice for air. *Tomorrow she will be out of our lives. He's going along with the plan. Technically speaking, this was my plan. To be unforgettable. He is being unforgettable.*

Dr. Harver toyed with Sam. He batted at her repartee. The program ended without altercation, though I nearly had a stroke holding back. Afterward, Sam introduced me to Dr. Harver as his assistant, which almost started another Great War, but I held my tongue.

"Your assistant?" I growled at him as we followed Dr. Harver to her car.

"Can we talk about this later?" Sam tried to silence me.

"At the first possible convenience." I assured him.

"I'm curious about this contraption," Dr. Harver said to Sam, first resting her hand on top of the movie box, then dropping her hand to his knee. I had to look away.

I watched the other passengers in the back of the motorcar. A handsome man, slightly younger than myself fixated on her hand skimming his leg, as I watched in my peripheral vision.

"I look forward to delighting you," Sam said.

The handsome young man spoke up, pointing to the lettering on the movie box. "Zeta, the assistant—are you his wife or sister?"

Sam laughed. "Premature perhaps. She's neither at the moment."

I waited for him to reinforce the status of our relationship. He didn't.

"Stop the car!" I said.

"Yes, do. We're here," Dr. Harver said.

I exited and headed straight for a row of shrubbery. There was a break in the tall hedge. A labyrinth. I heard Sam following me, calling me, so I started running trying to find a spot to breathe. I came to a dead end. Sam cornered me.

He held his hand out to me like he was trying to calm a wild animal. He put the movie box down. "Zeta, don't be mad. We're trying to get in with these people. Dr. Harver is influential. It's only one day, and I'm trying to make the most of it, for my family. Please, don't be angry. She means nothing, but we need invitations to the gala," Sam said.

"I know that. I know. I'm trying to hold this in, but you are mine. I don't share men."

"I'm not asking you to." He came closer.

"Stop." I held my hand up. "I have rules for you."

"Rules?" He stopped.

"To get through this night alive."

"Okay." He smiled.

"You don't touch her. Words, fine, I can choke it down, but don't touch her."

"What if she touches me?"

"Don't touch her back."

He nodded.

"Don't be alone with her and you're coming home with me tonight."

"What if she tries to get me alone?"

"She will. I know you can get out of a jam like that if you want to."

He nodded again.

"I'm going to need reassurances."

"Zeta, it's only been you, I can't even remember when it wasn't you, I've been wanting you for so long."

"More."

He started talking again.

"No, like this." I took his hands and put them where they needed to be.

"Oh. I understand." He took the lead and thoroughly reassured me.

"Good start. Spice the night with this and we'll be okay. Don't mistake this for insecurity, this is you physically calming my raging blaze, so I don't attack her."

"How am I supposed to calm this storm?" He moved in closer so I could feel the problem.

"Marry me and I'll take care of all your meteorological predicaments." I meant it. "What are the rules?"

"No touching, don't be alone, reassure." He recited, as he walked off adjusting his pants.

"Good. You alright?" I laughed.

"No, but I will be. I just can't look at you." He picked up the movie box and we went to join the others.

"Sam, if we don't get invited to the gala, promise you'll take me to dinner."

"I promise."

❦

"Thought we lost you." Dr. Harver put her arm on Sam's, and looked back at me, defiant.

I slid my tongue over my sharpest teeth. *War is unforgettable.*

The spacious salon was half solarium. Groupings of lounge chairs and small tables were sprinkled between lush greenery. Spirited conversations filled the room.

"I'd like to show you something Dr. Harver," Sam said.

"Lilith, please."

"Lilith." He set the movie box on a table and started the movie.

She looked both dazzled, and—did I detect—jealous? She didn't laugh with the others at the ending mishap reel. The movie attracted attention. The second time Sam played it, the first group remained, but a larger crowd gathered around. I could see Lilith studying Sam's parts of the movie but plotting instead of watching mine.

For years I've watched Sam with other women fawning over him. I've seen him charm and dazzle them, why does Lilith bother me so much?

Because Sam and I opened the box, and what came out won't ever fit back inside.

Sam played the movie many times, until everyone in the room had seen it more than once. Lilith got more familiar with his leg at every showing. With all eyes on the box, she could touch him as she pleased. Only the handsome young man and I took any notice.

Questions about the box itself were asked rapid-fire.

"I'm terribly sorry, please excuse me, I wasn't expecting to attend a gala tonight, but we've been invited, and I must prepare the check book." Sam laughed.

There were a few hearty laughs.

Lilith walked us out, arm in arm with Sam.

She has no idea how expendable she is.

Back in our suite, I was tempted to give Sam something to think about other than Lilith, but I restrained myself for the sake of my mother's rosary. Poor thing would be ground to dust if my mother ever knew, imminent marriage or not.

Sam dressed first because I wanted to take my time, to the last minute. He wasn't particular about sliding the doors to the bedroom all the way shut. I suspected this was on purpose. It took me a few moments to find a spot where I could face away from the doors but still see through the open space from the reflection in the opposing wall's mirror. I moved a chair two feet over to look casual and uninterested should he surprise me, or if Clive and Lilac returned.

I caught quick glimpses of him with pants, but no shirt—that had me swallowing hard. When it was my turn, I could offer him no such courtesy, I needed his astonishment later. He came out, shirt slightly unbuttoned, jacket over his shoulder, tie in his hand, swagger in progress. Thankfully his cuffs were at his wrists, or we would have faced delays.

I shut the doors completely and got to work. Even with the black sequinned shawl pinned at my clavicle and two black silk shawls obscuring my dress I looked classy. The long black satin gloves added to the glamor. When I opened the doors, Sam took a breath.

"You look beautiful, Zeta."

"You look edible," I replied.

"Let's go before we can't." He buttoned his top button and tied his tie in the mirror by the door. I watched the movements of his hands, confident to the last tug. "Okay, now—let's go now." He laughed.

⬤

The gala, held in the ballroom at the Waldorf-Astoria, was breathtaking. Tables surrounded a dance floor. On stage was an ensemble of musicians, and a lectern surrounded by flowers.

"What's this gala raising money for?" I wondered.

"Research. A university research department, I think. To tell you the truth, I'm not sure." Sam chuckled.

Several tables away, Lilith laughed at the right pitch to get Sam's attention. We both looked her way. She was wearing a floor-length heavily jeweled gown, sparkling and glamorous.

"You brought the music?" I asked Sam as Lilith sauntered over.

"Yes."

"How will you play it?"

"You'll see," he said quickly, before Lilith took his hand and pulled him into the crowd.

I worked the crowd myself, filling up on appreciative glances, picking my marks.

A booming voice came from the stage. "If you'll all be seated, dinner commences."

I found Sam. He was seated beside Lilith at a table with six chairs. She turned his chin back toward her as I found my name card directly across from him. I hid my fisted hands under the tablecloth. Her handsome young man was seated next to Sam, clearly, he'd been demoted. *It will be a miracle if Sam makes it out of this without a black eye. Unforgettable.*

I smiled at him. His jaw went from clenched to a smile.

Beside me, two more handsome men sat down. *She's gathered a crowd to adore her. I'm sure the only reason I'm here is at Sam's insistence.*

I hardly had time to introduced myself before the dinner service took our attention. Two of Lilith's fingers disappeared between Sam's shirt buttons.

I reached my foot under the table for Sam's. I couldn't find it.

I reached out my foot and this time found his. I took my first bite focusing my eyes on my food, but my heart on the feel of his leg against mine. His foot inched up my leg. I snuck a glance at him, he looked like he was having a hard time breathing, red blotches climbed his neck to his face. *He loves me.* Sam leaned back in his chair. His leg climbed higher, then was gone, and then back with the softness of his socked foot. I pushed myself as far forward as I could go, wanting more. I was afraid I'd choke if I took another bite. I looked at him again. He was tugging his tie. His foot explored further, it would never be enough, we were too far away, but still, I could hardly breathe, waiting, hoping. The attendant refilled my wine. I took a sip savouring every sensation.

Suddenly, Sam stood up. "Excuse me."

Whose foot? Lilith's main Magi caught my eye.

"Me too," I said, and followed Sam.

I heard Lilith make her excuses, following us.

We're at the gala, I doubt she has the power to have us removed. We've already made an impression. This ends now.

I stopped Lilith in the hallway. "No." I put my hand to her chest.

"Sam needs me to finish something I started." Lilith winked wickedly at me.

"Sam's a big boy he . . ." I started.

"Mmmmm, yes, he is." She smiled coyly.

Rip her face off.

"He's mine."

"Let the man decide for himself."

"You're out of your depth. I tell you this as a courtesy." I locked eyes with her.

She pushed my hand away. "If you don't trust him . . ." She continued on, walking Sam's direction.

"I don't trust you." I stepped on the back of her gaudy gown, stopping her.

Her dress was so tight she couldn't turn around as long as I was standing on it. She tried a couple times to pull free. I hoped her dress would rip.

"Excuse me." She lost her cool.

It brought me so much joy to see her struggle.

"Excuse me—" She tugged at it.

Wait.

She pulled forward. *Wait.* She pulled more forcefully. *Wait.* An admirable effort. I lifted my foot, and she stumbled forward, then to the ground.

Sam peeked out from a doorway, he shook his head at me, smiling then disappeared.

Lilith got to her feet and spoke an inch from my face. "Whatever you think you've got, you dirty immigrant, does not compare to me."

"Ladies, I believe the next course is about to begin. Shall we?" Sam offered his arms to escort us back into the ballroom.

"Yes, it is," she said through clenched teeth.

———◆———

Lilith's handsome young man—Magi One—watched my return to the table. I shrugged and sat back in my chair. I made entertaining conversation with the Magi, knowing I had an exotic factor Lilith couldn't hope to compete with. *Eventually, she'll remember one man is never enough for her narcissistic needs.*

Mid-dessert, Sam left the table, but this time not in a state, and Lilith didn't follow. In his absence, Lilith worked to regain control of the Magi, they seemed delighted to have increased odds.

Dinner settings were cleared, a brief speech was made announcing donation arrangements, then dancing commenced.

Magi One asked me to dance, which I accepted once I saw Lilith accept Magi Two's request to dance.

"I believe I may have misread the situation. I apologize," Magi One said as we began to foxtrot.

"Nonsense. I started it, I just didn't know who I was starting it with." I felt heat in my face.

"I'm sorry you were disappointed," he said as we maneuvered around an elderly couple on the dance floor.

"It was not a matter of your skill…" We turned, gliding through the required steps. "You clearly have undeniable talent." His eyes never left me, even as we danced in perfect time with the music. "It was a matter of my commitment."

We were silent the next few steps.

"Commitment means nothing to Lilith, I fear," he said finally.

"You can do better."

He shook his head. "I can't, I love her—she torments me."

"You can, that's not love," I said, as the last notes of the song were played.

"You should talk."

When Sam concluded a conversation with a group of guests and returned to our table, Lilith asked him to dance.

"I must dance with Zeta."

I wanted to look at her with victory in my eyes, but I resisted.

It was a waltz, so we were able to talk.

"She keeps asking me to dance, but I feel like that would fall under the no touching rule."

"Do we really need her at this point? We made a memorable impression, is she really the linchpin to success?"

"Probably not, but we'll have to leave now, I can't refuse to dance with her, or we'll make an enemy."

"I was thinking about that. An enemy can make you famous just as well as an ally, sometimes even better." I didn't want to think about his hands on Lilith.

"It's true, but I try to keep every relationship accessible, if possible. In the future we may need her help."

"I can't imagine it."

"This isn't a relationship we'll have to maintain for long. She mentioned an after-party. I'd like to go. This room is full of influential people. We can carve our names into the history books as real people, part of the scientific community if these people mention us in their correspondence, papers or journals. The more of an impression we make, the more viable our patents look in the future. It would be hard to deepfake, meaning artificially generate, references."

"Okay, you can dance with her, but don't let your hands wander, and hold her at a distance," I said.

"Like this, you mean?" Sam's hands wandered.

"Definitely not like that."

"Okay, so our plan now is to secure an invitation to the after-party."

"What about our tango? That might help."

"Oh yes, it will. Look in the corner, there." He pointed our hands to the corner. "I had them brought in. I think in half an hour we should give this crowd the show of their lives."

There were a dozen phonographs in the corner.

"Oh, I edited out the slow, middle section of the song. In the movie they had more story to tell. We don't have a story here exactly, keeping the tempo up will make more of an impact, I think."

"I agree, you keep me on my toes, Samso, switching things up at the last minute. Until then, what's the plan?"

"I'll dance with Lilith, you dance with anyone who asks, if you can get us an invitation, perfect. If not, maybe we'll just crash it." He smiled. "That would be memorable too."

Sam danced with Lilith. I worked the room. Most men asked me about the movie box. I didn't have to pretend I didn't know how it worked, I genuinely didn't, and I told them so. I kept the same rules as I imposed on Sam as far as my hands went, but I used every power of enticement I could to make an impression and land an invitation to the after-party. By the time Sam was setting up the phonographs, I had ten invitations, six indecent proposals, and two marriage proposals.

The Master of Ceremonies introduced Sam, who accepted the microphone.

"We offer you a gift, from Argentina, by way of Italy, by way of Virden, Manitoba .... The tango." Sam nodded to several waiters, who started the phonographs.

I made my way through the crowd to the dance floor while the introduction played. Lilith must have thought the gift was just the music because she imagined she'd be dancing with Sam. He stood tall, looking confident, and mouthwatering from head to toe. Lilith stood in front of him.

At the first dramatic sound of the violin, I bumped her out of the way with my hip. "My man, Lilith." I circled around Sam's body to his back, and pulled off his jacket, throwing it to the floor. He spun around, grasped my hand, and drew me in to his chest, leading me in a quick succession of our practiced moves around the perimeter of the dance floor.

Lilith, not shied away by Sam's rejection stomped diagonally across the floor and met us. Magi One followed her, whether he was hoping to save her from embarrassment or claiming what was his, I didn't know.

"Lucky us." I didn't smile, but I felt like it. Her hubris would make our tango a hundred times more memorable.

I turned to face her, blocking her access to Sam. She gripped my sequinned shawl. I dipped out of it, leaving it in her hand, and revealing the tight bodice of my red tango dress. I heard gasps around the room, but the only one that mattered to me was Sam's. I turned and winked at him. I dropped the shawls covering the skirt and heard another round of gasps at my red satin fitted skirt. Lilith made her move to cut in on our dance. Magi One made a move to stop her. I tango-stepped to a distance, Sam's eyes focused on me. I slowly pulled off my long black gloves, keeping in step, my eyes locked on Sam.

"Lilith!" Magi One grabbed her hand and spun her toward him.

I danced further away, stepping out of my shoes. I lifted my skirt to entice Sam with my red-painted toes. Sam stepped commandingly toward me, a moth to my flame. He dragged me by the waist, while I unbuttoned his top three buttons. He dipped me to the side with one arm, displaying me to the room. Lilith took her opportunity to step in, putting her arms around Sam's neck. I rolled off Sam's arm and saw the look on Magi One's face. *This will help both of us.*

I backed into Magi One forcefully, his hands went to my waist as a natural attempt to steady me. I looked to Sam and Lilith, then bent over, leaning against Magi One's crotch, and tore a slit up the side seam of my dress using the starting cut I'd put at the hem. I was sure they heard the stitches ripping in the hallway. Mouths were now agape as the audience was transfixed. I circled my freed leg around Magi One, causing him to turn away from Lilith. Sam spun Lilith so she could watch. I ran my fingers through Magi One's hair staring at her, taunting her, while the music buzzed like a frenzied hornets' nest.

"Lift me." I could feel he was strong enough to do so. I wrapped both legs around him, his hands on my buttocks. I pulled my hair loose, bounced it free, arching my back. I let out a loud cry then stretched my bodice to his face, staring Lilith down.

"Roooxxanne," the gravel pit belted out.

She didn't like that. Lilith marched over to claim what was hers, and I jumped down, and spun back to Sam. I motioned for him to roll up his sleeves. I saw him resist a smile. He shook his head. I took a few tango steps toward the Magi One and Lilith tangle, then glanced back at Sam. He let out a dramatic breath and rolled up his sleeves. I subtly shifted my shoulders, the fragile straps of the dress sliding to my upper arms. Biting my lower lip, sashayed with painted red toes toward him. The deep thump of the bass vibrated through floor, signaling the song's crescendo. I dropped to the floor with my hands up. Sam pulled me across the floor, then up into his arms, spinning us around. Incredibly, Lilith was moving toward us. I spun out of Sam's grip and stepped quickly to stand on the tail of Lilith's gown, and she screamed. I turned so Lilith and I were back-to-back. An unholy sound came from her as she tried to turn but couldn't. She tried to claw at me but couldn't reach me. I moved, dancing against her, and she howled—Sam and Magi One watched, spellbound. I could feel the power of what Sam and I had achieved. Lilith dropped to the ground, screaming in rage. *I think we've burned this Lilith bridge.*

Sam lifted me off Lilith's dress, Magi One lifted Lilith up and exited the ballroom. The room burst into applause.

I suspect many observers thought Lilith and Magi One were part of the show. Those who knew better, knew Lilith, and it was doubtful they'd hold it against us. Sam recovered the music machine and arranged for the return of the phonographs while I collected our various articles of clothing from the dance floor.

We danced and made connections until dawn at the after-party. All in all, the night was a raging success. Entering our suite, Lilac and Clive lay sleeping on the two couches. Exhaustion was our chaperone, with Sam sleeping on the floor, leaving the bed for me. I wanted to care, but sleep overtook me.

CHAPTER 15

Lilac

♫ **"Stand By Me"** ♫
by Tracy Chapman

In 1920, they hadn't heard of blackout curtains. The sun woke me about two hours after I went to sleep. We had one full day in New York before we had to get back on the train. I was exhausted, but my brain was up and there was no reasoning with it. Everyone else was sleeping, so I left a note, and went downstairs for breakfast. The hotel had a cozy restaurant. I sat by the window. Fresh orange juice was served in a crystal glass, probably full of lead, but I ignored it for the moment. I had coffee and toast with the creamiest butter, and I coated it with strawberry jam. If I did become stuck in the year 1920, the food was amazing. I always thought people's taste buds must get weaker as they get older, because I had heard older people complain that their favorite foods weren't as good as they used to be. They were right. All the more reason to make sure Sam succeeded.

"May I join you?" Sam asked.

"Certainly."

"Did you sleep well?"

"I slept well considering how short it was."

"Yeah, Zeta and I got in pretty late too."

"How did it go yesterday? Tell me everything."

"We did it."

"You better not have—Zeta is a proper lady."

"No." He blushed. "I mean, we made an indelible impression and met all the right people, we have a notebook full of addresses. We did what we set out to do." He looked truly happy.

"I'm so happy to hear that. You did good Sam."

"Honestly, it was mostly Zeta, she's everything." Stars twinkled in his tired eyes.

"She is." I thought so, too. "What's on the agenda for today?"

"I wanted to catch an earlier train this morning, but there aren't any, so I guess we have to wait the day, though I wish we could leave now. I want to get us home to Virden as quickly as possible. In the meantime, I'll start writing letters to the scientists I met."

"Nope."

He raised his eyebrows and pulled back his head.

"You're in New York, and it's 1920. Have fun today."

There was a long pause. It became uncomfortable. I'd been lighthearted, but it didn't look like Sam was into it.

"I have a job to do. You go play." He pushed his chair out scraping the hard floor, leaving the restaurant.

He's just tired and grouchy. He's going to wreck his chance at happiness with Zeta.

At home, I would have never followed someone and made a scene, but I wasn't at home. I caught up with Sam in the lobby. I pulled his arm and swung him around as hard as I could.

I'm tired and grouchy too.

"No, Sam. I don't know your mother, but I don't need to know she'd want you to be happy. She wouldn't want you spending your life trying to make changes without also enjoying your life. If she could go back and change one thing, she'd stay with you. She was overcome with sadness and frustration, but I guarantee you if she had the chance to think about it, leaving you would be her biggest regret. She couldn't change what happened, but she could have tried to enjoy what she still had. She would want you to love the life you do have, Sam, not spend it tunnel visioned on revenge." I failed to keep tears from escaping my eyes. "A little revenge is okay, but you have to be happy too." I whispered.

We stood, staring at each other. Anger and bitterness showed on his face. I half expected him to push me away.

"I don't want you to give up this project. I want to help you, but you need more than just revenge. You need people, fun, travel, and joy—and sunshine, and water, and dancing, and music, you know? You can't become the Count of Monte Cristo. And you can't expect Zeta to live that life of misery with you."

He hung his head a bit and sat down on one of the couches nearby.

"I know. When I first came back, it was all so fresh in my mind, and I was so hurt. I wanted to fix everything. As the years went by the pain lessened, but I was in this mode, and I just stuck to it. I'm not in that fresh torture anymore. We've already seen that we win. The family paper flickers mostly to us winning, so something you did, or are going to do, will make us victorious, Lilac. It's given me a tiny taste of freedom from revenge, but it's a hard habit to break. Zeta is reminding me of what life can be like. I didn't even let myself think about her because I thought she was just a distraction I couldn't afford. But it's nice, you know. It's nice to feel loved. It's nice to allow myself to love her."

He stared into the distance and paused. I let him have the time he needed.

"I want to accomplish this, this monumental thing, and I will. We have proof. That has to be enough."

He looked at the floor, just staring for a long time. I sat with him.

"You're right. I don't want to waste my life being unhappy, I don't want to waste her life by making her unhappy. The people who did this to my family live miserably. They're not making the world a better place. They add to the great human suffering." He choked back a sob.

"I don't want my life to sing in that choir. I want to help people live, but I want to show them what to live for. She's something to live for. Making her happy is something to live for."

I hugged him. "I'm so happy to hear you say that. Let's have a really fun day."

He bowed his head and said, "You're right. What do you recommend?"

I said the first thing that came to my mind, "Breakfast at Tiffany's."

"Of course. You know that was just a movie, right?"

❧

Clive and I, and Sam and Zeta strolled arm in arm, and heart in heart. It was about twenty blocks to Tiffany's. We picked up hot, fresh bagels from a street vendor on the way. It was a beautiful sunny day. Even though New York wasn't exactly a clean city, and the streets were filled with cars and horses, the air was still fresher than in was in my time in my sleepy little Virden. I enjoyed just breathing as we walked along.

A sign from across the street caught my eye. A broker was selling stocks for The Coca-Cola Company.

"Sam, Zeta, stop!" They turned around from a few strides ahead of us.

I pointed at the sign. "Buy some, for your family. Remember the red jerseys, maybe it's because they own stock in Coca-Cola?"

Sam's big grin was probably the first pure smile I'd seen on his face. "Yes!"

We waited outside while he bought as many stocks as they'd allow.

"Lilac, I think that was it. I think you've done it, thank you!" He high-fived me with the loudest high-five ever spanked. In that moment he lost the last hitch in his giddy up.

A little girl yelled out to us from some steps. "Do you wanna hear a joke?"

"I always want to hear a joke!" I said.

"Good!" She stood up and cleared her throat.

"What do you get when you cross an elephant and a rhino?"

It's an old joke, but I didn't want to spoil it for her.

"I don't know, what?"

"Elephino!" she said, laughing and slapping her knee. I doubt she understood the joke, which made it cuter somehow. She wanted to make us happy, even if it didn't make her happy.

"Thanks for making me laugh. What's your name?" I asked.

"Lucille Ball." She smiled, batted her eyelashes, and took a bow.

Of all the gin joints, in all the towns, in all the world, you walk into mine . . .

"You're Lucille Ball?" I asked then looked at Sam wide eyed. The other two knew something was up but weren't sure what it could be.

"Yes ma'am."

I handed Sam my purse. *How could I ask this?*

"Can you just remember this for us? I have a makeup compact in my purse, can you hold it up and Zeta can you see what makeup I should wear next time?"

Thankfully, Sam understood I was asking him to take a picture with my phone. *In a week, in the shower, I'll think of a smoother way I could have said that. Whatever.*

"Clive, get in here with us, you need makeup too." He had no idea what was going on, but he did it anyway.

Sam held it up and took the picture.

"Hmm, I'll have to think about it," Zeta said. "You both look beautiful just the way you are. No makeup needed."

"However, I imagine our young friend will have wonderful red hair when she gets older," Sam said, winking at us.

I looked at Lucy.

"Yes, I think so . . . Lucy, I'm a great fan. You've brightened my day, and I know you're going to brighten the whole world with your humor. You're going to be a star."

"Would you like some money for ice cream?" I asked.

"Golly, would I?"

"Here you go!" I gave her ten bucks, and her eyes turned to saucers.

"Thank you! I'll have ice cream for the rest of my life."

As she ran off, I said, "It was nice to meet you!"

"I can't believe we just met Lucille Ball!" I yelled, gripping Clive's arms and bouncing up and down. He just laughed at me.

"I have no idea what's going on here."

"She's a hilarious actress and comedian. *The Long, Long Trailer* is a classic movie. It's the story of my life," I said.

"Well, we'll have to watch it together then. I'd like to learn more about you."

"It's more the kind of thing you share after you're married, after you can't escape."

"Oh well, I like where you're thinking. I better see it quick so I know what I'm getting into."

Clive's words were like paper-thin bubbles floating in the air. We held our breath to see if they'd smash on the sidewalk, but they just floated away. We carried on, a little more solid, a little more satisfied.

"Would you like to see the picture?" Sam asked.

"Yes!"

He cupped the phone in his hand.

"I look terrible!" I said.

My smile was weird, one eye was closed, and my hair was a frizzy mess. Which I deduced it still was.

"I think you look beautiful," Clive said. I could see he did believe that.

"You're a keeper."

"I hope you believe that."

"I do."

We walked, arm in arm, taking in New York's glorious morning until finally—the words we all were waiting for ...

"We have arrived! Fifth Avenue and 37th Street. Tiffany and company!" Clive pointed to the Tiffany & Co. sign.

It was warm outside, thick with humidity, but when he opened the door, a new world opened up. The air was cool, and light, with a bouquet of hardwood floors, and class. It was cavernous and full of sparkling treasure.

Zeta, despite her strength and determination, looked as giddy as I was. She and Sam went off in one direction, and Clive and I in another. We had a lot of ground to cover.

"I'd like to find some small things I could take back," I said to Clive. "Tiffany is still highly sought after. It's a good investment."

"Whatever you like, Lilac. You could also just get things you like, treasures just for you."

It was a novel concept. I no problem spending money, but somewhere along the way subconsciously, I wouldn't spend over a certain dollar amount unless it would be an investment that would make money.

"Thank you. You're right. Maybe my mom would like something too."

I found a sale table. *Okay, well this is irresistible.* I picked out a few things I was sure I'd seen on *Antiques Roadshow* and confirmed with Clive they'd fit through the portal. We had them set aside as we continued browsing.

Wedding rings were displayed in the next case. I always feel embarrassed even passing by the wedding ring counter at a department store. Like I want one, but I'm scared I'll never get one. It felt worse this time because I was with Clive. I felt needy and humiliated all at once. I strode past with fake confidence.

"Just a moment," Clive said.

I turned around, trying not to let all my baggage show.

"Yes?" I smiled at him, turning away from the counter. Then a tear popped out. *No. Stop.*

"Are you okay?" He looked concerned.

"Mmmm?" I wiped the tear away. "Oh, must be a bit of dust." I opened my eyes wide and fluttered them a bit to confirm the problem was dust.

"Let's have a look at these rings."

"They're wedding rings." I now had my back to the case.

"You don't like wedding rings?"

"I don't not like them, but I don't have any." I laughed.

"Maybe you should."

Maybe? I only had two obvious choices: 1. Run out of the store crying immediately; or, 2. Go through a long, drawn-out psychological torture session featuring a non-committal vague conversation, turning Clive into the likes of Sam in my mind.

I ran my hands gently over his beard to get his full attention. "Say something meaningful or stop, do not mess with me about wedding rings, this is not a casual subject. I'm already in pain."

"I'm sorry. I didn't know."

"This isn't a casual topic for me. I'm sorry." I let him go and turned to compose myself.

"Lilac." He grabbed my hand. "Wait, won't you?" He took me to a quiet, dim corner and held both my hands. "Family isn't a casual topic for me either. I just didn't want to overwhelm you with intensity. Life is fragile and precarious, we don't know what tomorrow will bring, or even one hour from now. I do know I don't want to spend one more minute on this earth without you knowing how much I love you. I know there are things we have to work out, where we're going to live, what time we're going to live in, but I want to be with you. You make me feel good, and I want to keep you safe, and make a happy life for you. Am I crazy, or do you feel it too?"

I would have killed for a box of Kleenex.

"Just to be clear, are you adopting me?" Grabbing the hem of my dress, I smiled and wiped my face with it, like a lady.

He tipped his head to the side as if to say, "Are you kidding me?"

"Say it or don't say it Clive, I'm a ticking time bomb. Don't trifle with me."

"You're a bearcat." He laughed.

"Rraaaaawwwwwwrrrrrrrrr." I clawed toward him.

"Lilac, will you be my wife?"

It was hard to find a dry spot on the hem of my dress once the flood of tears ended.

"Yes." We held each other in the dim corner, laughing and wiping aways each other's tears.

"My lady, let's find you the perfect ring." I could see the uncertainty in his face. Like he wanted to spoil me with the best ring at that counter, but he was scared going over there would still hurt me somehow.

"Okay." I smiled.

He leaned into me. He looked at my eyes, my mouth. *Is this the moment? Is he going to kiss me? He already asked me to marry him, and he hasn't even kissed me yet.* I could feel the heat from his body.

When his hand touched my neck, then cradled my face, I tucked my thumb into his belt to steady myself. He backed me to the wall. His other hand came up to my face, warm and steadying. He leaned in further, stopping just before our lips met. I felt the tease of his beard on my skin, sending electricity to my toes. He kissed me lightly at first, but when I kissed him back, he dove in with something mind blowing and unexplainable. I put both hands on his hips, instinctively pulling him to me.

He laughed and kissed me again. "Let's find you a ring."

Baggage doesn't go away in a couple minutes, but I'd face it with him. I held onto his arm. As we got closer to the counter, I felt unworthy, worthless, lonely, hopeless. I squeezed his arm tighter like we were facing an ambush of wild tigers. I wanted to say, "I can't do this today," but I looked up at his face, and he looked so happy, he looked proud. His posture was confident. He was not going into battle—this was his victory lap. He had the sweat of relief on his brow. He looked like a man who knew everything was going to be okay, finally.

I caught a glimpse of myself in a polished metal case. *He's going to find out. For some reason he doesn't see me now, but he will, and all this will be over.* Tears streamed down my face, and I couldn't stop them. *I can't do this. He only asked me because I made it awkward. This hair can never look good, not ever. Ever. It will never, ever, ever, ever look good. He's a knight and I'm a pig.*

"Clive, stop. I have more problems than just Lan. It's not just my hair either. There's more. It's not just ring counters or cellulite or motion sickness or hallucinations. I've had so many failures and I'm never going to get better at them. I promise you I can't even try, there's too many, and I can't make promises I can't keep, I can't get in over my head. I can't be what you're imagining. I'm messy and tired, I get depressed, I have terrible periods, I'm getting a hunchback, my feet stink in sneakers, my ears aren't pierced evenly, and I'm not getting them redone because it might be too close to the other one and weaken the structure of my earlobe or make one, much bigger hole. I will never be whatever you want. I'm just not her. I'm so sorry." A salesman handed me a hanky, probably because the entire store was not ready for another flashing.

Clive smiled at me. "Lilac, I've had sisters and a mom. I already know all that. All of it. I know what a woman is. What you're talking about is the baseline of a woman. I'm afraid, don't get me wrong, because I know exactly, exactly what a woman is. You have all the ferocious subtlety of a woman, but you excel in compassion, forgiveness, loyalty, humility, generosity, appreciation, creativity, spontaneity, and you make me laugh. You accept me for who I am, how I am. You didn't run away scared. You're courageous, and industrious. You're everything my mom told me to look for, plus you're beautiful. I could not ask for more."

"I'm not beautiful, it's just dark in here."

"You're going to have to trust me on this one, you're perfect in every light, even when you're throwing up. I'm the expert on this—you'll have to defer to me." He laughed.

"I'm not always going to look this good though." The thought made me laugh.

"My dad used to say he gave my mom every laugh line and every grey hair, and he was grateful she spent them on him. Please, spend yours on me, I'll try my hardest to make them worthwhile." He kissed the corner of my eye, where my crow's feet will appear.

The hanky was nowhere near enough. *Panty time has come again.* I had to find a dry spot in the back of my skirt to wipe all my tears away.

"I love you." I kissed him.

"I love you too." He kissed me back, took my hand, and walked with absolute determination to the wedding ring counter.

Clive and the staff made me feel worthy. We looked at all the rings, but then, there was *the* ring.

"Do you like that one?" Clive pointed to a beautiful ring.

It was perfect. "I do."

"I like those words." He laughed. "Do you want to try it on?"

I nodded.

The salesman handed Clive the ring and he slid it on my finger. The hair on the back of my neck stood up.

"I'm getting married!" I yelled into the street as we left Tiffany's, carrying a pretty blue box. "We're getting married!" I held up Clive's arm like he'd just won the heavyweight championship title.

He grabbed me by my waist and spun me around. No more lonely, desperate, rejected, melancholy Lilac. I was happy, in love, and on top of the world. Until, of course, I had to get back on the train. The rest of the day was a blur. There was mad dashing to get everything packed up and ready to go, interspersed with passionate kissing. I remembered and brought a variety of medications for motion sickness, which proved useless, but at least I had tried.

CHAPTER 16

Zeta

♫ **"Breakfast at Tiffany's"** ♫
by Deep Blue Something

Sam and Lilac had a thing about going to the Tiffany store. Apparently, it's from a movie they've watched. It seemed to make them happy, so I went along, even though the hotel's coffee wasn't nearly strong enough to fully wake me up.

Lilac and Clive seemed to be having an emotionally intense time in the store, and I was so tired I begged Sam to find me some Italian coffee—correctly brewed. I could hear the sounds of my people in the streets, I knew they had to be drinking coffee somewhere. We found some at a café and the instant it touched my tongue, the remembrance of home revitalized me. I dipped my biscotti and tasted every good memory with my family. I'm not one to cry, but I was overcome with emotion. They were coming to Canada—my family. Our life wouldn't be the same as in Italy, but it would be even better because of Sam, and hopefully, our many mini-Sam bambini to come.

"Is it really that good—may I have a bite?" Sam asked.

"Get your own." I laughed.

He did and we went back to Tiffany's. Lilac was crying, lifting her dress showing her panties. It wasn't a tango, but Clive's attraction was undeniable. I envied the vulnerability of the moment.

Phillip would have destroyed her. Or maybe she would have hardened, like I did. No matter, she'll never have to worry about that with Clive.

"Would you like a wedding ring from here?" Sam asked.

I immediately started crying. "I've been spending too much time with Lilac."

Sam laughed and pulled me in for a hug. "It's nice to see your softer side."

"Yes, let's get rings, then book passage for my family."

I chose a plain band with no stones, utilitarian, fighting Lilac's influence.

"I see you more like this." Sam pointed to a very different sort of ring. "Strong and beautiful. Passionate and free."

I kissed him for seeing me that way. "I accept."

The ring I chose for myself was a man's ring, which Sam then chose for himself. Without intending to, he had picked my ring, and I'd picked his. We had them packaged up, Sam arranged to meet Clive at the train, and we left to book my family's passage to America.

"You know what these rings mean don't you?" Sam wiggled his eyebrows.

"We're really getting married?"

"Sex. They mean sex for you and me." He laughed.

We tried to arranged passage for my family, but in the end, it was easier to wire them money for the fare through Western Union and let them handle their own arrangements. We sent a list of train stops to bring them right to Virden. We sent enough money to get to Virden with luxuries along the way. I thought of my mother, and how this would most likely be the nicest time of her life.

"It's so much money, Sam. I don't like feeling indebted, but I appreciate it."

"Aside from you agreeing to be my partner in life, which would obviously mean this is our money, not mine, I did hire you to help me on this trip. You already earned every last penny of this money with your perfect performance last night." Blotches of red came up from his neck.

"I'm really looking forward to finding out exactly where this redness starts." I ran my finger from his chin to the bottom of the V of his button-up shirt. "Roll up your sleeves for me again."

"I don't understand your obsession with this." He laughed.

"You don't have to." I watched, breathless.

CHAPTER 17

Lilac

♬ **"Grow Old with You"** ♬
by Adam Sandler

The journey home wasn't as bad as the trip to New York. I didn't have any altered gluten in my system—and no ingested cocaine. Clive and I obtained our own cabby shack, and we kept the window open. It took us a while to secure everything that could fly around, but it was worth it. I felt ten percent better than on the way there. Once again, Clive showed me what a spectacular man he was by holding back my hair while I puked, rubbing my back when I cried, and talking me down off the ledge from wanting to end it all by jumping from the train.

Just five days later we were home. When we arrived, he still wanted to marry me. Bless that man.

CHAPTER 18

Zeta

♫ **"The Gambler"** ♫
by Kenny Rogers

We had four days of train travel before we crossed the Canadian border and could get married. We didn't have to wait, but we figured in the long run it would be better, and surely, we could wait four more days.

Clive and Lilac got a cabby shack again, but I couldn't take the vomiting anymore, so Sam and I opted for open seating. Vomiting would have to be Clive and Lilac's chaperone.

Two days in, I heard a voice that made my blood run cold. *Phillip.*

I opened my eyes. Sam was gone. Phillip was sitting across from me.

"Look who's all dressed up," Phillip said.

I stood to leave—he grabbed my hand and pulled me back down.

"Sit."

I reached in my pocket, but my gun was gone.

"Looking for this?" He flashed the gun at me from his jacket pocket. "No locked door here to keep me out."

"What do you want?"

"For starters, that ring. I heard you're pretending we're still married, and I'm lost at war," he said. "It doesn't suit you. Barbed wire would be more fitting."

"I'm not giving you my ring."

I heard a click from his pocket.

The ring is replaceable.

"Fine, here." I handed it over.

"Thank you, that wasn't so hard, was it? You're looking fine, Zeta. I've missed you."

"You got what you wanted, leave."

"I didn't get everything I wanted." He put his knee between mine.

"Never again."

"I disagree. Right now. Get up." He pointed down the aisle. "Go that way."

I'd rather be shot where I sit. No. I'd rather have this over with and have Sam and my family for the rest of my life. It isn't the first time anyway.

I stood and went toward the back of the car. Phillip followed with the barrel of my gun shoved into my back.

"In there," he said.

I tried the door, but it was locked. "I can't open it."

He pushed me forward and tried himself. "Go."

I scanned my surroundings for ideas.

"I figure, if you were able to buy yourself this ring, you must have more money, and I need money right now."

"In trouble?"

"None of your business." He shoved me harder.

"I don't have money."

"I don't believe you, is your family in Virden yet?"

"No." I thought about what a vengeful man Phillip was.

"Well then, I know you're still saving for their passage. I'll take that money for passage of my own. Maybe I'll look up my in-laws in Italy." He laughed.

I laughed. "You suddenly want to travel? I thought immigrants were animals? You know immigrants come from the places you'd be visiting."

He shoved me through an open door and slammed it behind us.

"Are you running?" I probably shouldn't have antagonized him.

"You just never gave me the proper chance for children, and neither did Bonnie." His mind was clearly elsewhere.

"Did Bonnie run you off too?" I laughed at him, trying to gain the upper hand.

He pointed the gun at my head.

Well, that didn't work.

"No, I shot her in the head, just like I'm going to do to you, after I get you pregnant."

He's missing basic education. "We don't have ten years."

He hit me hard across the face with the gun, and pulled up my skirt, forcing me back onto some luggage. I leaned back and kicked him hard in the shank. He howled, holding his shin falling back against the wall. I grabbed my gun and aimed it him as I backed out of the door. In the aisle, I put it back in my pocket, and hurried to look for Sam. I almost made it to the end of the train, still no Sam in sight.

Phillip caught up with me. He grabbed me by the hair. I kicked back at his kneecap. He let go for a second, but I knew he'd never really let me go now. I turned and held my gun on him, without concealing it at all. "Time for you to go. Out."

"The train is moving." He looked down the steps to the door.

"You should have thought about that earlier."

"You're not going to shoot me on a train."

"No?"

"If you do, you'll be wanted, like me."

"Open. The. Door."

"Zeta." He started pleading, as if begging would change my mind.

"Open it!"

"I'm not going to." Phillip sat down at the bottom of the steps.

"Zeta?" Sam looked at me, my gun, and Phillip wedged between the bottom step and the door.

"Phillip," Sam said.

"Sam," Phillip replied.

"He took my ring," I said.

"Phillip?" Sam held his hand open.

"Immigrant slut," Phillip said. "How long did you wait, or were you in his bed when you weren't in mine?"

"The ring," Sam said.

Phillip handed him the ring.

"I think this problem will take care of itself." Sam turned his back on Phillip to put the ring back on my finger.

Phillip grabbed the door handle to pull himself up, but the door flew opened, and Phillip yelled, not able to hold on, rolling down the hillside.

"I should invent train doors that open inward," Sam said, pulling the door shut.

When the train stopped at Winnipeg, we were able to marry, finally.

Sam arranged for a cabby shack at the end of the train. We let loose eight years of pent-up lust. The porter knocked on our door and told us to be quiet or we'd be removed from the train. It was hard to do, because Sam was hard from head to toe, but we reduced our volume. Sam said I was the one making most of the noise, but I said he was responsible. By the time we got to Virden, I could hardly walk, and Sam wasn't fairing much better.

Back at my house, which was now to be our house, we found that our bodies had recovered enough to resume newlywed shenanigans. "Should we sleep so we can get to work tomorrow?" I asked.

He did the thing I now love, and we just did that for a while, then some other things that felt good. Then we ate and did all that again. It was like my mind was a cloud with a silhouette of Sam's body burned through in pure sunlight. I couldn't think about anything else, no matter how hard I tried. Phillip, even in the first month of our marriage, never sent a jolt of Eden to curl my toes and transfix my brain, like Sam did for me again and again.

By morning, some of my sense had returned. Not much mind you.

Sam leaned against the counter, holding his cup of coffee. "Coffee's not as good as it was in New York, what are we missing?"

"Biscotti." I laughed. "You got any?" I winked.

"For you I do." He winked back.

"At this rate we're never going to get anything done." It was impossible not to think about every good thing hidden by his clothing.

CHAPTER 19

Lilac

**♫ "All My Only Dreams" ♫
by The Wonders**

I went directly to the doctor's office as soon as we were home, and sat in the waiting room, hoping for a cancellation. I figured, there was no way I could be in worse condition than after five days of train travel. They fit me in, and the doctor gave me a note for another two weeks off of work, which I texted to Jane, and then went home and slept for thirty-six hours straight.

CHAPTER 20

Zeta

♫ **"A Little Less Conversation – *JXL Radio Edit Remix*"** ♫
by Elvis Presley and Junkie XL

Sam and I eventually found a rhythm. A work rhythm!

We plowed through documents quickly.

"I can't believe how fast you are at this," Sam said.

"I have a confession."

Sam laughed. "I feel like this is going to be a life of daily confessions between us."

"Do you have things you'd like to confess?"

"Not at the moment." He kissed me and peeked down my top.

"Hey, I'm trying to work." I laughed.

"Confession, go."

"There are three subscriptions to the Canadian Gazette in Virden. In order to divorce me Phillip had to run a notice for six months, twice weekly outlining his reasons for divorcing me. He charged me with adultery with a fictitious man. The subscriptions came through the post office. One comes to the postmaster. I always read it first, to tell you the truth I don't think he reads it at all, he just keeps them on his desk as more of a status symbol. I was shocked to see my name. I pulled out the page and put the other two copies in my bag."

"Isn't messing with the mail a federal offence?" Sam laughed.

"I said this was a confession."

"Carry on, my child." He grinned.

"For six months I intercepted all three papers, twice a week and spent the night altering Phillip's name, my name, and Virden. Then, replacing them as if they'd arrived the following day. It's not easy to pull up the ink on newsprint and then reprint it."

"No wonder you're so fast. This ain't your first rodeo." Sam winked.

His compliment hit me in just the right spot.

"Speaking of rodeos . . ." Sam might not have been thinking what I was thinking, but he was easy to convince.

CHAPTER 21

Lilac

♫ **"Lifting the Building"** ♫
by David Holmes

The documents Zeta and Sam created while I slept were spectacular.

I spent my days ordering supplies on the internet, printing and collating information from the database, and hanging out with Clive. I had everything delivered to the house—my groceries, vitamins, everything. I felt a little bit bad about continuing to put my job on hold, but I really didn't know how things were going to turn out, and it was good to have the job security, for when the portal ever closed . . . something I didn't like to think about because Clive and I hadn't quite worked out the future yet.

Sam and I ordered things online and talked about where we were, as far as the plan went. We'd accomplished a lot. Per the timeline, Sam's family was safe and sound. It seemed as though the Coca-Cola money allowed Sam's family to scare off the GM company, but in fixing Sam's family's problem, a similar scenario happened to one of his neighbors. It could become a never-ending rabbit hole.

"I get that you're still vengeful toward GM seed companies in general, but is it a battle that can be won? It seems like no matter what we do, or even think about doing, they pop up and are horrible anyway. We have a few weeks left. What if you just go deliver the Coca-Cola shares to your family, and then you and Zeta can come back to the future?"

"First, Zeta's family is coming, they won't get here in time, and honestly, I think the 1920's might be better for us. Second, I do feel a responsibility toward my neighbor's family," Sam said.

"What if you gave them some shares too, and then we just didn't check the news anymore. You and Zeta pack up and be ready to go the instant her family arrives." I suggested.

"Then there will be two of me in the future, how's that going to work?"

"Okay, we buy more Coca-Cola shares for you and Zeta, and we buy you documents, and you live your life somewhere else under a new name, you could even keep Sam Gabler, why not?"

"I want to do this."

"Of all the problems in the world you could fix, and knowing your family is okay now, why this one, Sam?

"The family in that picture isn't my family. It's my mom and dad's DNA, but it's not them, not *my* mom and dad. I can tell just by the way they're smiling. It's literally not even their crooked teeth. They didn't have to work hard like my parents did. They didn't struggle like my parents did. No matter what Google says, my history happened. It happened to me. They tortured and killed my parents. They're torturing and killing farmers every day. These are my people—I will fight for them. I have nothing to go back to, everything I love now is here, and I want to fight for my people."

I could see where Sam was coming from. I wouldn't do it, but I wasn't him, and I'm in no place to judge. It was noble. *A noble, losing battle.*

"Fair enough. Since we only have a few more weeks maybe we need to light this firecracker at both ends, working in the past and in the future." Whatever Sam and Zeta were doing was up to them, but I wanted Clive and I to be guilt free in Hawaii recovering soon.

"What do you mean?"

"Let's get all the work you've completed over to Ben now, because you've accomplished everything on the list, but obviously it's not enough. We're still in a GM seed mess, only further along than we were when we started."

"So, we get Ben's professional advice beyond what he's already given us?" Sam asked.

"Yeah, when he sees everything laid out—as he builds a case with it—hopefully he'll be able to see where the holes are. Obviously, there are holes, or the timeline affecting GM seeds would be fixed. His team seems to be the most likely people to be able to find the holes. What do you think?"

"It is worth a try. We're running out of time and ideas. Any help would be appreciated."

"I think Ben and his team will help give you a clearer map to follow for the rest of your life. As long as you hit all the destinations, you can be confident it will work."

"Let's do it."

We tried burying the documents in 1920, and then digging them up in my time, but it didn't work, so we brought them back to the shop, and tried to think of other ways to transfer them to the future without just taking them through the portal. Aging them was hard. Google had some ideas, but mostly, we just ended up burning through the pages, wrecking them by trying to age them.

We thought about mailing them to ourselves in the future. Contrary to what Hollywood might have you believe, no company would take a package with such a distant future delivery date.

We held another brainstorming meeting with the four of us, I brought Cokes with ice, and Hawkins Cheezies. *Brain food. Ha ha.*

"Who would have these documents stockpiled, and not realize

the value of them, so we could suddenly discover them and bring them to light?" I asked.

We all wracked our brains.

"The museum!" Sam said.

"Yes!" I pumped my fist. "They have loads of things they don't have room to display. A pile of scientific documents would easily be stored and forgotten about!"

"Okay, well, I know the Buchanan family is prominent in 1920, and when I was living in Virden in your time, they were still a prominent family. When I was first traveling to the past, I went to the museum to see what I needed to do or wear to fit in. I didn't have another time traveler to so kindly pave the way." Sam smiled at me.

"I never thought about what it was like for you when you first came to 1920. You found me within half an hour and have looked after me ever since. All of you. It would have been hard with no help. I imagine you weren't in a good headspace either."

"No, I wasn't, but I did okay. The people of Virden were kind to me. It's a good town. Very quickly it became home. After the portal closed, I met this guy." Sam punched Clive's shoulder. "And everything got a lot better. Until he went to war, of course."

"And when I came back, you saved me." Clive play punched Sam's shoulder.

"So, we just have to intermingle our documents among the Buchanan family's papers?" Zeta asked, referring to a prominent Virden family.

"Yeah," I said.

"We don't exactly run in the same circles," Sam pointed out.

"How many circles can there be, there's like 400 people in this town," I said.

Zeta shrugged. "You'd be surprised."

"Okay, well, what would get you in?" I asked. "Are they throwing a party at their house you could crash, and slip away to the attic, and put your envelope inside a big trunk of family posterity?"

"Not that I know of," Sam said.

"Does anyone have anything in common with them, sports, book club, charity?" I asked.

Nobody offered anything.

"I doubt it." Sam tapped his pencil on the table. "He's a rich investor. He loans money to businesses in the whole region. From what I hear, he charges slightly higher interest, but then again, qualifying for a loan is slightly easier than at the bank. I've never met him, but I know where his office is."

"Maybe you could seek advice, or get a loan? Who else is in the family?" I asked.

Clive pulled a Cheezie from the bag. "He has a son who is often overseas working on investments there, though it sounds like he spends most of his time hunting big game. Mrs. Buchanan is really involved with the church, I know that. They have a daughter who plays the piano for the plays at the Auditorium Theatre."

"Is there any church connection?" I asked.

"I haven't been going to church—might look suspicious if I joined now," Sam said.

"I'm Catholic, there's no Catholic church here," Zeta said.

Clive shook his head, no. "Not anymore."

There's more to that story, but maybe this isn't the time.

I reached across Clive's arm and snagged a Cheezie. "It isn't unusual for people to take a sudden interest in religion?"

"I guess I could try . . ." Sam said, scratching his head. " . . . but how long would it take before I was invited over to their house? I mean, what would the wife ask me over for?"

"Dinner. She's probably hospitable. Or maybe there'll be a picnic at her house, that would be a great chance. Any of you could try," I said.

They all agreed to the plan.

By the next morning Sam had an invitation.

"What happened, she just invited you over out of the blue?" I was so excited the plan was actually working.

"Well, as a matter of fact—I was talking to her daughter. I was locking up the shop, and walking back here when I ran into Baby leaving the Aud."

At this point, I should have realized there was trouble . . . her name was Baby? *Pullease!*

"I told her Clive and I wanted to go to her church, and I asked her when they held their services. She asked about you, but I knew direct conversation between the two of you might be a problem, so I said you weren't interested in coming. Instead, she invited us over tonight!" He was so proud of himself, and I was proud of him too. "I was thinking you and Zeta are probably much better at quietly sneaking around than Clive or I would be, so while we're distracting them at dinner, you guys could put the envelope into the attic, or a suitcase, or the library, or something like that."

We thought about hiding the documents somewhere solid like behind the baseboards, because nobody ever moves beautiful baseboards, but in the end, we decided that would be too loud. It would be easier to slip one set of the papers into a book in the library, the least likely to be read, and another set into the attic somewhere.

Since the Buchanan house was now a museum, I went to their website, found a floor plan, and a bunch of pictures of the house. I printed everything so we could plan our reverse heist. The library was on the main floor, as was a bedroom, the formal dining room, and parlor. We hoped they used the rooms as intended. Since most of the shelving was built-in, it was likely they did.

We packed up some B&E equipment and tried to anticipate how it would all go down.

"What if we just took the documents in with us, and made the excuse of using the washroom to slide them in somewhere?" Clive asked.

"Well, you could, except if you got caught, it's going to make life here really awkward for you, unless we can think up a good reason for snooping in their library," I said.

"Well, I could say I was looking for a Bible, and I had a couple questions." Sam suggested.

"Good idea." It sounded good and saved me from the heart attack of breaking into their house and piddling on their carpet—I had no nerve for that sort of thing.

"But if you aren't successful and get caught, you can never go back there, so we can never try again," Zeta said.

In the end, we decided we'd each take a set of documents in with us and do what we could. If there was a very clear, safe opportunity for any of us, we'd take it. Sam and Clive's main mission would be to distract, Zeta and I would plant documents, but if Sam or Clive had a clear opportunity, they'd take it.

We packed up our criminal things. I started with Lycra pants. *Criminal.*

By the time evening came I was sick. The stress was unbelievable. "I don't think I can do this."

"We can. We have each other." Zeta grabbed my hand and gave it a squeeze. "If it doesn't work, we can try again. If we get caught, I'll say you went into hysterics, and were searching for your husband, and I was trying to catch you to calm you down."

She was on to my mental instability.

"Believable. I like it," I said.

Clive and Sam looked a little too handsome to be sent over to a rich, piano-playing young woman's house for dinner, but it was for the greater good. I had to deal with it.

Clive must have seen the panic in my eyes. "We can do this.

Everything is going to be okay." His whispering breath on my neck gave me chills. He kissed me, and I tugged his beard, pulling him back for one more.

"You promise?"

"I promise." He kissed me again. Clive and Sam left. Zeta and I followed, not far behind.

CHAPTER 22

Zeta

♫ **"Hollaback Girl"** ♫
by Gwen Stefani

L ilac and I snuck through the bushes and climbed up into a treehouse while Sam and Clive distracted the Buchanans at the front door. The treehouse had a window facing the house. I could see Baby, flouncing around her room in a red corset, and little else.

"Aarrrrgghh." I couldn't help it, I'd just gotten rid of Lilith, and now Baby?

"Shhh," Lilac whispered. "What?"

The window was only big enough for one of us to look through and I wanted to see. "Nothing."

Baby lay across her bed opening her legs, then closing them.

Do not react.

Sam will not be interested, he has me.

She's ten years younger and a virgin.

Baby rolled over to straddle an imaginary man laying across her bed, tantalizing him before having her way with him. *She would not.*

I opened the hatch, ready to claim what was mine.

"What are you doing?" Lilac asked.

"This was a mistake."

"Hang on. Hang on." She tried to stop me.

"Look!" I pointed to the window.

Lilac looked through and said over her shoulder, "What?"

I looked. Baby was gone.

"Sam and I are married—I should be in there."

"Zeta. Take a breath. We have a plan. We can do this. It's going to help Sam, and by extension you in the long run. Please . . . just breathe. We gotta stick to the plan. We have limited time, let's get this over with tonight."

"Fine. Fine."

We stayed in the treehouse until it was fully dark. I looked back through the treehouse window. Every window on our side of the house was dark. "I think we can go now."

We crept around to the back of the house and tried the back door. It was open. *Of course.* Unfortunately, it creaked when we opened it. We heard someone coming down the hallway. I darted to the back stairs, and Lilac ducked into a closet.

As soon as I turned the corner on the stairs, I froze in place and waited. Someone came into the kitchen. I heard the sound of dishes, a stove opening, closing, then they left. I quickly scampered up the rest of the steps, two at a time, only stepping on the sides, never in the middle. I waited at the top of the stairs, listening for sounds. Nothing.

I pulled the rope on the attic door, and folded down the ladder, gently climbed the steps, and then closed it all up behind me, trying to be quiet. I used the portable light Lilac had given me to take in my surroundings. There was a cedar chest, but it was locked. There were several travel trunks, likely holding young Mr. Buchanan's hunting trophies. Thankfully, they too, were locked. *All of this will be sorted through at some point between now and a hundred years later.*

I tiptoed to where the wall met the floor, counted ten beams from the back of the house and slid the document bag between the crack. *Hopefully, they never have a leaky roof and have to do repairs.*

I hurried out of the attic, ready to make my way downstairs. When I grasped the newel post at the top of the staircase, I heard Baby and Sam talking in the kitchen. I stood completely still, holding my breath.

"Thank you for volunteering to help me prepare the tea," Baby said.

"I feel more like I was volun-told, but you're welcome."

"It's going to take a little while to boil the water. I thought maybe you could tell me a little about yourself."

"Uh . . . not much to tell, I'm just an inventor . . . a botanist, interested in learning about God."

"I think God is in everything, don't you?"

"I'm not sure," Sam said.

"I think we feel Him in all the gifts He's given us."

"Uh, Baby, I don't think we should . . . No—that's not a good idea."

"Don't you want to feel all of God's creation?"

"I don't think any man should feel *all* of God's creation."

She laughed coyly. "Shouldn't we experience as much and as many of the pleasures there are to enjoy on this earth?"

"I don't know much about church, but I'm pretty sure that's exactly not what we're supposed be doing."

"Am I teaching you, or are you teaching me?"

"I'm married," he said.

"Lilac doesn't seem right in the head, you poor man, and she isn't here to learn about God."

"About Lilac . . . Baby, no—you have to stop, that's not right. Baby!"

She just giggled. "You can just look, you don't have to touch, but you can if you want to."

"No."

"I know you want to. Here, like this . . ."

I bit my knuckles hard. The kettle started whistling. It whistled far too long, telling me they were indisposed.

I'm going to murder him. I opened the landing window and dropped to the ground, twisting my ankle. The pain was a distraction from my blind fury.

CHAPTER 23

Lilac

♫ "Unpretty" ♫
by TLC

Once the dinner service and tea were finally over, and I hadn't heard anyone walk by the closet door for about ten minutes, I was able to exit the closet.

I heard Baby excuse herself to powder her nose. I panicked and went through the first door I saw and scrambled into the closet. She came into the room I was in. I hadn't closed the door to the closet so I could see her through the crack. She was clearly not getting ready to teach Sam and Clive about the Bible, I can tell you that much. She was strutting her stuff in front of her mirror like she belonged in a tawdry production of *Moulin Rouge*. She undid her top, revealing a red lace corset. I was furious. She pouted and curled her hair around her finger then giggled into the mirror. I wanted to scratch her eyes out. She sprayed a puff of perfume between her plumped up breasts. *As if he's going to be sniffing there!* She pinched her cheeks and kissed her reflection. Then she ran her hands around her luscious, but fake silhouette. I had to look away before I knocked her out. By the time I'd regained my composure, she had retied her church-approved dress and gave her butt one last look in the mirror, winking at herself as she closed her bedroom door. Tramp!

According to the floor plan, the library was the next room over. I waited until things were quiet for a while before I made my move. It was a long wait. My imagination about what was going on in rooms unseen was dastardly. I started worrying dinner would be over, and the men would retire to the library before I'd had a chance to get in there. I had no idea how much time had passed. Finally, I figured it was quiet enough—I took a chicken-like run down the hall and into the library. I saw Baby at the piano and Clive, Sam, and Mr. and Mrs. Buchanan heading for various chairs in the parlor. I hoped to heaven she was a lousy singer. I had to pause a minute to find out.

I heard a sound so beautiful—I was shocked it could come from such a wicked heart. I looked at Sam and Clive's faces, I could see they were startled into true love by it. *The three of them can just go off and get married in Hawaii already!*

I stomped quietly to the library shelves because someone had to remember to save the world, even if the stupid men's pants were pointing them in another direction.

I had a flashlight, which if I was caught with, would be really hard to explain, so I tried to move quickly through the books hoping I wouldn't be caught. I really didn't know a lot about the Buchanans, so I didn't know which book they wouldn't be likely to look in. I also had to consider which books were big enough. Science books? Business books? Music books seemed like they would be used.

The piano stopped. I panicked a bit and looked toward the window and considered jumping out. There was some shuffling, and then the voices were clearer. I thought about the floor plan and figured they were standing in the front entrance. I heard the door open and then more voices. More company! What if they wanted to come into the library?!

I opened the window, so I could make a quick escape if

necessary. Beside the window there was a Japanese screen with some kind of dragon war scene on it. I hurried behind it and sat tight. The louder the voices became, the more I wished I'd jumped out of the window.

The piano was playing again, and there was a chorus of voices this time. I felt fairly safe, until I heard noise in the adjoining room. The drawing room.

Must be nice to have all these rooms.

I heard Clive's voice. Then Baby's.

"What do you mean?" Clive said.

"Don't play coy with me."

I peeked through the keyhole like Bob Dylan. Stupid Baby was whispering in Clive's ear.

"I don't think that world be appropriate," he warned, leaning back.

She took the opportunity to lean forward.

"Baby, come play us another!" I heard in a loud voice coming from the other room.

"Maybe later," Clive said to Baby, totally enraging me, and satisfying her, the harlot.

"I'll be right there—just showing Clive my porcelain collection," she yelled, totally unladylike. She untied the front of her dress giving Clive two eyes full, and he looked! He looked at her porcelain collection! I was done.

I moved from behind the screen and found the biggest book on the shelf, and slid the documents in, careful not to slam it closed like I wanted to. I was halfway to the window when the door handle for the library turned. I hit the deck and hid under the desk, which was useless because it just had four spindly legs, but I didn't have time to make it to the window. I held my breath.

As quickly as the door opened it shut again, and I heard footsteps coming toward me.

"Lilac?" Clive whispered, while Baby wailed in the parlor. "I thought you'd be gone by now. What are you still doing here?"

"Not getting a free peep show, 'Maybe later!'" I punched him in the chest.

"I only looked, please. We have to keep our options open."

"Pig!" I felt a tear pop out as I turned to the window.

He grabbed my arm and turned me around. "Options to come back here, not to contract a venereal disease." He kissed me and held his face against my cheek while he whispered in my ear, "Nothing compares to you Lilac. You're my girl, forever."

I was filled up by that, I wanted to shout to everyone in the parlor I had the greatest guy in the world, but I decided, for everyone involved, my time would be better spent going back to my apartment and acting like Baby in my mirror.

"I put the papers in a book already."

"Which one?"

"That one." I zeroed my flashlight in on the biggest book on the shelf.

It was a Bible.

Just then, shoes were clicking down the hall, and there was contact with the doorknob. I literally dove through the window and had an excruciatingly painful landing. As I rolled into the bushes, I heard Clive say, "I just needed some fresh air." He closed the window and went back to the party.

I hope that worked or Clive saw Baby's boobs for nothing.

Meeting up with Zeta, she looked like hell on wheels and limped from a sprained ankle.

The guys came back not too long after that.

Zeta stared Sam down.

"You guys got back early," I said.

"Yeah, Clive told them he was feeling a bit lightheaded, he needed to rest," Sam said.

"I figured it would go with the needing fresh air; besides, I wasn't going to get anywhere tonight."

"Well, if Baby had anything do to with it, you could have gotten *all the way*." I laughed even though it wasn't funny.

"Seriously, Baby's got nothing on you. You're saving the world!" Clive said.

"So, after we save the world, you'll run into Baby's arms and just rub your face in her boobs?" I needed one more reassurance.

"The only boobs I'm dying to rub my face in are yours. I assure you." He kissed me. "As soon as you'll let me, just say the word."

"You looked—you didn't close your eyes." *Okay, two reassurances.*

"It was a split second. It's like watching a train wreck . . . there's confusion about what you're seeing. I'm much more curious about what you're holding back than by what she offers to every passerby," he said, reaching for me.

"I'm holding you to that."

"I hope so." He winked at me.

"I put my documents in a huge Bible. We might have to go retrieve it. They're churchgoers, it's probably a dumb place."

"Something tells me they never crack the thing open," Sam said.

"That's true. Hopefully it's just a show Bible."

Through our entire conversation Zeta stared at Sam, with death in her eyes.

CHAPTER 24

Zeta

♬ "Royals" ♬
by Lorde

I tried to storm home, but my ankle was the size of a grapefruit and throbbing. I started down the road with an angry limp.

"Please, let me carry you," Sam said.

I only agreed because he'd get me to my gun faster.

"I was at the top of the stairs, while the kettle was boiling," I said, our faces nearly touching.

"I didn't touch her."

"It sounded like you did."

"I didn't. She definitely wanted me to, though." He laughed.

I pushed out of his arms pain shooting up my leg when I hit the ground. I took a few hobbling steps toward home.

"Zeta, please. Stop." He held my arm—I wasn't in a position to fight him. "You have to know she's got nothing on you. I was just trying to buy you time. She's a girl, you're a woman. I could not have been less interested in her. She gave Clive the same peep show I got. I'm pretty sure there's four showings a week, plus matinees. Where's the challenge in that? Now you—you make me work for it."

"You're handsome and you know it. Women love you. She won't be the last to throw herself at you, but I'm warning you Samso, if you cheat on me, it will be the last thing you do." I spoke right into his face.

"See what I mean?"

"I was happy when Phillip left, not so with you. You spoke your vows to me, and I expect you to keep them."

"I have and will always keep them, and right now—especially the one about looking after you in sickness. Please let me carry you." He cautiously picked me back up.

"What exactly did you see?"

"Do you really want to know?"

"Yes."

"I'm not even really sure. Udders?"

I burst out laughing. My anger broke the surface of the ice, and I got a breath of air.

"A dairy cow requesting milking? Unclear."

We both laughed and it felt good.

I put my head on his shoulder and enjoyed the scent of warm spice that came from behind the collar of his shirt with every step.

By the time we got home, I was in a much better mood. "I don't think I've ever shown you how I think the tango should end."

"The grand finale?"

"In three parts," I said.

"Three?"

"Three."

I showed him, staying off my ankle.

"You are the undisputed goddess." He dropped to the bed, exhausted.

CHAPTER 25

Lilac

♫ **"Free Fallin'"** ♫
by Tom Petty

Sam wouldn't go through the portal, and I couldn't go retrieve the documents from the museum because I was supposed to be sick, so Zeta and Clive were up. Sam said he'd prep them.

I went back to my apartment to print more of the database and keep in touch with my family. I called Mom, and my brother, just to shoot the breeze.

Zeta and Clive came through the portal to go to the museum. Zeta's ankle was still swollen, but she'd wrapped it and said she'd be fine. They changed into some of my clothes. I had no idea how much unisex clothing I had until we needed it. They both left in T-shirts and drawstring shorts with Crocs. I imagine they both felt like they were in their underwear, but I assured them nobody would bat an eye. Zeta had to mess her hair up a little, because she looked too perfect, I didn't want them to stand out. They were nervous, but courageous.

After they headed out, I waited for a while, but I was too anxious, so I went down to be with Sam. Carrying a few textbooks, and the last stack of database printouts, was substantial, so I took it right to his lab.

Baby was bouncing down the stairs just as I got to the door.

"Perfect timing," she said and winked at me.

"Oh, what can I do for you?" I asked, thinking she actually wanted to talk to me.

"No, your husband did it all," She winked again wickedly and was off.

I really hate that girl.

I tried not to be mad because I was ninety percent sure she was just trying to divide and conquer, but Sam was whistling when I opened the door, and so I was naturally transformed into a protective old bag.

"What was Baby doing here?" I demanded.

"I think she's lonely."

"Then she should volunteer."

He laughed. "Zeta has nothing to fear from her. Baby's like an empty plastic bag and she's a trunk full of treasure."

Sometimes, guys say weird things are actually awesome.

"She is. Remember that. The documents I had from before the portal opened were in her writing, so you two were going to be together even before all this extra help started. She was willing to help you even when you hardly had any concept of how to make your plan work. Even when your team was losing. Don't jeopardize your relationship over stupid Baby's manipulation."

"Yes, ma'am."

I handed him the two-foot-high parcel.

"This is great! How much more is there to go?" Sam asked.

"That's the last of it."

"Hopefully, all this is enough for whatever Ben suggests. I think it's enough for what's on the list already. Any word on the museum front?"

"They're still over there. I was getting too anxious—I left them a note to meet us here. I needed company."

"Great, until then I have something for you to do." He pointed to a stack of books. "Can you go through that stack, and write down all the scientists and researchers names, and then later google when they were born, when they died, where they lived, where they went to school, and whatever else you can find out about them that you think might be helpful. If any of them are living now, maybe making an effort to correspond with them will make a difference."

"Good plan, what are you going to do?" I asked.

"The same thing, only with that stack," he said, pointing to a pile of scientific papers.

We copied names and chatted, drank a couple pots of tea, and he made us lunch.

<hr>

I was beginning to get anxious because Clive and Zeta really should have been back by now.

"I'm going to go check on those guys, make sure they didn't get into trouble."

"What about people from work seeing you?" Sam asked.

"What if they're in some kind of jam though?"

"Good point."

Of course, as soon as I walked into the back alley, I saw my boss getting out of his car, obviously returning from lunch. I should have known. He called out to me. I thought about pretending I didn't hear him, but it would only make things more awkward the next time I saw someone from work. Living across the back alley from your place of employment is convenient, but super stupid.

I waved and he jogged over to my car.

"How are you feeling?" he asked.

"Exhausted. I appreciate you asking. How are things at the office?" I tried to change the subject.

"Good. We all pitched in and got you some flowers. Jane tried to deliver them this morning. I guess you were resting."

"Yes. I'm supposed to be on total bed rest right now. I'm just running out to get…" *Not something he would be willing to run out and get for me* … "An enema bucket. Apparently … chamomile is very soothing … to inflamed rectums." *That should do it.*

"Okay then. Get back to bed as quick as you can and rest up. We miss you." Off he went back to work to spread the news of my infected butthole.

Zeta and Clive were coming down the street, so I went back inside to wait for them.

"We got them, we got everything!" Zeta said.

I hugged her. Then I hugged Clive, a little bit more.

I couldn't believe we'd gotten away with it. I couldn't understand why burying it didn't work, but maybe we'd just chosen a lousy spot? Hard to know.

We all crawled back through the portal, and went to Sam's lab, leaving the papers in my time because we didn't want to mess things up.

"Got 'em," Clive said.

"Everything?" Sam seemed surprised.

Zeta told him all the nitty gritty details.

"This is a relief," Sam said. "Lilac can take these documents to Ben, we'll find out where the holes are in our plan, and we can work from there."

"I'm on it." I turned to leave.

"Wait!" Sam looked at Zeta and Clive. "We should still have some time before the portal closes. How about we all go on a road trip? We deliver the documents and then take a fun road trip together in the future while Ben does his thing. We'll take a week. That will give him time to see what's possible and allow us a break.

A little bit of happiness in the middle of evil. What do you guys think?"

"I could take a few days. My family won't be here for months. I'd like to see where you come from," Zeta said to Sam.

I was totally speechless. Sam hadn't been through the portal at all since I'd arrived. My first thought was to ask questions or protest, but why would I do that? *I'd love to relax and go on an easy vacation with Clive. Take the good.*

Nobody protested, I think everyone was relieved and ready for a break from all the intensity.

"I'm driving!" I said.

Everyone laughed.

Sam and Zeta left to pack their bags.

"Can I come help you pack? I want to see where you live." I asked Clive.

"Certainly."

We didn't worry about propriety; we just walked together. He lived in an apartment over a shop, just like me. In fact, the layout was very similar. I suspected there was probably only a few sets of plans, and only a few builders during the time when the majority of Virden was built.

Things weren't in disarray, but they weren't super tidy, either.

"Sorry, I would have cleaned up if I knew you were coming. I've been a little distracted lately," he said as he grabbed a plate and cup and put them on a small counter.

"I didn't come here to check up on your cleanliness. I just wanted to see your stuff, see who you are." I laughed.

There was a sketchbook on the table. "May I?"

"Um . . . I suppose so." He turned red.

His drawings were strong, angular, like him, except for the last four, they were soft and round, like me, because they were me.

"Oh." I could feel myself blushing.

I wandered around while he packed. He had books and games, drawings and puzzles. There was a line of plants in front of his windows. His bed wasn't made, but his clothes were hung up. There was a dresser with every drawer open, but the clothes inside were neatly folded. There were a few dishes in the sink, but no half-eaten food laying around. He had tools, cowboy hats, wood carvings, and several pairs of nice-looking boots.

I loved him, but as I looked around, I realized I hardly knew anything about him. I liked what I saw, and I was looking forward to learning everything there was to know.

"I think I'm about ready. I'm not really sure what to bring."

"We have money, if you forget something, we'll buy it on the trip."

He hugged and kissed me. "I feel like I just want to keep you here. Let's just go to the courthouse now and come right back here." He kissed me like he'd never kissed me before.

The heated feeling was building in me by the minute. "Sam and Zeta are waiting, and we're going to have lots of time together on this trip." I kissed him quickly, with finality.

There was a warm summer breeze blowing as Clive and I walked down the street holding hands, heading toward adventure.

We met Sam and Zeta at the shop looking as excited as we were. Clive, like a true gentleman helped me up through the portal first, and when I turned around to grab his bag—the portal was shut.

I was confused at first. I'd never seen the thing totally shut. I pushed it with my hands, gently at first because I didn't want it to fling in Clive's face, but then I was pounding on it. I turned around and kicked it with my feet. Nothing.

No, no, no. This is not happening. Clive is coming and we're going to be happy forever.

I grabbed a flat head screwdriver and a hammer from my toolbox and destroyed the inside of the cupboard. Behind the wood was brick. I scratched at the brick with my hands, my knuckles scraped and bleeding. I begged the portal to open.

Please, please. I need him. I need to be happy. I finally found someone who loves me. I need this, please, please, please.

Inside the cupboard was hot and stuffy, and I was sobbing. I started to feel nauseous and then I felt a crack on the side of my brain. It opened into a huge overpowering darkness. Nothing had ever been real. I was in an abyss of blackness, unknowing. I was too scared to cry anymore.

I lay on the floor of my craft room and looked up to the skylight at the illusion of protection, the illusion of shelter, but was any of it real? *How do I even know if I'm alive?*

The picture of Clive's face flashed in my mind, and I felt an overwhelming sadness, but I couldn't react to it. I didn't have any tears. I ran to the washroom and threw up repeatedly. I dry heaved long after my body had no more to give.

I fell asleep on my bathroom floor and woke up in the middle of the night freezing. I wanted to get up, and go to bed, or get a blanket, but I felt weak and sick. Eventually I fell asleep, shivering.

In the morning, I woke up to a pounding head, and the overwhelming urge to barf. I tried; there was nothing there. I wanted the pain to stop, and I thought eating might help. I went to my craft room instead and tried to force the bricks through to the shop. They were solid. I sat on the floor staring at the cupboard and imagined Clive's face appearing. My eyes were red, but no tears came out. I closed my eyes and woke up when the sun was right over the skylight beaming directly in my face. It felt warm and I liked the light, but as soon as I looked back over at the cupboard, I felt empty.

CHAPTER 26

Zeta

♫ "Angel" ♫
by Sarah McLachlan

The hardest part about the portal closing was watching Clive fall apart. Eventually, Sam and I had our own issues about it, but seeing Clive retreat back into who he was after the war, and before Lilac, was painful. He went back to not looking anyone in the eye. He spent months not leaving bed. If we hadn't brought him food, and forced him to eat, I'm sure he would have died. Ultimately, he wouldn't allow Sam to come around, so I just brought him food, and watched him eat it in silence.

CHAPTER 27

Lilac

♫ **"Chandelier"** ♫
by Sia

I left the craft room and closed the door. I poured a glass of juice. Before I could finish the glass, it started coming up. I knew I was beat.

"Mom?"

"Lilac! I'm glad you called."

"Mom, I'm having some trouble eating." Suddenly all the tears in the world started.

"Oh sweetie, what's wrong?"

"I can't eat anything—I keep throwing up."

"Do you have the flu?"

"Maybe." *Flu of the brain.*

"Did you try a capful of Coke?" She asked.

"I totally forgot about that. I'll try it. Hang on, okay?" I got a bottle of Coke and drank a capful. "It seems to be holding."

"Just take one capful every fifteen minutes or so. Eventually, you'll be able to get back on track. Did you have a bad night?"

Where do I start? How can I tell her? Should I tell her?

"Mom, so much has been going on. I just don't even know where to start."

"What do you mean? With work?"

"Not really."

Should I tell her? She's my mom, it sounds like a crazy story, but maybe she'll believe me.

I told her the whole story. I mean everything. She was supportive. She said she was going to come and help me. I asked her if she thought Dad would be able to open the portal, she said if there was a way, he would find it.

I felt a lot better after I got off the phone. I fell asleep on the couch and woke up to a crazy idea.

Maybe Clive left me a note somewhere. He said a great spot to leave a note would be . . . what did he say? In the baseboards! He said, "Nobody moves fancy baseboards."

I grabbed my screwdriver and hammer and got to work removing the baseboards.

I wanted to keep them as intact as I could, pulling off whole lengths at a time, but there were years of paint and stubborn nails. Every one splintered in half, which made me fairly committed to the project. I had gotten myself in too deep to quit. It was hard work and my body was weak, but my mind was determined. I hammered the screwdriver behind the top of the baseboard, then wedged a doorstop under the screwdriver, and pushed until I heard the satisfying sound of the wood peeling back, then I'd go six inches over and do the same thing. Once I had an entire length off, or a busted half, I'd search in the cracks for anything Clive might have left for me, some kind of a sign.

The phone rang a few times, but I ignored it.

I was almost done in the living room when there was a knock at the door. I ignored it and kept working. The knocking got louder, but I kept working, I knew Clive would tell me how to get back to him.

There has to be a way, we are meant to be together.

Finally, I heard the door being unlocked. I eyeballed around the corner to see if the chain was in place and it was. I kept working.

"Lilac! Are you okay? What's going on in there?" It was Jan, my landlady. She wasn't going to be happy with my remodeling.

I ignored her and focused on the last four feet of baseboard. By the time they were able to get into the apartment, I only had two feet left to remove.

Jan took me to the hospital. Well, Jan, and Buck, and a policeman. I wasn't cooperative. I felt bad about that in retrospect, but I was desperate. I took the medication the doctor gave me. I'd been in this show before. I knew if I cooperated, I'd be released sooner. All night long, I dreamed about Clive, and the last two feet of baseboard. I dreamed I pulled it off, and there was another portal, and I knew if I could squeeze through the space, I could live with him in the past, and I wanted to. I just had to get skinny enough to squeeze through.

When I woke up my doctor was there.

"Lilac." He felt my forehead, pushing my hair back off my face. "I'm sorry to hear you're having a bad time. I would like to run some tests on you."

I didn't have any fight in me. I was feeling physically stronger, but so mentally confused it was hard for me to tell if I should fight him or not. Most of me thought not.

The sooner I get them to believe I'm normal, the quicker I get back to my apartment and to the last two feet.

He ordered a lot of tests, earnestly trying to figure out what was wrong with me.

"Do you feel like you've been in another time recently?" he asked.

Seriously, just let me back to my two feet of baseboard.

"I don't know. I don't feel like I know what's real sometimes."

Dang, I wish I didn't say that.

"What do you mean?" he asked.

How do I even backtrack out of this? What will get me out of here as fast as possible?

"Sometimes my dreams are very vivid. Maybe I should stop eating mushrooms before bed?" I tried to laugh it off with him.

"What about this—pulling the wood off your walls?"

Oh, somebody told him about that.

"Don't you ever wonder what's under your carpet or behind a mirror? I was just curious."

"Why didn't you stop after one baseboard?" he asked, not letting me get away with it.

"It was just kind of addictive. Once I started doing it, I didn't want to stop."

Our conversation went on like that for a long time. He asked me a perfectly normal, concerned question, and I answered him with what sounded to me like the most normal answer I could give him without getting into time travel or anything else that had happened.

He kept me overnight. They watched me swallow pills that made me sleepy, but the pills didn't take the reality of my experience away from me, because it really did happen.

The following morning though, I was less sure it happened. Mom and Dad came in to visit. I didn't want them to be there. I knew the reason I was in the mental health wing was because of my mom, and to be fair, she did it because she loved me. Jan had gotten the ball rolling initially, and to be fair to her, I had been destroying her apartment.

Mom sat beside the bed. "How are you feeling?"

"I've been better." I wanted to add I'd never been worse, but I also wanted to go home as soon as possible.

"We went by the apartment."

"I was looking for something from Clive." A nurse walked by, and so I lowered my voice. "I don't know what's going on with me. Am I losing my mind?"

The first step to getting better is admitting you have a problem, right?

"No. You're not losing your mind, sweetheart, you're just under a lot of stress."

I wasn't under a lot of stress—everything was going great until I found the portal.

"Your body finally had the break it needed. You've had a hard few years, I think it was just telling you it wanted rest." She sounded so normal, and right.

I was inclined to believe her. I'm not sure if it was the pills or what, but really, wasn't it more likely my body was enforcing rest, than I'd been time traveling?

I slept most of the day and into the night. Mom was in and out with Dad and Uncle. Everyone looked worried, but loving. I felt crazy, but safe. The blackness was there, but I could pretend it wasn't for longer periods of time, it wasn't forcing me to look at it anymore.

The next day I was released to go home for a few hours. Dad made new baseboards to match the original ones and painted them perfectly to match. I eyed the last two feet. Mom caught me.

"Lilac. Dad worked very hard to fix this room."

"Thank you, Dad. You did a good job. I'm sorry I made all that work for you."

"Well, it's not every day I get to put my carpentry skills to use for you. I was happy to do it." He really was the best guy ever . . . except maybe for Clive.

"Look. I feel like I'm crazy, but at the same time, I don't feel crazy, and I feel like it's real. I want to go look at the portal." It sounded stupid when I said it out loud.

"Okay, sweetie."

We all walked into the craft room. There were bits of wood all over the place and a brick wall at the back of the cupboard.

Mom made the sound she makes when she feels sorry for some small animal. I started gagging. I went to the washroom and threw up all of my good hospital food.

Mom came in and held back my hair while I threw up and cried.

"I just need to know."

"What?" Mom said.

"I need to know what's behind that last two feet." I looked at Dad, pleading with him. "Please, I don't know how to get over this, I need to know."

"Okay," he said.

I could tell Mom didn't think it was a good idea, but I could also tell she was grateful Dad was willing to do it. There may have been a small part of her that believed me, and also a small part that wanted to see what was behind the baseboard.

Mom hugged me as we all sat on the floor, and Dad did the honors on his freshly painted masterpiece. He cracked back the board. There was a tiny space between the floorboards and the wall that ran the length of the two feet. It was conspicuously empty.

"I *am* crazy. I'm losing my mind. I really thought there would be something there," I said. "What about all my stuff from 1920? I gave Uncle a license plate!"

"Lilac, didn't you find it in a suitcase?" Mom asked.

"I only said that because I didn't think he would believe where I really got it from. Wait, I have dresses." I went to my closet and showed her the dresses, shoes and ribbons.

"Lilac, these look like they could have come from New To You."

"No, look at the sewing, it's so well made!" I was sure the sewing would prove it.

"This is beautiful work. Lots of the Mennonite women around here are excellent tailors," Mom said.

I went to the documents compiled for Ben that Clive and Zeta had left on the counter. "What about these?"

"These do look like they're from a long time ago, but they wouldn't be aged like this if you brought them through a portal from the past."

"That's because in the past, I broke into the Buchanans' home, and left them there in an old Bible, and then just went a few days ago to the Buchanan Museum and got them." I was really not helping myself at all.

"Lilac. You have to let this go now. There's no message in the baseboards; there's no portal in the craft room. For you, for your life, you need to let this go. You have to trust me, okay? I care about you and your future." Mom smoothed my hair back behind my ear. "You've had a bad episode. Have you been eating wheat?"

"No. I don't think so." *I mean I did, but after I went through the portal.*

"I think you just need some rest. You need a real vacation. You need to just totally relax."

"Maybe I should go to Hawaii," I said, more to myself than to them.

"There. Now that's a good idea. Just go to Hawaii, and relax for a few weeks, no, for a month. Then you can come home, and slowly get back into things, maybe start half time at work for a couple of months and then go back to full time. That would be good, don't you think, Dad?"

I followed Dad's line of sight to a four-inch piece of baseboard that was somewhat unevenly installed on a tiny lip at the corner. I quickly looked back at my mom before either of them noticed I was looking at what he was looking at.

It's there, I know it's there!

I couldn't do anything about it in the moment, but I would.

I spent days telling all of them what I thought they wanted to hear, I'd been tired, and seemed to have a delusion, but my head was a lot clearer with the medication. Taking the medication didn't affect me, except it made me tired, and somewhat numb, but my determination to get back to Clive was as strong as ever.

Mom and Dad stayed at my apartment while I was in the hospital, and Dad refit the craft room cupboard with a new piece of wood and painted it so you would never be able to tell it was the site of such a bitter parting.

I was off of work on stress leave, which curried pity from my officemates who sent over a nice gift basket with gluten free treats, jams, cheeses, and a sudoku book. It was noticeably missing a bottle of wine. I knew it was Jane who put the whole thing together, and I wished I could be a better worker for her; she truly cared about me.

Mom booked my ticket for Hawaii, took me to get my travel insurance, and then over for some retail therapy to Shari Lyn Fashions. The owner helped me pick out a couple bathing suits that made me feel comfortable, a couple beach cover ups, some sandals, a new purse, a skirt, a dress, and some sleeveless blouses. I wanted to make everyone believe I was dedicated to the idea of going to Hawaii.

Mom and I had an extended talk about where the money came from. I still had some of the $66,000 from the sale of the one-hundred-dollar bill. Actually, I had lots of it—more than thirty grand. I knew if I told her I found the hundred-dollar bill in the suitcase it would make her feel better, but if I told her I got it from Sam, not only would it make her nervous, but I would probably end up back in the hospital. I couldn't really expect her to believe in the portal, especially since I had a history of hallucinations with my gluten allergy. I don't exactly have a clean history of mental health in my family either. It hurt that I wouldn't be able to share it with her, but that's the way it was. I told her the suitcase story, and we celebrated my good fortune over lunch at Gopher Creek.

After three or four days of total mental repentance, Mom and Dad felt comfortable leaving me alone to have an afternoon nap, while they went out to Uncle's to look at a tractor engine. *Is there anything Dad can't fix?*

Once I was sure they were gone, I got out the screwdriver and the hammer, and very carefully pried the baseboard away from the wall. Sitting innocently in the crack between the wall and the floorboards was a rolled-up piece of paper in a slip of plastic. I briefly wondered where he got the plastic from but then realized it could have been from the computer packaging or any number of things I'd taken down there. I was so excited to read his note, to find out how to get back to him. I was sure he would have a plan.

Just so I didn't get locked up again, I carefully put the baseboard back and touched up the paint so it looked better than new. I put everything away, then went to my bedroom, closed the door, got into bed, and carefully unraveled the note.

Lilac,

It's been fifty-eight years since the portal closed. I waited a while, then I got married to Baby. I'm kidding. Too soon? It isn't for me. I bought the shop and have checked the portal cupboard every single day of my life hoping to see your face, praying to see it. I thought maybe it would open up again in four years, like it had before. I had a bag packed at the store, ready to go the instant it opened. Every day was a bitter disappointment. Even as I write this, I have a lump in my throat.

I did get married to a nice woman named Mary. She was the wife of a good friend of mine. He died in a train accident, and left her with two small children, Henry and Edward. I adopted them and did the best I could to raise them right. It isn't that I don't love Mary, we've had over thirty years together, but ours is a marriage of friendship. I loved her husband, and I try to love her how he would have. I try to love her how I would have loved you, but my heart still holds out for you somehow. I am an old man now, but my heart is still young and wants you, though I have resigned myself to the fact I will never see you again. I think of our time together and how you worked with us to save Sam's family and really, all of humanity. I hope we have been victorious. I hope you live in a healthy world. I wonder if you will even remember me, maybe in your timeline none of this has happened. I wonder if Sam, Zeta, and I have just been mentally ill, poisoned and delusional imagining the future and you.

I just wish I could hold you one more time. I wish I had enough life to live right through to your time, and be with you, but I'd be so old, and you would be perfect you. I want you so much, but I feel my life slipping away. I don't want you to question what happened, to question our time together, but most of all I don't want you to wonder if I ever really loved you. I loved you with all my heart and I love you still. I don't know why time ripped us apart, but I know you will be my last good thought.

I know you probably think I wish we'd spent the night together, and I do, but it was the days I missed you the most. I never met another person like you. After the portal closed, everywhere I looked there was something missing. I get teased about talking to myself, I'm content with that, because, really, I'm talking to you.

I'm at the end of my life and I know we have never reunited. The portal never opened again. We've come to the conclusion that maybe it was on a cycle and your visit was the last. Maybe it was astrological, and it will be hundreds of years before it opens again. All I know is, it hasn't opened again, you haven't come back. Please don't spend your life trying to get to me. You must move on. You have to let go of me. Don't forget me, but make your life full without me.

The internet never worked after the day the portal closed. I'm so glad you went to the trouble of printing everything out. By the way, I never got to my Sandwich Islands, I hope you can go for me. I will die happy if I know you'll go and think of me.

With all of my true love,
Clive

He had a small map drawn at the bottom with a clue.

There was so much pressure in my face it felt like it was burning. I read his letter again, sobbing. I was so sure he would have a plan. Why didn't he figure out a way? I felt violent. I wanted to blow up the apartment, and the portal, and the brick wall. I wanted to smash every dish in my kitchen.

I heard the front door open. *Mom and Dad.* I covered my head with the blanket. I heard Mom open the door to peek in on me. I held my breath and tried desperately to stop crying for one moment. The door carefully close again. I grabbed some Kleenex from my nightstand and tried to wipe up what I could without sounding the trumpet by blowing my nose.

Clive is dead now and there's no way to get to him, ever.

You told me you loved me, and you wanted to be with me. You said you were going to marry me. Where are you?

Eventually, I exhausted myself to sleep. I woke up with a blazing headache and a crusty face. It took me a few seconds to remember what was going on. As soon as I did, I felt a pit of sadness—with a trace of intrigue—over what Clive had hidden for me.

It was still early afternoon. I could hear Mom and Dad talking in the living room. I left my room, and headed straight for the bathroom to make myself look normal. I did the best I could then came out to the living room.

"Hey guys, how's it going?" I asked, so very nonchalantly.

"Good, they got the tractor going," Mom said.

"Was there ever any doubt?" Dad stuck his chest out in mock, but real pride.

"How's Uncle?" I asked, to be normal.

"Good. He says hi."

"Did you tell him I'm going to Hawaii?"

"I did. He wants to go too."

"He'd never come with me. He's just blowing smoke." I sort of hoped he wouldn't since I still wasn't sure I was really going, but if there truly was no way to get back to Clive, what would be the harm?

Maybe I do need a break. Besides, he wants me to go.

I figured I would never stop talking about Clive like he was alive. Really, as long as time travel exists, everyone is alive, all the time, at some point in history. Eternal life. Not the kind of eternal life I'm after, but interesting to think about. How to find portals is the next thing. *Maybe I could find another one?*

I stood there, having a normal conversation with Mom and Dad, but inside I was stewing.

Will I become mad with determination, and destroy the rest of my life by being a crank who chases time travel? Will I feel so committed to Clive's love that I will spend every last minute trying to find a way back to him? Even if I got to him, what if it was after he married Mary? Could I spend my life trying to be with a married man? I have no control over the portal, or any others I might find in my lifetime. If it closed on us, why would it suddenly open for us later? Was it intentional, intelligent, or was it just a random rip?

It closed on Sam before, and then opened again, but Clive said he checked it every day for the rest of his life, and it never opened again. Why? Was he telling the truth, or lying to protect me? He seemed awfully determined to let me go.

"Lilac?" Mom and Dad were both looking at me. I was pretty sure I'd missed a part of the conversation.

"Sorry. I'm not quite myself," I said, and in an utter Freudian reflex, looked at the last little bit of baseboard I'd pulled off and repaired. Dad's eyes followed mine.

"You did a good job repairing it. Did you find anything?" he asked.

Dang.

I wanted to say yes to vindicate myself, but there was the chance they would think I wrote it myself in some delusional state.

"No, but I had to look. Now I know for sure. I was crazy, but I'm not anymore, I can move on," I said with all the confidence I could muster.

"Good," Mom said.

"I really appreciate you guys coming out here. You don't know how much it means. Whenever I really need help, you're here for me." I meant it, they couldn't help what happened to me was so unbelievable. For them to stick to me even after all I told them was great. I was glad to know there really wasn't anything that would make them turn their backs on me. No matter what I faced in the future, I could rely on them. I wanted to have Clive too, but we don't always get everything we want.

"We love you," Mom said, and we had one of those family moments with tears, and hugs, and stuff. It was horrible, but also great.

"So, what are we doing tomorrow?" I asked.

"Well, we were thinking about going up to Clear Lake, what do you think?"

"I think that sounds like a great plan. I can wear my new bathing suit!" I said, sounding excited, because I was.

"Great." Mom clapped her hands in her cute little way, where she does it really fast and close to her face, so she looks like a little chipmunk clapping. I love her so much.

I told them I was going for a walk. I wanted to think about some things, and I thought fresh air would help. They didn't love the idea, I could tell, but I think they wanted to trust me a bit, so they didn't make a stink about it.

— ✦ —

I went to my room and grabbed the map.

I walked to the old cemetery. I was looking for a headstone marked "Simpson," but couldn't find one. Then I saw the monument style headstone with the name Amanda Hugankis, and I knew I'd found it.

Sam must have helped him with this.

I felt down the right side—there was a hinge, so I pulled it open from the left side. The stone was hollow inside and held a metal box. I pulled it out and closed everything back up. I sat in front of the headstone staring at it for a long time. Clive was my man to hug and kiss. I wanted to hug and kiss him right then. I felt someone looking at me, and I turned around, sure I would see him, but he wasn't there. I started crying, because I knew I would never see him again. I knew for sure in that second it was truly over. I cried over the grave like Clive was buried there.

Clive's actual headstone is probably here.

I collapsed crying until it was starting to get dark, and the last thing I needed was for Mom and Dad to send out a search party, so mustered my strength, carried the box home, and put it in the trunk of my car. I was curious about what was inside, but it felt disrespectful and vulgar to just open it without some kind of ceremony.

That night, after Mom and Dad were in bed, I crept down to the car, brought the box to my craft room, and sat in front of the portal cupboard. I lit a couple candles and took a few deep breaths. I opened the cupboard door. It was just a cupboard, no portal. I sat the box in front of me and quietly opened the metal lid.

My eyes blurred with tears as soon as I saw the assortment of things. There were beautiful old post cards with letterpress text and a greeting card with scalloped edges.

He knows me so well.

There was a photograph of handsomely refined Sam, Zeta and Clive with Albert Einstein, and a small note from Sam: *It's amazing who you can meet before they're famous.*

There were newspaper articles congratulating Sam and Zeta on scientific achievement. There was a gold chain and a rectangle pendant, embossed with a bursting heart. It was wrapped in a slip of paper from Clive. It read: *The portal that brought you to me.*

The portal that took you away.

I put it on, grateful Clive was able to appreciate the good in life, even while surrounded by evil. I hoped I would be able to feel the same way someday. As I held it between my fingers and thumb, I could feel the love Clive put into making it, or having it made, and I felt grateful for the portal bringing us together. There was a medal from the Society of Canadian Scientists for discovery, and a paper certificate congratulating Sam and Zeta for their work in the field of genetics. There was a stack of patents I'd have to inspect closer later.

There was a picture of Clive with my grandfather as a young man. It took my breath away. Obviously, they'd only lived a couple hours from each other, but I just never considered them meeting. I searched their faces for meaning, but I didn't know why Clive would seek him out, unless it was just to be close to me. I wondered if my grandfather remembered Clive. I wondered if the history of my grandfather was different now. I didn't have any new memories of him, but I wondered if anyone else did.

There were two more one-hundred-dollar bills, which was a huge bonus, but I would have to wait a few years to bring them to auction, or whatever, because their value would be brought down by how many there were on the market at the same time.

I have lots of time.

It was a lifetime of collecting things for me. It broke my heart. He really knew me and cared about me, and I had no way to get to him.

Probably the only man on earth who will ever really love me, and he lives one hundred years in the past.

At the bottom there was a letter from Sam.

Lilac,

By now you've probably figured out I lied about the eight-week opening. I'm truly sorry. It was selfish of me. It's the biggest regret of my life. I put my family's happiness, and my desire for revenge ahead of your family's, and in the end, it cost you and Clive the happiness you both deserved. I was so relieved when we got back from New York and the portal was still open. Honestly, I had started to believe my own lies. I thought we could take that road trip. You know it's bad when you drink your own juice. There really was another woman, and she really wouldn't help me, but I have no idea how long the portal was open that time. I was too much of a coward to go through and do the work myself. You did so much for me, and you deserved better. I'm sorry. I'm truly sorry.

Sam

I could have killed him, but he was already dead. I felt so much rage, but there was nowhere to direct it. *My bangs are getting it for sure.*

I went to bed and googled the GM seed situation. As far as I could understand, Sam registered all the patents, first- and second-generation seed patents, by the end of 1920. A huge seed corporation now claimed their designs were stolen, and deepfaked, to have been registered in 1920. They claimed nobody from 1920 could have possibly designed them, the scientific community simply wasn't that far advanced. The company re-registered the patents as their own. They were currently selling first generation patent seeds with fifteen years left on this round, and another twenty years with second generation seeds. Situations like the one with Sam's family were popping up everywhere. Gabler Consulting was trying to prove Sam Gabler was in fact a genuine, accomplished scientist, and did have the capability in 1920 to design the seeds he did. *Interesting development. The patents from Clive should help with that, hopefully.*

It was overwhelming.

I thought about googling Clive, but I didn't think I could handle it. Instead, I just cried under the covers.

I wonder how much of my life will I spend crying in bed?

The next morning, I grabbed a gluten free muffin and a tea, and went back to bed before Mom and Dad were up, which was unusual, because Dad never sleeps late.

There was one more thing in the metal box I had left to open, a letter from Zeta.

CHAPTER 28

Zeta

♫ "Falling Down Blue" ♫
by Blue Rodeo

*L*ilac,

First, I'm sorry. I'm sorry Sam lied about how long the portal would be open. It was a big problem between us for a long time, but when my family arrived, safe from Italy, and Phillip came back with revenge in his bones, I understood doing anything, justifying anything and believing anything to protect the ones I loved. It's no excuse, but it's a reason. A delusional side takes over. If the lawman hadn't caught up with Phillip, I would have done worse to him than anything Sam's ever done. Still. What you and Clive had was beautiful, and I'm sorry.

I've tried my best to do right by Clive. And I tried to do my best by you, too. You helped us so much, I hope some of what we tried to do for you made a difference. I hope Lan is alive. It took me a while to think of something that might help, but if it didn't, please know I did try.

We have a big family. Nine children! They just started coming, and I never wanted to stop. They've helped with the cause. My brother married, and my kids have eight cousins. They're all grown up now, we have thirty-four grandchildren. My parents died happy. We're aiming to do the same.

I destroyed the seed timeline and Sam's family papers. They were driving us mad. They'd flicker to disaster, and Sam would turn moody and selfish. For our sanity, I had to destroy them. Hopefully, we were successful with his family, but I take comfort in knowing we tried the best we could.

I'm including a map to our crowning achievement. I hope it helps—we worked hard at it.

I'm sorry for how things turned out with Clive, but I hope you can find forgiveness for Sam, and I hope you find love again, and have the happiness we have had. I sincerely wish that with all my heart for you.

With love,
Zeta

CHAPTER 29

Lilac

♫ **"My Heart Will Go On"** ♫
by Celine Dion

Lan was alive—but even though I remembered growing up with her in the current timeline, we'd never gone to school together. She was a singer now. I figured she was fundamentally the same person, so I hoped to meet her one day, and build something new. I still lost my best friend, but she was okay, the mental torment of her life never happened. *Thank you, Zeta.*

I convinced my parents that even though none of the time travel stuff was real, I still wanted to deliver the documents I had found to Ben at Gabler Consulting. I had a severe gluten allergy, and if they could do something about how we grow our food, and to defend and protect farmers, I wanted to do it. I'd been doing pretty good for a couple weeks. I was trying hard to look and speak normally, and just generally behave myself. They agreed with me but insisted on driving me to Gabler Consulting to meet with Ben.

I put the map and patents in among the documents from the Buchanan Museum and arranged for us to meet Ben at the location on Zeta's map. I thought if we could find whatever Zeta hid with Ben there to witness it, it would be much more credible.

We arrived with shovels and a metal detector.

I laid out the map on the hood of the car.

"What do you think?" I wanted Ben to take the lead so he felt more attached to whatever we found.

"This looks right to me." He pointed. "That way? Two hundred and eighty steps."

We followed one another in single file, counting silently. Based on our step strides, we all ended up at different spots.

"Everyone, find a branch and push it into the ground where you ended up," Mom said.

"Good idea."

We did that, then metal detected around each area. We found a coin and a button, but no strong signals. We dug at each spot. Nothing. We dug a wider radius around each spot. Nothing. We looked for markings on trees or on rocks but couldn't find anything.

A few hours and a hundred holes later, we were all covered in sweat and dirt. I plopped down. "Maybe we got something wrong?"

Mom and Dad probably think I made the map myself.

"Maybe there's a different starting point," Ben said.

All of them sat down too. I lay back and looked up at the sunlight, filtering through the trees.

I started laughing.

"What?" Mom asked.

"Look!"

The trees all around us had giant peach and purple flowers with silver leaves. I'd never seen trees like them in my life, and I knew for sure they were not native to Manitoba. We were in a hidden grove of GMO trees. Designed by Sam and Zeta. Absolute proof they were the genuine article. We could cut a tree and count their age by the rings, proving their patents were valid . . . even though, of course, they weren't.

We all lay there, exhausted, but in awe of the beautiful blooms, and what they meant.

Small consolation, but I'll take it.

I wished I could turn and see Clive lying next to me, reveling with me in the moment.

Four years later

♫ **"The Power of Love"** ♫
by Huey Lewis & The News

I traveled to meet Lan, we did hit it off, and I'd go watch her shows when she was in the general vicinity. I did some trips to her shows too, LA, Las Vegas, Houston, Miami, mostly places I'd always wanted to visit anyway. When she did a show in Hawaii I went, my second trip for Clive to his Sandwich Islands.

When I was at home, I usually started my morning by setting the kettle to boil and then couldn't help but check the portal. I knew I'd never find it open, but my heart raced a little every time. I had the picture of Clive, Lucille Ball and myself and his letter to me taped to the inside of the cupboard door. My family was convinced I'd made it with AI.

"I miss you." I'd kissed my finger and touched it to Clive's name at the bottom of his letter.

I would crawl in and push on the back of the cupboard.

One morning, unlike every other morning, it opened. My heart skipped. It was quiet.

"Clive?"

"Lilac!" Clive's face popped up. "I'm coming, right now."

Thank you so much for reading!

If you enjoyed this story, please consider leaving a review. It doesn't have to be long—just a sentence or two helps other readers discover the book . . . and means the world to the author.

About the Author

Theory Knight writes what she knows: love, laughter, and the beauty of second chances.

After sidestepping her share of romantic plot twists, she found her own happy ending—and now channels that hard-won joy into feel-good rom-coms filled with klutzy charm, smart banter, and endings that make you believe in love all over again. Fans of Emily Henry, Lynn Painter, Helen Fielding, and Sara Desai will feel right at home in her world of awkward heroines, comedic disasters, and swoony heroes who get it right—eventually.

When she's not writing, Theory is likely thrifting for treasures, road-tripping with a playlist that deserves its own fan base, or daydreaming on a sun-drenched beach (real or imagined). She's a lifelong collector of rocks, stories, and stationery, and believes the best inspiration often hides in the most unexpected places.

Her heartwarming rom-coms are the perfect escape for readers who like their love stories with a dash of chaos and a whole lot of heart.

You can stay current on Theory's projects via her Instagram profile (@theoryknight) and via her website www.theoryknight.com

Other Rom-Com Novels by Theory Knight

Tiger in My Tank

Inklings Afire